PRAISE

"Letters in Time is like a wonderful meal with a delicious balance of engaging characters (both sweet and bitter), a fascinating peek at history, a captivating community, and a slow-burning romance for dessert."

—Donna Weaver
USA Today Best-Selling Author

"Susan Reiss captures the magic, mystery and charm of that quintessential Eastern Shore town – St. Michaels. Secrets lay hidden for generations among the stunningly beautiful estates along the Miles River. Can't wait for her next …"

—Kathy Harig, Proprietor,
Mystery Loves Company Bookstore

"[Susan Reiss] will transport you to the Eastern Shore of Maryland, but will remind you of whatever town has a special place in your heart… It leaves me wondering what other secrets this quaint little Eastern Shore town is hiding and I'm waiting for Susan Reiss to tell us."

—Barbara Viniar, Retired President
Chesapeake College, Maryland

Letters
IN TIME

BOOK ONE

SUSAN REISS

INK & IMAGINATION PRESS
an imprint of Blue Lily Publishers

ISBN: 978-1-9498764-7-5

Cover Design by Rachael Ritchey, RR Publishing
Interior Design: Jennifer Jensen

Website: www.SusanReiss.com
Instagram: SusanReissAuthor
Twitter: @SusanReiss
Bookbub: Susan Reiss
Goodreads.com: SusanReiss, Goodreads Author
Facebook: Susan Reiss

Dedicated to

Elizabeth Dorbin

For your patience in answering countless questions
For your captivating family stories and historical tidbits
For your inspiration and steadfast support

This one is for you.

CHAPTER ONE

"I hope the symbolism of the butterfly of renewal and courage works for me here at the Cottage." —*Emma's Journal*

They sat me down in an antique dining chair and parked me in the middle of the gravel driveway leading to the Cottage. Inside, I'd take up space as the movers wrestled things in and out. Sitting here under the towering pine trees, I was out of the way. Sidelined with my crutches. Away from the action. The way I'd been since the accident that almost took my leg and my life.

At least, I reminded myself, *I'm still alive.*

But my rightful place was in the thick of things, whether surrounded by exuberant children in a kindergarten class, counseling their parents, or supervising the painting of a hallway mural. I was always dashing around on the playground or running classroom activities in the school environment I loved. My husband—my ex—said I was happiest around children and that I preferred them to adults. Maybe he was right, but things had changed.

Now, my job was telling the moving men where to put my

belongings—and which of Uncle Jack's things they should remove from the Cottage.

A puff of air blew off the saltwater creek. It brought a moment of relief from the August humidity and the heat of my frustration, but the tears of impatience, yearning, and self-pity threatened to come once again.

No, this was not the time or place to cry. I decided to come to the Eastern Shore, to live in Uncle Jack's Cottage that was now mine, to make this big step in taking back control of my life. It was better than staying in my city condo where my past life haunted me—when I could do what I wanted, whenever I wanted.

I took in a deep breath and wiggled my body around so I could sit up straighter in the antique armchair that belonged inside as I did. Now, all I wanted was to be independent. Since I was a little girl, the Cottage was the place where exceptional things happened. In the silence of my heart, I whispered, *I hope it will again.*

Thankfully, I had myself under control by the time I heard the crunch of footsteps on the gravel. *Boss,* as he was called, was the big, burly man who owned the moving truck. He lumbered toward me, wiping his forehead with a red print bandana. The thick beard that covered the lower half of his face glistened with sweat.

"Miss Chase," he called out. "I'm sorry, but I gotta tell ya, this ain't gonna work. There's not enough room in that small house for everything."

A moment ago, I wanted something to do, a problem to solve. But I didn't want this one. "I thought if we took out—"

"Yes, ma'am. We already took out the furniture going to charity, but that place is packed. There's no room for you to get around on those crutches."

I pushed at those instruments of torture that labeled me an invalid, at least in my own mind. My chest tightened. Panic. Another side effect of the accident that almost killed me. "What can we do?"

"S'cuse me," the young man who worked with Boss

interrupted. He was so thin he looked like he'd blow away in a stiff wind, but he hefted furniture as if it were made of matchsticks. "During our break, I went for a walk and found an old building right over there in the woods." He pointed toward a path through the trees.

"The old garage," I said. "I'd forgotten all about it. Do you think it will work?"

"It's dry, empty, and has plenty of room. There's a lock in the truck we can put on the door. Out there, I don't think nobody will bother your things."

I started to maneuver myself to my feet, looked at the path again, and fell back in the chair. "I wish I could see it."

The two moving men looked at each other and smiled.

"I think we can make that happen," Boss said. "You'll be fine if we do this."

He balanced my crutches across my lap and together, the men swooped me up in the air, chair and all. A giggle escaped my lips. This was the way to travel. I floated through the woods like a bird. At the garage, they whisked me inside and placed the chair gently on the concrete floor. The young man was right. It was big and empty and perfect for storage, except for the tall thing standing in the corner, covered by a marine blue tarp.

I pointed. "What is hiding under there?"

Before the words were out of my mouth, they pulled on the tarp and uncovered a treasure. It was a desk, but not just any desk. It was massive, about three feet wide and six feet tall. The dark wood was scratched here and there, and the dull finish was thirsty for some furniture polish. The large writing surface could accommodate a laptop computer and notes. Above that surface was a large door that hid cubbyholes, slots, and shelves for everything from research books to paperclips.

It was perfect. Just what I needed to put my secret plan into action. I hadn't breathed a word to anyone about the lifelong dream I wanted to make come true.

I wanted to write a book.

A book for children that would transport them to a different world, far away from the day-to-day routine, and fire their imaginations. I'd spent the last six years teaching kindergarten, so I had a good idea what they would love. Teaching the little ones how to read was so exciting and rewarding. Of course, I didn't have the germ of an idea or characters yet, but I thought if I relaxed here at the Cottage, sat next to the waters of the Chesapeake Bay, miles away from the demands of modern life, the story would come to me. And this desk could help channel those thoughts and help me get things done.

Boss inspected the desk. "I haven't seen one of these in years. I think it's an old plantation desk."

"A *plantation* desk? Here in Maryland? Don't you mean a farmer's desk?" I asked. "Plantations were down South."

"This whole area of the Eastern Shore was small farms and plantations," Boss countered.

"Uncle Jack probably picked up the desk in an antique auction somewhere," I said.

"Could be. Or maybe it's always been here on this land." Boss gave the desk a little shove. "It's old and it's solid." He pulled out a drawer and showed me the dovetailing in the corners. "It's well-built. Can't figure why a good piece like this would be stored in the garage under a tarp." He shook his head and sighed. "Well, Miss Emma, do you want to leave it here or—"

"I want it in the house," I declared quickly. "If it fits. The doors—"

"We'll make it fit. Don't you worry," Boss said with confidence.

Thinking about their long drive back to Philadelphia, I added, "Once we get the extra pieces stored out here and the desk moved in, you gentlemen can be on your way."

"I hope you're not leaving." Another man with a deep voice tinged with a bit of a Southern accent spoke behind me. "You just got here."

Still skittish from the accident, I spun around and wobbled. One of my crutches tumbled to the floor. The stranger had scared me and he knew it. His suntanned face was full of regret.

"I'm so sorry," he said. "That's a bad habit of mine, charging into a conversation like that. Are you all right, Emma?"

My eyes narrowed as I stared at the stranger. "Who are you?" I challenged.

"Whoa." He took a step back and held his hands up, palms out, in surrender. "Easy there." Behind him, a blur of white zoomed to his side and growled. Calmly, the man held out his hand and pointed to the floor. "Ghost. Down." The large white dog laid down immediately. "Good girl. Friend."

"How can I be your friend," I snapped. "if I don't even know your name? And how do you know me?"

"Well—" He ticked off each point on the fingers of his right hand. "Mr. Saffire, the lawyer in Easton, said that Mr. Jack's niece was moving into his cottage today. There's a moving van outside. Two big men are pushing things around. You're a woman I've never seen before. You're sitting down and supervising these gentlemen while holding on to crutches." He retrieved the fallen one from the floor. "Ergo, you must be Emma Chase."

He paused, then said softly, "My condolences, ma'am. Mr. Jack was a wonderful human being. I'm going to miss him. He wanted me to look out for you."

I realized that this was the man Mr. Saffire had hired to help with things around Uncle Jack's Cottage. "Then you must be Mr. T. J. Dorset."

"It's TJ," he said gently.

"What?" I asked.

"I go by TJ as if it's one word, not T. J. with periods and all. I like to keep it simple."

I was too tired to play games. "Well, TJ without periods, thank you for coming by, but I have everything under control here."

"Then I'll say good afternoon." He nodded as he backed away. "Come on, boy." The Labrador retriever, with fur the color of snow, bounced up and stood next to him.

TJ touched the brim of his ball cap and was about to leave when my cell phone rang. Boss took my crutches making it easier for me to work the phone out of my pocket. I groaned when I read the caller ID: Lawyer-Heinrick.

"Great, just what I need. If you could give me a minute…" I took a deep breath and was determined to sound friendly as I touched *Accept*. "Hello, is that you, Mr. Heinrick?"

"Of course, it is, Ms. Chase. Who else would it be?" he said with a bit of a sniff.

"Well, sometimes it's your secretary." I didn't add, *poor woman*. "What can I do for you today?"

"It's more like what could you do for me…days ago. I sent an email, an important one. You have yet to respond."

Great, I thought, an attorney and a disciplinarian, all in one package.

"Ms. Chase, I was given to understand that you preferred email, but I must have your prompt reply. Without it, how I am to do my job and represent you properly is beyond me."

I looked down at my leg and wished I didn't need representation. I remembered running barefoot here at the Cottage. Running with Uncle Jack's Labrador retriever Prince. Running to climb in Uncle Jack's boat to go crabbing. Running after fireflies. The doctors still weren't sure I'd be able to walk normally again, let alone run.

"Ms. Chase? Are you there?"

"Yes, yes, Mr. Heinrick," I said quickly. "You are absolutely right."

"Well…" he said with a huff of self-satisfaction. "I'm glad to hear you say that. I'm not used to being ignored, Ms. Chase."

"Oh, I certainly wasn't ignoring you." If the man hadn't come so highly recommended as the best personal injury lawyer in Philadelphia, I would have fired him long ago for his condescending and controlling attitude. "I've been having some trouble with my email account, but I can assure you that I will respond soon."

TJ walked into my line of sight and gave me a quizzical look that bordered on comical. I waved him off, afraid I'd laugh.

"See that you do, Ms. Chase. I can't have my work undermined—"

"Oh, I'd never do that." I hoped he wouldn't notice my supercilious attitude. "I will be in touch soon."

"See that you do." And with a click, he disconnected the call.

I looked at my phone in surprise. Did the man act like a dictator with all his clients or was there something special about me? Well, this was not the time to figure it out. I put my phone back in my pocket and stretched a little. My body ached. The day's activities were taking a toll. I wasn't as strong as I'd hoped, but if I let it show, everyone would bustle around, making me feel even more like an invalid. Invalid. A horrible word. Pronounced differently it meant the same thing: Invalid. Null. Void.

Worthless.

I caught sight of TJ giving me a cockeyed smile. I didn't want him to read my deepest thoughts. The last thing I needed was pity. "What's so funny?" I barked. I closed my eyes wishing I could take back my harsh words. I didn't mean to take out my frustration on this well-meaning stranger, but I couldn't let him or anyone else see how defenseless I was. And he was such a convenient target.

He jerked back. "Nothing, ma'am. I was just surprised that you got cell service and held it long enough to complete a call."

"What do you mean?"

He shook his head slowly, his hazel eyes smiling. "We don't have good cell coverage down here. The phone companies won't put up more towers. Guess some big ole cloud bounced the signal for you this time. Don't depend on it, is all I'm saying."

As he walked away followed by his dog, I noticed a small magazine sticking out of his back pocket. I wondered what he was reading. "I'll check on you tomorrow," he said.

Before I could tell him that it wasn't necessary, he'd slipped away.

It took Boss and his helper less than an hour to swap things around and move the desk out of the garage in the woods and into my writing room. Wait, I decided to call it my writing *den* to remember Uncle Jack who loved his den. Virginia Woolf said it was important for a writer to have a special place to work and now, I did.

Seeing the desk nestled in the corner by the window, I felt a strong sense of accomplishment. Not that I'd done anything really, but I did make the decision to move it into the Cottage. After everything that had happened in the past months, with all decisions taken out of my hands, I felt like I'd taken another step forward. This desk would inspire my book, I just knew it. I hoped that the decision to come to the Shore was another positive one.

By the time the moving truck crunched over the gravel driveway out to the main road, the sun was dipping toward the horizon. The water in the creek that ran by the Cottage barely rippled as if it was exhausted by the heat. It wasn't the kind that you waded in to catch salamanders. The creeks of the Chesapeake Bay region were sometimes wide and deep enough for a twenty-foot sailboat and the rivers were two miles across or more.

The land on the far side of the creek was once an island but was now joined to the mainland by a one-lane road to make it easier to farm the acreage there. I was happy to see that one of my fondest things from childhood still lived on the island: a large… no, a *huge* oak tree known as The Lone Oak. Its stately limbs were impressive. The lower ones had welcomed me to climb, swing, even stretch out and lean against the trunk to read a favorite book. My mother was terrified that I'd fall and break my head, or at least an arm, but when she wasn't around, Uncle Jack let me be a kid.

During those days with Uncle Jack, we'd spend hours together. At the end of each day, we would sit quietly and watch the sun sink in the west. The moment it disappeared, I believed there should be a sound. We'd try out different pops and glissandos as we made our way inside the Cottage.

I gazed out the window into the growing darkness and whispered, *Here I am, Uncle Jack. I wish you were here.*

I didn't want to wallow in sad thoughts, so I gulped down a sandwich for dinner and went back to my new writing den. I couldn't identify the different woods used to create its natural richness of tone and pattern. Why had Uncle Jack banished this beautiful piece of furniture to the garage in the woods? That was one of many questions that would go unanswered. Fortunately, the moving men had found a rag and some furniture polish to wipe away cobwebs and the thin layer of dust. I don't think I could have managed it by myself and I didn't want to wait until the housekeeper came. I was too excited to make this desk my own.

I opened the large doors above the writing surface and my breath caught. Cubbyholes and shelves waited for my things. Could there be a hidden compartment or two? I decided that no bills or medical instructions would be kept there. Only notes for the book and drafts. Vertical slots would keep file folders neat. I dragged a box of office supplies over to the desk and dove into it to find places for ballpoint pens, places that had once held quills. There were cubbyholes for a stapler, scissors, and a ruler. Drawers for stashing away thumb drives and chargers, all those things that take up space until you need them. A couple of shelves could accommodate a few books, including the one about punctuation a friend had given me, because I never used commas in the right places.

The challenge would be to remember where I put everything. Supplies were incidental until you needed something. I checked the bottom of the moving box and found a stack of white printer paper. I decided it could sit on the corner of the writing surface until I found the printer. That clean white paper was begging for words to appear. I was tempted to take a pen and start scribbling, but prudence and caution prevailed. I needed what energy I had left from a long day to get upstairs to my bedroom. But first, I had to put my mark on my new home.

I reached back into the box and retrieved a small pile of origami paper. Origami—creative paper folding-- was a favorite pastime. It didn't take long to do and it could put the whole world on pause for a few minutes while I made something lovely and meaningful.

I chose a square of Wedgewood blue paper to signify the open sky and water of this area, but what form should I fold I wondered, then smiled. It only took a few minutes for me to create a delicate blue butterfly, the symbol of change and growth. A caterpillar had to change to become beautiful. That's what I had to do--change to become self-sufficient and independent again.

I set the butterfly on the edge of a cubbyhole, to remind me of my goal and a way to mark my creative space. This desk would be an inspiration.

I straightened the stack of paper sitting on the writing surface, ready to record my new story starting tomorrow. Tomorrow. The beginning of my new adventure.

It was time to put the Cottage to bed as Uncle Jack always called the nighttime ritual. I turned out the lights one by one and checked the windows and doors as well. City ways died hard, even in a beloved cottage in the country.

Now that the Cottage was tucked in, it was my turn. I stood at the bottom of the staircase and stared up at the top step that looked miles away. What was I thinking, leaving a modern, one level condo and moving to a historic old cottage with two floors? I reached up to my neck to touch a necklace, a gift to celebrate a major accomplishment. I always wore it to remind myself that I could do tough things. But it was no longer there, lost in the emergency response to save my life.

This was your idea, I lectured myself. *So, you better haul your sorry body up these stairs or you're gonna sleep on the sofa without a soft pillow or blanket.*

I grabbed the banister with one hand and jockeyed the crutches around with the other. Who would have thought that shifting my 120-pound body would be so hard? Panting from the effort, I began the climb that I thought would be so therapeutic.

I felt every muscle stretch, every nerve twitch as I stepped up. At this rate, it would be time for breakfast when I finally got to the top. My kindergarten teacher instinct kicked in. What would I tell a child to make this fun? Of course, my old fallback. Sing a song! A counting song. But singing one I used in the classroom would make me miss the kids even more than I already did. I'd make up my own. That would distract me.

The first line that came to mind was *Here's step one. I wish I were done.*

That was too pessimistic when I faced so many more steps. I teetered on the first step from standing there so long. Then inspiration came.

"Here's step one," I sang. "I've just begun."

Oh, this wasn't working. I looked around thinking that I should sleep on the sofa when something caught my eye. Outside, near the Lone Oak, a light was dancing around. The kids in my kindergarten class would think it was a fairy dancing in the blackness of the night. More likely, somebody was holding a candle or flashlight. By the old tree? In the middle of nowhere? I squeezed my eyes shut and opened them again. The light was gone. The painkiller must be playing tricks. I needed to get some sleep. I wrapped my hand around the banister again and pulled myself up another step.

"That's step two to make just a few, but it's one more than when I'd begun." The singing sounded more like grunts and the rhyme was awful, but I was making progress.

After only six steps, the tears started to flow. My shoulders hurt. My leg hurt. My pride was in tatters. Why did I think I could do this? Not only live alone in the Cottage but recover the use of my leg?

I can't do this alone, Uncle Jack. I need you.

He always said, "Emma, you can do anything you put your mind to."

I smiled remembering how that brilliant, accomplished man always let that one preposition dangle at the end of that sentence. He said it would help me remember what he said.

And that's what l have to do…remember.

I wiped my cheeks with my sleeve, took a big breath, and climbed my way to bed. I only had enough energy to make my nightly entry in my journal.

The next morning dawned bright and clear with a break in the summer heat and humidity. Going down the stairs was a little easier. I was in the kitchen in no time and grateful it was small and compact. Soon, the toaster hummed. The coffeemaker dripped. The Cottage was beginning to work its magic, making me feel like I was home.

Anxious to begin work and make my mark on that stack of white paper, I hustled through breakfast. The dishes could sit in the sink for now. With a fresh mug of coffee placed on the computer table with wheels, I carefully pushed through to my writing den for the first day of work on my new book. I refused to let it rattle me that I had no clue about the storyline or characters.

As I approached my magnificent writing desk, I looked at the stack of paper I'd left there and gasped. Words were written on the top sheet.

My Dearest Emma,

CHAPTER TWO

"A good short letter is better than a poor long one. The language of a letter should not be...too dry or abrupt. It should be easy, flowing, graceful."

How to Write Letters: A Manual of Correspondence Showing the Correct Structure, Composition, Punctuation, Formalities, and Uses of the Various Kinds of Letters, Notes and Cards by J. Willis Westlake, A.M., Professor of English Literature, State Normal School, Millersville, PA 1883

I rocked on my crutches from the shock. It would be better to sit down than fall down, so I got myself into the chair and dropped my crutches to the floor. I couldn't believe someone had addressed a letter to me in such an intimate way and left it on my desk. Almost forgetting to breathe, I slid the page in front of me and read:

August 22, 1862

My Dearest Emma,

If I may still call you my dearest since you must think so badly of me for not writing sooner. It is not a lack of desire to contact you. It's about having the ability to write.

This war has brought such deprivations down on us. I have sat here at my father's desk, as if chained to it, waiting for that most precious commodity, paper.

Now that it has appeared and in abundance, I shall be able to tell you what has transpired and assure you of my faithfulness now and always. I often think of you walking by the water, watching the osprey, and breathing the salt-tinged air. It brings me such comfort.

Your obedient servant,
Daniel

My dearest Emma? Who is this Daniel? How did he get into the Cottage?

I held my breath, listening. Was this Daniel still here? Could he be in the living room or watching me from the hallway? I spun around in the chair, but no one was there. The letter fluttered to the floor.

Okay, calm down, I told myself. If he was here, there would not be much I could do to defend myself. My phone, where was my phone? Not in my pocket. Not on the desk. Idiot.

I'd left it on the kitchen counter by the sink. So near, yet so far. There was nothing else to do but get up on the crutches and get to the kitchen as fast and as quietly as possible. Hopefully, I wouldn't run into the intruder.

The rubber tips on the crutches made squeaky noises as I tried to tiptoe across the hardwood floor. My ears strained to hear any other sounds. There was nothing except the hum of the fridge and the tick-tick of the old hallway clock.

It felt like it took hours to get to the kitchen. I reached for my phone. My hands trembled as I tapped out 911. I needed the police to come.

Only there was no call, no bars on my phone. No Service.

What should I do? Get out of the Cottage!

This wasn't a horror movie where the starlet waits around for the Slasher to appear. I moved to the patio door as fast as I could. I pulled, but I couldn't open it. The door was locked.

The intruder, this Daniel, must have come in another way.

Ever so carefully, I slid open a drawer and pulled out a steak knife. If this Daniel came at me, I could wave it around to threaten him. But how was I to use the crutches, carry the knife and not stab myself? No time for an elegant solution. I had to move. I stuck the blade between my teeth, the sharp edge away from my lips.

I held my breath and listened. Still nothing, but the fridge and the clock. Slowly, I made my way down the hallway to the front door. One glance at the deadbolt showed me that the front door was locked, too. Did Daniel come in, write that letter, leave, locking the door behind him?

I stood there like a dummy trying to figure it out. Then there was a light scraping sound at the door and the deadbolt handle slowly turned.

He was back.

Fear glued my feet to the floor. I watched with growing panic as the lock clicked. The door handle turned. The door began to open.

"Emma, it—"

SLAM! I threw my body against the door. The crutches clattered on the floor. My fingers scrabbled to close the lock again.

I rested my face against the door, panting. A fist struck the wood from the other side again and again. The solid knocking thumped against my face, sending the ugly vibration through my head. The deadbolt knob started to move again. I grabbed it to keep it in place, my fingers squeezed against the metal.

"Who are you? What do you want?" I demanded, my voice breathless and pathetic.

The response came from two inches away on the other side of the wood panel.

"Emma? It's me, TJ. Are you hurt?" He sounded as terrified as I felt. "I'm coming in."

"Wait!" I swallowed my fear. "Wait. You'll knock me down." I flipped the lock, picked up the crutches, and collapsed on a step.

"Now?" he asked.

"Yes, now," I called out, my heart thundering in my ears.

At first, the door opened an inch then flew back in a rush. His head swiveled around, taking in the situation. Seeing that all was quiet, he knelt at the bottom of the steps.

"Emma, are you okay?" His soft words, spoken with a Southern caress, were meant to comfort a frightened child. "What's wrong?"

What could I say? Somebody—somebody named Daniel—broke into the house while I was asleep, wrote me a love letter, and left, locking the door behind him? It sounded ridiculous to me, even though that is what happened. I was sure of it. This country boy would think I was a skittish female from the city who jumped at every odd sound that came with living close to nature. The man would resign from the caretaker job before he started. Or worse yet, he'd be at the Cottage all the time. My mind whirled with the possibilities, but the one that didn't occur to me was about to happen.

"Emma, I'm so sorry. I was trying to be considerate. Mr. Saffire gave me a key so you wouldn't have to run to the door every time I came by." He glanced away and sighed. "Look, I thought I'd open the door and yell out to let you know I was here. I meant to save you some steps, not to scare you."

He didn't factor in that my nerves would be jangling from finding a letter from an unknown admirer inside my locked house.

I wasn't ready to reveal its existence, but I was hell-bent on preventing it from happening again.

TJ slipped his John Deere hat off like a courteous schoolboy. His light brown hair, streaked blonde by the sun, fell over his ears. He took out his key ring. "Here, I can give you my key to your front door. I can't promise it's the only key outstanding, but at least you'll have mine."

The perfect solution. "I have a better idea. You bring up an important point. There might be other keys out there in possession of people who are not as honest as you are. What do you think about changing all the door locks and making sure the window locks work? Can you do that, TJ?"

He looked around and twisted his mouth a little as he considered the situation. "You only have two doors, including the one out to the patio. Yes, ma'am, I can handle it. No problem, but I'll have to go into town to get the locks."

"Can you do it today?"

He nodded as he held out a hand to help me stand up.

"Oh, that's okay. I can do it myself. I have to do it myself if I'm going to get back to normal." I put my hand on the newel post and, using one crutch, I struggled to my feet.

"May I hand you the other crutch?" he asked carefully.

I hid my burst of frustration as I reached out to accept it. "My lawyer said you're supposed to be my go-to man for things around the house, is that right?"

"Yes, ma'am, that would be me. I'm your handyman and an active local farmer. Anything you need, let me know and I'll take care of it." He pulled an index card out of his shirt pocket. He wasn't wearing a T-shirt like so many other men did on the Shore. Instead, his pale-green cotton shirt had a buttoned-down collar and long sleeves rolled up his suntanned arms. "I wrote down my name and cell number. I'll put it on the refrigerator door where you can find it when you need it and have reliable phone service," he added as he took off down the hall to the kitchen.

I followed him, swinging my crutches, sometimes hitting the wall. "I should write down my cell number for you."

"It's okay, ma'am. Mr. Saffire gave me all your contact information," he said with a smile.

"He did, did he?" I felt a little exposed. This guy looked nice enough, but…

He must have read my thoughts because he said quickly. "I have your number right here."

He patted his shirt pocket on his rather broad chest that I couldn't help but notice. I chuckled to myself that I must be getting better.

"I always have my cell turned on, but I'll stop by to see if you need anything."

"Oh, I don't think that will be necessary. I'll call you when I want something." I needed to be clear that I didn't want neighbors and new friends dropping by. I'd come to the Cottage to do certain things, and I meant to accomplish what I'd set out to do, as always.

"Remember, cell coverage is spotty here. There's a great signal on Route 50 for people heading to the beach."

"But down a country lane, coverage isn't so good?" I said.

"Don't worry. Mr. Saffire arranged for a landline to be installed in the house. The phone company should be here any day now."

"There's no specific time? Like today?"

"Well, I don't want to speak for the phone company, but there is such a thing as Eastern Shore time."

I began to nod slowly. "I see. The installer will be here when he or she gets here?"

"I'm afraid so."

Our conversation petered out. The silence felt awkward. I grasped for the first thing that came to mind. "Your name is TJ? Is that short for Tom Jr. or something?"

"Not exactly." He laid on a thick Southern drawl. "But my family does have deep roots in the South, Miss Emma."

I couldn't help but laugh, something I hadn't done much lately.

CHAPTER THREE

"I took an old mahogany Bureau to the shop for repairs… I found this inscription on the bottom written in the varnish in a firm large way July 16, 1792 by L. Tarr for James Dawson, Baltimore, MD. We have given the piece to…"

—*100 Years of Change on the Eastern Shore: The Willis Family Journals 1847-1951, Edited and Annotated by James Dawson*

"That's better," TJ said with a big grin. "Maybe we could start over." He took a step back. "Good morning, Miss Emma." He made a deep bow from his narrow waist. "Thought I'd drop by and see if you had a good night. I hope this fine morning finds you well."

I could feel my smile slowly melt off my face as I remembered the letter from Daniel on the desk. "Of course. Why wouldn't I be?" I hoped he couldn't hear the crack in my voice, but he did.

He turned his head slightly to one side and frowned. "Well, I don't know, right now you seem jumpy, like a spooked filly that had seen—"

I rushed to interrupt. "No, no, I'm fine."

He waited and the silence stretched between us again.

I quickly added, "I slept very well. I always do when I'm here at the Cottage. Been that way since I was a child." If only my voice sounded more convincing.

"What's got you so…" The rest of his question dangled in the air between us.

This was the moment. I almost blurted out that I'd found a letter from a stranger named Daniel. But something made me pause. What if TJ had written the letter? No, I'd better keep it a secret for now. If he had, I would be smart not to let him know that he'd frightened me so easily. I needed to buy time to figure out what to do.

I pointed to a machine on the counter. "Would you like some coffee? It's always fresh and perfect every time."

"I have a machine like that," he said with pride. "It was a gift. Never would have bought it for myself. Now, I can't imagine living without it. May I?"

I nodded and sat down. He selected a coffee pod of a dark blend and set the machine to brew. "I really like how it works. I can dash into my office between chores and make myself a mug. Morning comes pretty early here and coffee is the fuel that keeps me going."

He made a fresh cup for me and I watched him over the rim of my mug as we sipped our coffee. He was tall, my guess about 6'2". Under his fresh shirt, his arms and chest were well-developed from working hard on the farm, not hours in the gym. I suspected that if I touched his arm, it would be rock solid. His face suggested gentleness. His hazel eyes, tending to green, reflected the land where he made his living. Could he be a man who would threaten a woman living on her own with a letter? It was hard for me to believe. Everything and everyone suggested that I could trust him. I opened my mouth, paused, and closed it again.

"Yes?" TJ said.

I didn't think he was watching me that closely. His extra

attention made me uncomfortable again. Maybe his word to describe me was correct: skittish.

"What?" I snapped. "I mean, what?" I repeated in a softer tone.

"It's just that you looked like you were going to say something."

"Why would you think that?" I looked away, feeling defensive.

"Well," he said with a chuckle. "You were sitting there with your mouth open, looking more like a fish gulping air than ..." He shrugged. "Maybe it was my imagination." He put the almost-empty mug down on the counter. "I guess I'd better go and get those new locks if I'm going to get them installed today." He pushed his hair back off his forehead and settled his hat in place. "And when I come back, I'll honk my truck horn and knock, so you can come and let me in."

Feeling a little foolish, but more comfortable with the arrangement, I nodded. "Thank you for coming by this morning," I said, feeling centered again and eager to get back to my plans for the day.

He moved down the hallway. "And again, I'm sorry about the trouble." He poked his head into the den. "It looks like you're settling in." His back went straight and he charged into the den. "Wow! Did you bring that with you?"

I followed him into my new writing den. I pushed down some growing resentment that this stranger was so comfortable wandering around my house. But TJ had been a great help to Uncle Jack as he got older so it must have come naturally to the man.

Boundaries, I thought. *I need to set boundaries.*

"I found the desk in the garage. Uncle Jack must have thought it was too big for the room since he liked to watch TV in here."

"I'm not surprised. Nothing goes to waste here on the Shore." His eyes were bright as he ran his hand over the satiny finish of the writing surface. "What a great place to work!" There were slight indentations from someone's work long ago, but all in all, it was smooth. "You've got all the cubbyholes to hold notes, a flat surface to scribble on and a view of the water. It's a perfect place to write a story."

"How do you know I'm thinking about writing a book?" I demanded.

"Um, Mr. Saffire said you were going to try your hand at writing. Kind of a far cry from your old career, isn't it?"

"What do you mean, *my old career*?" I was getting agitated.

TJ looked like he would rather be back in the fields than talking to me. "Mr. Saffire said something about ..." He seemed to struggle to remember. "Yes, he said you were a kindergarten teacher in Philadelphia."

"Yes, I was... and I still am." My hackles were up. Why was I so defensive every time someone mentioned teaching? Did they know something I didn't know? Was I that afraid that my injury wouldn't allow me to return to the classroom I loved?

TJ's eyebrows shot up in surprise. "Oh, sorry. I was under the impression that you'd resigned and moved down here to the Cottage permanently."

"I love my job," I assured him. "I've taken extended leave until I finish my rehab."

"You need to get your body back in shape if you're going to keep up with kindergarteners," he said with a bit of admiration I thought.

"Don't I know it." I didn't want to be reminded how much work I still had to do to get ready for the classroom. "I love my job. I love the children."

"You must miss them."

I nodded with a soft smile. "You have no idea." I touched the hollow at my neck for the necklace. I swayed a bit and leaned on the desk for support.

TJ pulled the chair up behind me. I sank into it gratefully. Then spotted the mysterious letter where it had landed on the floor. I didn't want the inquisitive TJ to see it so, I scooted it under the desk with my foot where I could retrieve it later. "Thanks for your help, but I really don't need to sit down."

He shrugged. "Moving takes a lot out of a person and I mean anybody. Might as well rest while you can." His eyes wandered over the desk. "This desk seems perfect for writing. If you look, you might even find a hidden compartment or two."

"You seem to know a lot about this desk," I said.

"I recognize the design. It looks like an original desk used by a plantation manager. He'd work here to keep the books of crops planted, costs, market prices, slaves—bought and sold."

"Slaves?" My eyes grew wide. "No! Maryland was a Northern state, part of the Union."

"Officially, yes. In reality, the part of the state east of the Chesapeake Bay had plantations as self-sufficient as they were in the South. They raised everything from corn and wheat to chickens, cattle for meat and dairy, even tobacco. The Eastern Shore had more in common with the rebellious South than the Union North. The landowners had slaves who took care of it all, everything from crops to the owner's daughter. Who knows what secrets this old desk is keeping?"

His next question caught me off-guard. "What are you going to write?"

It was an innocent question, but my defenses went up again, stronger than ever. "I'm working on several ideas," I hedged.

"Maybe I can help," he said, with a smile. "There are—

"I don't want any help." *Boundaries.* "I'm sorry. That was rude. I think I need to see what bubbles to the surface of my imagination."

He held his hands up in submission. "Okay, then. Don't want to step on your creative toes."

"Thanks. I appreciate that."

He headed toward the hallway and the front door. "Well, I guess I better get to the hardware store and get those new locks. I'll be back this afternoon if that's okay."

I nodded, afraid to open my mouth again. How many times could I bite his head off before he went away?

He paused. "They say that writers need writer friends. There's a nice group of ladies you might want to meet. Think about it." As he headed down the hallway, he called out, "And don't forget to set the deadbolt."

I heard him close the door. *Please, just change my locks so I can keep out unwanted visitors, especially a man named Daniel.*

CHAPTER FOUR

"I did not visit the place of execution but went from the Easton Gaol to my office feeling sad over the scene. This has been a lovely spring day. The frogs, leather winged bats and spring birds have made their appearance." March 12, 1875

—The Willis Family Journals 1847-1951
Edited and Annotated by James Dawson

I leaned over and found the letter from Daniel that I'd pushed under the desk. Yes, it was still there, not a product of my painkiller-fueled imagination. Maybe closer inspection would give me a clue to the man's identity. The words were scratched on in a sheet of my white printer paper in an odd shade of brown ink. The writer hadn't used a pen with a smooth modern nib. A bell was ringing from a corner of my memory. Had this Daniel used a pen with a metal nib that he had to keep dipping in ink? It all reminded me of the time of Daguerreotypes and ladies in hooped skirts. Plantation days.

That's ridiculous, I scolded myself. I was about to drop the letter in the wastepaper basket and paused. *No, I think I'll keep it for now.* Standing, I reached up and slipped it into the cubbyhole on the top row. I plopped back in the chair, feeling satisfied that I was in charge again. But that feeling didn't last.

Once again, there was loud knocking at the front door of the Cottage. It didn't sound like a polite neighbor bringing muffins. Somebody wanted my attention, *now.*

"I'm coming," I yelled out as I fumbled with my crutches. As I made my way down the hallway, I realized I hadn't heard TJ's truck horn. When I reached the door, I didn't open it.

"Yes, who is it?" I asked.

"Miss Emma, it's TJ and a friend."

When I opened the door, I was surprised to discover his friend was a member of law enforcement.

"Sorry to bother you again. This is Officer Conklin. There's something he needs to talk to you about."

I opened the door wide. "Why don't you come in?"

"No, no need. I just have a few questions for you." The officer looked young, but something about him suggested that he had seen more, done more, trained for more than I wanted to know.

I moved over to the step to sit down. Who would have thought the stairs to the second floor would be a convenient resting spot. "Hope you don't mind. Standing tires me out quickly."

"Of course, ma'am." He moved into the doorway. "I'm glad you're here, too, TJ. Saves me a trip to your house."

"What's going on?" he asked.

"Has either one of you been over at the Lone Oak, digging around?" He glanced at me and, seeing the crutches, quickly dismissed me as a candidate for a digging expedition. He redirected his attention to TJ.

"No, I haven't been over to the old tree for a while." His face filled with concern and his speech took on a bit of a Southern lilt. "Is it okay? Do I need to bring in the tree doctor?"

"No, the tree isn't the problem," the officer said. "There are holes dug all around the tree. It doesn't make sense."

"Sounds like someone was looking for something," I suggested.

"More like *someones*. I figure there had to be at least one other person," he said.

"Why do you say that?" I asked.

"Because someone hit Kid Billy in the face with a blunt object, maybe a shovel. We found him this morning, lying with his body in one of the holes. He's in the hospital and it doesn't look good for the boy."

I gasped. "How old is he?"

The detective shrugged. "Only seventeen. This is one of life's cruel jokes."

I looked at the tree across the creek, out in the middle of nowhere. "How did you find him? I imagine not a lot of people go over there."

"We got an anonymous call on the Tip Line, probably from somebody who was there or heard someone talking about it afterward."

"Drugs?" I asked.

The officer looked at me quickly. His eyes narrowed. "Why does everybody from the Western Shore jump to that conclusion. Sure, we have problems here, but it's not like *over there* where you're from."

"I only meant—"

He folded his arms and spread his feet apart. He was spoiling for a fight I didn't want. "How do you explain all the holes around the tree? Think they were going to bury the drugs for safekeeping?"

Both TJ and I stared at the officer.

With a great huff born of frustration, he dropped his arms by his sides. "I'm sorry. We don't normally get this level of violence. If that call hadn't come in, the kid would have died out there in the field."

I glanced across the creek again and shuddered. If I'd left the windows open the night before, I might have heard voices, angry

27

ones. If someone hadn't called it in, I could have been looking at a corpse while I had my morning coffee. Was Daniel involved? A shudder ran through me.

"I've got almost nothing to go on," the officer continued. "Did either of you see anything?"

TJ shook his head. "If it happened late at night, I wouldn't. I go to bed really early."

I piped up. "I don't think it means anything, but I saw a light late last night across the creek. It was there for only a minute then it was gone."

The officer pounced. "What time did you see it?"

I had to think. "I'm not sure. I'd say around midnight. I saw the light as I was going upstairs."

"Where did you see it? Can you show me?"

"Sure, I locked the front door and saw the light through one of the living room windows." I pointed.

The officer and TJ exchanged looks.

"What? Did I see something important?" I wanted to know.

A message passed silently between the two men then the officer said carefully. "No need to jump to conclusions." He reached into his pocket and pulled out a business card. "If you see a light again or anything unusual, you give me a call or call 911, okay?"

I stifled a laugh. "I'm sorry, officer. TJ tells me that I need to rely on smoke signals until the telephone installer comes."

He looked at TJ. "Dead spot?" My handyman nodded. "Well, maybe I can get them to rush the order along. A person out here alone and in your condition should be able to call for help, if you need it."

I'd feel better if I had access to the outside world. I should never have cancelled Uncle Jack's service, an unnecessary expense, but who knew I'd be living here.

The officer said, "Well, I'd better get going, I have other stops to make. Nice meeting you, ma'am. And don't forget to call if you see or need anything…when you get a phone, that is."

I thanked him and watched as TJ walked him back to his car.

Even though the officer was trying to speak softly, I heard him say, "She's a sitting duck out here all alone."

I bristled and called out. "No, I am not." To add gravity to my declaration, I got to my feet. Sadly, it took a lot of effort and emphasized how weak I was. I didn't let that hold me back. "TJ is going to change all the locks today."

TJ shrugged. "I was on my way to the store when I saw you turn in."

"I'll have the only keys," I announced. "So, no one will be able to get in unless I open the door, sir. And I'm not opening the door for anyone I don't know." I gave him a big smile. "Anyway, I need to be here. You know these old houses need care, especially as the weather gets cooler. We don't want any broken pipes, now do we?"

The officer shook his head slowly. "Ya know, TJ can take care of things like that. Maybe you should go back to where you came from. No disrespect, ma'am."

"Of course, but I'm not going anywhere. Uncle Jack left me the Cottage." I felt my face getting hot with irritation. Did everyone believe they knew what was best for me?

The officer assumed a more conciliatory tone. "What I meant, ma'am, was that you might go back home until we get this figured out, for your own safety."

"Nice idea, but I can't go home. I don't have one to go to." Both men looked at me. "I sublet my condo. The new tenants wouldn't appreciate an uninvited guest."

The officer adjusted his belt with all the gadgets necessary for policing today. "Fine, be careful and lock your doors, at least until we find out what happened and why."

He got into his car and while he drove down the long lane to the main road, TJ sprinted up my front steps. "Don't worry. It was probably kids roughhousing." He flashed me a big plastic smile.

"A shovel in the face sounds like big trouble to me," I said.

"Well, if you need anything, remember, I live just up the road."

"Close enough for me to holler, at least until I get my phone?"

He took off his cap, ran his hand through his hair and pulled the cap down tight again. "Tell you what, if you need anything, turn on all your lights. The Cottage should shine like a Christmas tree in the dark. If I see that, I'll come running. Deal?"

I smiled. "Deal." Somehow, this handyman had a knack for making me feel better.

CHAPTER FIVE

"In Memoriam"

—*How to Write Letters*
by Professor J. Willis Westlake, 1883

With TJ on his way to get the new locks, I swung myself on my crutches back to the desk and sank into the comfort of the soft leather chair. I willed myself not to look up at the cubbyhole that held the letter.

I'm here to write a book and get strong, not *worry myself into a tizzy about a childish prank.* My chuckle sounded weak and unconvincing. Despite my best intentions, my eyes wandered toward the letter. I clasped my hands together and squeezed hard to keep me in the here and now. I took a deep breath and took out a small stack of papers that needed attention concerning Uncle Jack's affairs.

I made a note to get the boiler checked and arrange a fuel oil delivery schedule for the winter. I'd be here until March when the sublease on my condo would end. There were legal documents that I set aside.

At the bottom of the stack was an envelope addressed to me. Mr. Saffire said Uncle Jack had written me a letter when he signed his will. I'd put off reading it, not feeling ready for the emotional ride it promised. Now, it seemed like an easy thing to do in comparison to starting a book or tracking down my secret letter writer. I carefully tore open the flap and unfolded the handwritten letter inside.

My Darling Emma,

If you are reading this letter, I'm gone from your life, but not forgotten, of that, I am sure. You are my one constant I could always depend on.

No matter how many playmates or soccer games you had, no matter how many courses and assignments you had to complete, and the boyfriend demanding your attention, you always had time for your Uncle Jack.

With due respect to your mother, my sister, I've always thought of you as my daughter. Whenever she came to the Cottage in the summer, she'd stay inside with the air-conditioning turned up, while you and I played at the water's edge in our bare feet, watching the soft crabs molt out of their shells. Remember how we'd stand in the mud and squeeze it between our toes? You said it tickled. Your mother was appalled at the mess when we walked back into the kitchen.

I whipped a tear away with a flick of my hand. I'll never forget the look of dismay on my mother's face that day. She never got dirty, not ever.

How we grew up in the same family, I'll never know. I guess we're together now and will spend eternity hashing it out.

I blinked away another tear and read on.

Memories like that have made my life rich. That is why I've left the Cottage to you, and only you. It is a place that feeds your soul as it has fed mine. I never contaminated it with visits from my law partners or clients. I only welcomed those who felt its nurturing atmosphere. Every time you came, it was a joy. Though you tried to hide it, I saw the regret on your face when it was time for you to go.

Remember the time when your mother came to take you home? You didn't want the summer to end, so you crept down to the dock and climbed into my rowboat. I'm not sure where you thought you were going, but you untied the line and pushed off. It was the flailing oars that caught my eye as I poured some lemonade in the kitchen. By the time I got down to the water, the current had grabbed you and was taking you out to the river. You weren't afraid. I used the small sailboat to capture and tow you back. Thank goodness I'd put an outboard motor on it though it seemed like overkill.

You said the sailboat was like a knight's steed riding to the rescue of a damsel in distress. You always had an active imagination.

Now, darling Emma, I won't be there to save you, but I'm not worried. You've turned into a grownup I respect and admire. I hope you rediscover the joy you felt at the Cottage when you were a child. It will always be there for you.

> With all my love,
> Your Uncle Jack

P.S. There's an old desk in the garage.

My breath quickened.

> P.P.S. It is a Plantation Desk, used by the manager back when local farms were big operations. The plantation manager kept track of everything from that desk. When I bought the Cottage, the owner of Waterwood – the farm that surrounds my land – offered it to me at a sinfully low price. I couldn't turn it down, but I should have left it at Waterwood. Emma, the desk seems to be connected with a man named Daniel. That's all I know. it would be better to leave it in the garage.

Uncle Jack's letter slipped from my hand.
Daniel!
"Too late, Uncle Jack. Daniel and I have already met."

CHAPTER SIX

"Pleasure, interest, and duty equally demand that our friendships and social ties should be maintained and strengthened. In many cases, this can be done only by means of letters. No one would willingly lose out of his life the joy of receiving letters from absent friends, nor withhold from others the exquisite pleasure."

— *How to Write Letters*
by Professor J. Willis Westlake, 1883

I don't know how long I sat at the desk staring out the window at the ospreys zooming above the creek. Slowly, anger started to burn deep inside. Anger? No. Resentment. I resented how my life had been upended and how I was bouncing around like a tiny boat in a storm. It had started with a truck driver who was texting. He drove straight into me, demolished my car, and sent me flying on a helicopter to Shock Trauma.

For weeks and weeks, I was at the mercy of the doctors, their dour expressions, and the endless cycle of pills and surgeries. I had no choice but to follow their orders. They were working hard to save my life and then my leg. Those missions accomplished, they were determined to get me back on my feet, even if I thought it would kill me. When I shifted to the rehab center, it was a different kind of torture – physical torture in the excruciatingly painful therapy sessions and the mental torture of boredom. The painkillers wouldn't allow me to concentrate on reading a book, let alone teach children.

When I was allowed to go home, I felt like a convict let out on parole. If I didn't behave by taking things slowly, going to physical therapy sessions, doing the exercises, they'd throw me back in rehab.

The thought made me shudder. The joy of moving back home was short-lived. It was hard to sit at home with nothing to do, not that I could manage much. The aide took care of cleaning and cooking and getting me to appointments.

At first, I was happy to sit on the balcony of my city condo and feel the sun on my face. Then I started watching the people down below, clutching their briefcases and phones as they dashed around with someplace to go. I had no idea when I'd be able to slip back into my life again. That's when depression set in. I'd never been in analysis, but suddenly, I was sitting across from a stranger who asked, *Why do you think you're sad?*

I wanted to scream. *A troop of monkeys would know. Why don't you?*

When he offered me a prescription for even more medication, I knew I had to get away and focus on getting better... my way. The doctor was resistant, but his office found an outstanding physical therapy practice fairly close to the Cottage. The rest was a matter of organization and money thrown at the problem.

Now, sitting at this beautiful antique desk, an unseen adversary was trying to wrest control of my life away from me, again.

Not on your life, Buster or Daniel or whoever you are. You're messing with the wrong woman. This is my desk. I won't share it.

I pulled open a small drawer and took out my Waterman rollerball pen, another gift from Uncle Jack. I slid a small stack of paper in front of me to protect the wood while I block printed the words.

DEAR SIR,

WHO DO YOU THINK YOU ARE? I AM NOT YOUR DEAREST. YOU MUST NEVER WRITE TO ME AGAIN. DO YOU UNDERSTAND? NEVER!

EMMA CHASE

Under normal conditions, I would slide this note into an envelope, address it and stamp it for the mail. But this situation was anything but normal. How do I address a letter to an unknown person...or a ghost?

GHOST?

My skin went cold as if a chill breeze had blown over me. Ghost? Where had that idea come from? The rational part of me replied: What other explanation is there?

I sat very still in the chair. Who would know for sure? Thoughts of a medium, tarot card reader, even a priest, raced across my mind. Outside the window, a blue heron squawked its arrival on the creek. Its distinctive cry, like fingernails on a chalkboard, jerked me from those mystical thoughts.

No, I decided. That approach will only invite more strangers to the Cottage. Gossip would spread like wildfire. Whatever I did, I'd have to do on my own.

How do I send the letter to a ghost? I reached for the original letter from Daniel. Maybe if I put the two letters together on the desk, they would find their way back to the original sender.

I couldn't help but reread his original words:

If I may still call you my dearest...think so badly of me.
This war...deprivations...waiting...paper.
Assure you of my faithfulness now and always.

I scanned my terse response and crumpled the paper into a tight ball. Even though this stranger, this Daniel, was intruding on my life, he didn't deserve to be chastised. I'd accused my physical therapists of taking out their frustrations on my battered body. Now, I was about to do the same thing to someone else.

Never mind. He didn't deserve it. I took a blank page and wrote:

Dear Sir,

Please, who is writing to me?

Respectfully,

Emma

That was better. I put the pages together and placed them where his letter had first appeared. What happened to the two letters would tell me a lot. I sat back. I knew I was right when I told the doctor I didn't need the anxiety medication anymore. I bet he'd flip if he knew what I was doing now. I—

Two toots of a horn outside interrupted my revelry. Time to get back to the real world. TJ was back with the new locks. I pressed my palms to my eyes. Thank goodness I didn't say anything about the letter to him. It would remain my secret. I looked back at it and my response and wondered if I would hear from Daniel again.

CHAPTER SEVEN

"I am not at all in a humor for writing; I must write on until I am."

— *Jane Austen*

I was at the door by the time TJ walked up, juggling the new locks and his tools, followed by his enormous white dog.

"That didn't take very long," I said, trying to be gracious. "I appreciate you doing this so quickly."

"It's not a matter of choice now. We need to make sure you're safe."

I thought I saw him wince as if he didn't mean to be so honest. Somehow, the mysterious light I'd seen the night before didn't worry me as much now that TJ was taking care of the locks and I had dealt with Daniel.

"I'm sure I'll be fine. Again, I appreciate the work you're doing." I set off down the hall. "I'll be in my writing den if you need me."

"Have you started your book already?" He sounded impressed.

"I wish. I drafted a note or two. It's a start." I hid my smile. If only he knew my secret.

It didn't take long for frustration to replace my confidence. My computer and printer were connected and working perfectly, except for one minor detail. I had no connection to the internet. I didn't want to interfere with TJ's work so I went back to the desk and gazed out the window while some anti-virus scan ran on my computer.

"You're deep in thought."

I nearly jumped out of the chair.

TJ added his apology. "I'm sorry. I'm used to creeping around quietly because your Uncle Jack often fell asleep in his chair. I didn't like to wake him. I'll try to remember to make noise so you know I'm around."

And I had to remember that even though I'd lost my uncle, TJ had lost a friend. "That was considerate. I'm sure he appreciated it. I know I do."

He glanced at the whirling icons on my computer screen. "I thought you were working."

"I'd like to, but I need internet access."

"Don't worry," he said. "You'll be connected soon enough and I don't mean with dial-up."

"Thank goodness for that." We both laughed. He was easy-going and I liked that he treated me like a normal person. Not an invalid.

He went on to explain. "When the telephone guy comes to install your landline, he'll hook you up."

"I was beginning to think I'd have to use carrier pigeons."

He shook his head. "No, it's not that bad. Well, I'm done with the locks." He held out his hand. "And you need these." A collection of keys tumbled into my hand. "Those are the keys to all the locks." Slowly, he reached into his back pocket, pulled out a crammed key ring, and began to work one of them off the ring.

"What are you doing?" I asked.

"You said you wanted all the keys." He kept working the key off the ring. "This is the key to the garage. Now, you'll have all the keys. I'll come to the front door so you can let me in." He handed me the key. "Your Uncle Jack was a good man and a good friend. He wanted me to look out for you and I will, if you let me."

Oh dear, did my face betray my concern? "No, I didn't mean I don't trust you. I'm used to being on my own, that's all."

"Yes, and being in control. I get that. Out here in the country, it's good to have friends looking out for you. Now that Jack isn't here…" His voice trailed off.

"In a way, he's still here because of my happy memories," I said with a sigh.

"I know what you mean." He looked away for a moment. "Well, anything you need, let me know."

I followed him to the front door and leaned heavily against the wall. I felt like I'd moved around more this one morning than during my entire stay in rehab.

"Thank you, TJ, for doing this work. Don't forget to give me the bill."

"Mr. Saffire has things under control." He opened the door and stepped outside. "The harvest starts next month, so if there's something that needs doing, it would be better to let me know soon."

He skipped down the steps and whistled. The white streak flashed through a forest of chestnut brown tree trunks then Ghost scampered to his master. After a vigorous scratch behind the ears, they headed toward the truck. That's when I had the feeling I was making a terrible mistake. Without thinking, I called out. "TJ! There's one more thing."

He came back to the bottom of the steps.

"I'm sorry, I…" I took a deep breath and started again. "A woman is entitled to change her mind. I just did. I'd like you to keep the key to the garage on your keyring," I looked into his hazel eyes and I was sure. "And a key to the Cottage." To lighten the moment, I held out the abundance of keys he'd handed me only moments ago. "Only you're going to have to figure out which ones they are."

He picked through the collection, pulled the padlock key, and one more. "I believe this is the one to the front door." He tested it. "Yes, got it in one."

"Now, put them on your keyring," I said, trying to sound very serious, as if I'd never doubted him for an instant. "And use them whenever you need to."

"Yes, ma'am. Whatever you say," he said with a wink.

A cloud of dust making its way down my gravel driveway caught my eye. "More visitors?" I groaned.

A sleek white Jaguar sedan stopped behind TJ's truck and a small woman wrapped in an ensemble of white silk emerged. Yes, it was an ensemble – a snowy-white tunic top and flirty skirt of the palest gray. She could go to lunch at any New York City restaurant, but it was more than expensive clothes that made her remarkable. Her flawless skin had the luminescence of the inside of an oyster shell. She paused, no, posed by the car for a moment, then waved.

"Hello! I'm here, TJ," she called out as she stepped gingerly over the gravel, careful of her white high heels.

"A friend of yours?" I said so softly only he could hear.

He took a deep breath and waved. "Hello, Catherine. Good to see you again."

She tiptoed to the steps and gave him an air kiss on the cheek then flashed a million-dollar smile at me. "You must be Emma. I'm Catherine Carmichael from the writing group. TJ told me you're here working on a book and may be interested in some feedback. Our group is very good at that."

I shot TJ a dirty look while she took a breath. But he missed my reaction by looking off in another direction.

"I thought I'd pop by, introduce myself and invite you to come to our next meeting." She reached into her white straw tote and pulled out a large envelope. "I took the liberty of printing two of the pieces we'll review soon so you'll be able to join right in." She handed me the envelope with the complete confidence that I'd want them.

"I suppose you'll need a ride to the meeting." She flung her hand in the air to bat away a fly. "I'll be glad to pick you up."

TJ added, "And I'll give her a ride home afterward."

"Perfect. I'll send TJ all the information." Again, her hand touched his arm. "Do come, Emma, it will be fun to have new blood. Now, I must run." She called out over her shoulder. "Who knows, maybe we'll be reading your work soon."

As we watched her drive away, I hissed at TJ, "Blabbermouth."

"I have to go, too," he said. He sprinted to his truck before I could say anything else.

Boxed in, again.

CHAPTER EIGHT

"All wars are follies, very expensive and very mischievous ones: when will mankind become convinced of this, and agree to settle their difficulties by arbitration? Were they to do it, even by the cast of a die, it would be better than by fighting and destroying one another."

— *Benjamin Franklin*

My first full day at The Cottage was so busy, what with visitors, changing locks, the tedium of unpacking, and the fear and excitement of finding Daniel's letter. I made the tortuous climb up the stairs to bed right after dinner. My journal entry would have to wait.

The next morning, the sun streamed in the window at a very early hour, because I'd forgotten to pull the bedroom curtains. I turned over and put a pillow over my head until I remembered that an answer to my letter to Daniel could be waiting on the desk downstairs. I'd wanted a reason to get up in the morning that wasn't a medical appointment. *Now, I have one,* I thought with a sigh.

It felt like it took me hours to write my journal entry, shower and dress, but I had to get ready for the day first. There would be no running upstairs for me to change or get something. At least, not yet. When I thought I had everything and was ready to start the day, I went to the stairs and mumbled to myself each time I stepped down, *Go slowly. Don't fall.*

When I reached the bottom of the stairs, I was winded. It was going to take time to get my strength and stamina back. But there might be a letter waiting for me. *Slowly, slowly,* I repeated to myself. When I entered the den, I stopped in mid-step.

There, on the top of the stack, was a letter in flowing copperplate handwriting. I moved into the desk chair and reached for the letter.

Dear Emma,

Have you forgotten your childhood friend so quickly? Have you thrown away the love I offered you so truly? Have you buried the feelings you told me you would treasure for your whole life?

This war has killed so many young men. Even though I live, is our love and friendship only another casualty?

I did not leave your side by choice. I hope you know that in your heart. When your father told me that he felt he had to stand by his convictions and join the Confederacy, it was a dark day. When he asked me to attend him during the journey to the other side, I could not say no.

I wanted to stay with you, protect you from the cruel aspects of this war, but no matter what my conviction is, I had to stand with him. After all the things that your father has done for me and my father, it was the right thing to do. You said you agreed with me. You said it brought you comfort that I would be with your father, attending to his needs and protection during this difficult time. Have you changed your mind? I know it's been a long time since I've been able to write to you, but I am here now. I hope you will accept me into your life again.

Your humble servant,
Daniel

It had happened again. I guess I should have been terrified of such a bizarre happening. Instead, I settled back in the chair to consider the contents of the letter. There was no question in my mind now. I was not the Emma who was the object of Daniel's affections, but who was she? It didn't feel right that he was writing to me in such an intimate way. And who was Daniel? Uncle Jack's postscript about the desk kept me calm as I read the letter from a ghost. Because a letter from a ghost was exactly what I held in my hand, I was sure of it.

All good questions to consider, but not without coffee. As I nibbled a slice of cinnamon toast and sipped my second cuppa, I marveled at the difference in my reactions to Daniel's letters and this incredible situation. Yesterday, I ran around the house screaming—well, screaming in my head—looking for an intruder. This morning, I hurried down the stairs in anticipation of finding a response to my letter.

I looked out the window at the water, sky and majestic oak tree with its limbs spread wide and its green leaves fluttering in the breeze. It was a view that always gave me a sense of security. *I am vulnerable*, I admitted silently. *The important thing is, what are you going to do about it?*

The plan for physical therapy would help rebuild my body. What about Daniel? I could tell this Daniel person – or ghost – to Go Away! Would being dismissed make Daniel angry? Could he retaliate in some harmful way? I could have the desk moved back to the garage. I looked at the cubbyholes, slots, and small drawers and liked what I saw. Something about the organization and neatness appealed to me. Besides, if I buried the desk and its ghost under the tarp again, I'd deprive myself of something that might inspire my story. I could feel my lower lip want to jut out in a pout. It was time to admit that I had absolutely no ideas for the book. A nurse had suggested writing about the accident and my recovery. "It might inspire others," she'd said. A shudder ran through me. The last thing I wanted to do was relive any moment of the past months.

I shifted my thoughts back to Daniel. I had to make a choice. Fear wasn't the emotion pushing me toward a decision. It was curiosity. Who was this man? Who was Emma? What had happened to them?

While I was pondering these questions, I heard strange scrabbling noises coming from the front door, quickly followed by intense knocking. Resigned to another onslaught of visitors, I called out. "I'm coming!" and assumed the position with the crutches firmly under my arms. The knocking continued until I threw the deadbolt and flung open the door.

"Yes, yes, what's so urgent?" I barked.

The short woman with her strawberry blonde hair pulled up in a bun on the top of her head jumped back. Her pear-shaped body made me think of the children's rhyme about something wobbling, but it wouldn't fall down. I had to fight the urge to laugh.

"Oh, thank goodness," she sputtered. "I thought I'd been

locked out and I ask you, how am I to do my job if I can't get into the kitchen."

Her non-stop talking made me think that no amount of coffee would have prepared me for the arrival of this magpie. She hustled past me with grocery store bags dangling from her arms. She was half-way down the hall, when she suddenly stopped, turned around oh so slowly, and looked at me.

Her voice cracked with a mixture of fear and embarrassment. "You're not Miss Emma, are you?"

Not every out-of-the-way house has a person on crutches standing at the door. I didn't want to scare her away, if she was Maria, hired to shop, cook, and clean.

I gave her a weak smile. "Yes, I'm afraid I am."

Her eyelids closed slowly and she looked like she wanted to sink right through the floor.

"Let me guess, you're Maria," I said gently.

All the bags rustled as she held her arms wide and announced, "Yes, that would be me."

"I understand you're my angel of the kitchen and all things domestic. Welcome!"

She smiled with relief. "I don't know about that," she said. "But I'm here to take care of the house and your meals, Miss Emma." Her rising comfort level showed as her sentences got longer. She seemed like one tough lady, but the glittery eye shadow above heavy black lashes showed she had a girly side. She cocked her head and narrowed her eyes in confusion. "So, if you know who I am and why I'm here, why did you lock me out? I can't do anything standing outside."

"It's my fault. I had TJ change the locks on the doors yesterday." I shrugged. "It wasn't personal."

"Well, I'm sure glad you're home. I thought I was going to have to take all this food back to my house. It's not cold enough yet to leave it on the steps." She huffed and turned toward the kitchen with her bundles. "People in my town always leave the kitchen door unlocked, so a neighbor can drop in or get something like I did last night. I was making a pot of chili only to find I was out of chili powder, so I went next door to Helen's, took her chili powder, and finished up my dinner, but don't you worry, because I'll replace what I took. That's the way we do things here on the Shore."

I could tell it was going to take some effort to decipher those long, run-on sentences. As they kept coming, she bustled around the kitchen, reporting on the items she'd brought as she placed them in cabinets and the fridge.

"I wish I could help you put away the groceries," I said.

"Ha! This ain't nothing. There are more bags in the car. And Honey, if you could carry the bags and put away the food, I'd be out of a job. You do your stuff and I'll do mine. We straight on that?"

"Yes ma'am, we're straight."

She took the bottle of painkillers from the table. "What about these?"

I stepped forward without thinking and started to wobble. It was embarrassing for her to see how unstable I was, but she was at my side with a firm grasp on my arm.

"Thank you," I mumbled.

Maria ignored my moment of weakness and shook the pill bottle. "Where do you want to put these pills so you remember to take them on time because you need to stay in front of the pain as the nurses like to say." She inspected my face. "You did take your pills this morning, didn't you?"

I wanted to say yes, but I braced for the lecture that would come when I shook my head.

"No, eh?" She tapped the top of the chair, the unspoken instruction to sit down, and she pulled a glass from the cupboard.

Dutifully, I sat down. Instead of a lecture, Maria handed me a full glass of water and the pill bottle minus the top. I took the pill with a sip and tried to hand her the glass.

"Nope, drink it all. It helps it work somehow, I don't know how, but it does." She watched as I did. "Now, you must have a Smartphone of some kind, right?"

I pulled the useless telephone communication device from my pocket.

"Now, set an alarm for your next pill, so we won't have this problem again," Maria instructed.

Sometimes, good ideas come from the most unlikely places. I did as she suggested while she launched into a story about one of her uncles.

As I listened with half an ear in case there was a quiz, I realized that I'd missed something important about Daniel's letters. Hopping up on my crutches, I interrupted Maria's endless flood of words. "Thank you so much for coming. I'll get out of your way so you can get your work done."

I swung myself down the hall to my writing den and closed the door. Sitting at the desk, I laid the letters side by side. Yes, there they were, the clues I'd hoped to find.

In the first letter, he wrote about war: *This war has brought such deprivations down on our heads.* And again, in the second letter, he wrote: *This war has killed so many young men…join the Confederacy.* It was the time of the Civil War.

His reference to *my father* suggested that Emma was the daughter of the plantation.

His connection to the desk was clear: *I have sat here at my father's desk.* His sense of loyalty was strong: *After all the things that your father has done for me and my father, it was the right thing to do.*

These clues could lead to the identification of my ghost. I had to smile. Yesterday, Daniel was the source of fright. Today, I'd claimed ownership and the relationship between long-ago Emma and Daniel intrigued me.

I turned on my computer, opened my browser to start a search… and brought my fist down on the desk, hard. No connection. Maybe there was a coffee shop on the way to the physical therapy place.

Physical therapy!

My first appointment was today! If I didn't live up to my promise to show up for every appointment and follow the regimen, the doctor would insist I return to Philadelphia. If I deviated from the plan, the insurance company could cut off my coverage. And I wouldn't heal so I could resume my normal life. No, there was no option. I had to go to P.T.

I checked the printed schedule and looked at the clock. The driver Mr. Saffire hired to take me to P.T. appointments was late. I called out to Maria, who rushed in out of breath.

"Yes, what's wrong? Are you okay?"

I smiled as I shook my head. "I'm fine, but I'm going to miss my physical therapy appointment." I glanced at the clock. "Unless you drive me. Can you?"

"To where?"

"It's someplace in Easton." It was the county seat and center for medical services. "Where all the medical offices are, I think."

Maria stepped back and shook her head slowly in a wide arc. "No, no, ma'am. I can't do that."

"You have a car…"

"Yes, but I don't drive everywhere like you people on the Western Shore," she insisted. "I only go certain places. I do not go into downtown Easton where people drive like maniacs. Ever since all those stores came in—what do they call them—oh yeah, big box stores. It's getting to be a regular big city around here. Nope, I'll drive out here on the Bay Hundred and go to my grocery store, but not on those roads where everyone is in such a hurry or in those big busy parking lots with people fighting over spaces. No, ma'am."

"I'll pay you extra," I said, hoping she had a price I could afford.

She came over and stood right in front of me with one hand on her hip. "What part of *NO* didn't you hear? Now, if you want me to stop bringing in your food and— "

"N-n-no," I said quickly. I didn't want to lose her help. "No, I understand. And thank you for all you do."

"I haven't done much yet. Now, if I can get back to work." She headed out of the room but made a quick turn toward the front door. "But Mr. TJ might take you."

TJ? How did she expect me to contact—

Deep, rich tones floated in from the hallway. "Hello? Did I hear my name?"

The man had a sixth sense of knowing when to show up at the Cottage. He walked into the writing den. "I hope you don't mind. I honked."

"I'm late for a physical therapy appointment and need a ride. Could you—"

With a sweep of his arm toward the door, he said, "Let's go."

I looked down at my loose-fitting top and slacks. Not really what I'd usually wear to go out, but the thought of wrestling my way up the stairs, let alone the time it would take, spurred me into action.

"I'm ready," I said. "Let me get my wallet with all the insurance cards."

Maria had dashed out and appeared with it in hand.

"Okay, now we can go," TJ urged.

I glanced at the desk and saw that the two letters were sitting out so anyone could read them.

"Thank you, Maria. And TJ, I'll be right with you," I said, leaning against the desk, trying to hide the letters behind me.

"I thought you said you're late?" TJ insisted.

"Why don't you go and start your car."

"Truck," he corrected softly. "I have a truck."

"Fine, whatever. I'll only be a minute." It must have been the expression on my face that sent them moving in opposite directions.

Carefully, I stacked the letters and slipped them into a large cubbyhole with a few blank sheets of paper on top, in case someone got curious.

CHAPTER NINE

House Calls: "I sent for Doctor Matthews... who prescribed rubbing the extremities and down the back and on the stomach with whiskey and repeat it every half hour." March 10, 1862 "Doctor Matthews came to see Cassie who is sick in bed." February 9, 1863

—The Willis Family Journals 1847-1951
Edited and Annotated by James Dawson

TJ had to help me get up and into his truck. It wasn't like a sedan. I had to climb in, but once inside, I was surprised it had all the comforts of a town car. With the crutches stowed in the back seat with Ghost, his dog, we made our way down the drive.

"Sorry about how hard it was for you to get into the truck and all," he said. "I work on farms and need a rugged vehicle to drive into the fields and off-road. I could borrow a car if I need to drive you around."

"No, don't change things for me. With your help, I made it in fine. Maybe someday soon, I'll be able to spring into the cab all by myself."

"For your sake, I hope that day is soon." He made a wide turn as we swung onto the main road. The momentum gently threw me against him and I got a whiff of his good, clean smell. No sweet cologne or sweaty odor for this man.

He braked softly. "Sorry about that."

The movement of the truck unnerved me a little. I still wasn't comfortable being in a car, or truck, no matter who was behind the wheel. I tried to breathe and concentrate on my hands. I caught him trying to catch a glimpse of me. Once, twice.

Finally, I had to ask. "What, what is it? Why do you keep looking at me?"

He took a deep breath and blew it out slowly. "Sorry, I was trying to figure out if you'd mind if I said something."

"Go on, say it, say whatever you want." I was getting nervous as we headed to P.T.—physical therapy—or as I called it, Pain Today. I turned toward him and was struck by the sad, almost puppy-dog-look on his face. "I'm sorry. I'm nervous about starting with a new therapy practice. All they seem to do is hurt me. I didn't mean to take it out on you."

He glanced at me again, then grinned. "Maybe what I was gonna say is good for you to hear."

"So…?"

"Okay, first, I want to say that you don't have to hold on for dear life. I'm a good driver and we'll be able to see any trouble coming a mile away on this road if it's gonna come at all."

Beating down my fear, I peeled my fingers away from the bar and clasped my hands in my lap.

"That's better. Now, what I was going to say was that I'm impressed that you didn't blow off the appointment. You could have. You had lots of reasons for not going, like being late, no driver, too tired from the move—"

I stopped him. "I can't do that. I hate not being able to do what I want to do. This is hell for me. I'm used to being on my own, relying on myself. I want to get better. I have to get better.

That's why I came down here, and to preserve my sanity. Make me a deal. If I ever try to back out of P.T., make me go. I might not appreciate it at that moment, but I'll thank you later. I promise."

His tanned face moved into a big smile. "You've got a deal."

"Good."

I nestled into my seat to try and enjoy the ride. The Cottage was a magical place to be, but it wasn't immune from giving me cabin fever. Out here, there were no buildings of concrete and glass to block my view of trees still green with the life of summer and the gentle waters reflecting the blue sky. In spots, I could see for several miles. The land had been ground flat by the massive glaciers of the Ice Age. When they'd finally melted, they flooded the Susquehanna River and created what we know today as the Chesapeake Bay. Here, it was free and open. A wave of happiness went through me, something missing for a long time. I felt like dancing, but that would have to wait until I could stand on both legs.

A memory cropped up that might be very appropriate to share with TJ. "Going to P.T. like this reminds me of the times my dad took me to see the doctor when I was a little girl." A giggle escaped. "That's how I knew I was going to get a shot or something equally awful. Mom would always cry when I cried, so Daddy always took me. Then he spoiled me terribly."

"What did he do?" TJ turned down the air-conditioner.

"Oh, he'd buy me a toy or..." I hoped to plant a suggestion. "Or he would take me someplace special afterward, like the ice cream parlor, the playground, someplace that would make me forget the *trauma* I'd just experienced."

"That's nice," TJ said.

The guy couldn't take a hint. I tried again. "Since you think I was so good about coming to P.T., what about a reward?"

"Okay, I didn't think you'd be interested in a playground, but there's one—"

"No," I cried, "Not a playground!" Was this man dense... or teasing me?

"Okay, okay, I was just playing. Where would you like to go?"

"Is there a place where I could learn about the history of this area?" I asked.

He shot me a strange look. "What kind of history? Do you want to go to the Talbot County Historical Society?"

I stared at the road, trying to think. "That might be a possibility."

"No, that won't work. They're moving or something. I heard all the files are packed away."

Why is everything so hard, I almost screamed?

"Would the library do?" he asked. "There's a special reference area called the Maryland Room. You might find what you're looking for there."

I wanted to cry out with delight but, hoping to sound only vaguely interested, I said, "Yes, that sounds fine."

His next words made me tense up again. "What are you looking for?"

I could handle myself in the classroom, but I was a lousy liar in social situations. I wasn't going to tell him about Daniel and the letters. "Oh, I don't know," I began, hoping to sound nonchalant. "I'd like to find something out about this area and the people who lived here." I looked away toward the passenger window so my face wouldn't betray me.

"Well, I can tell you that *this area* is called the Bay Hundred. That comes from the Revolutionary War. The—"

I interrupted. "What about the Civil War?"

Way to go, Emma. That was about as subtle as a sledgehammer.

I tried to backpedal quickly. "I mean, I was surprised to hear that Waterwood was a plantation and had slaves. Somehow, I only equate that with the Deep South."

"Oh, there were plenty of Southern sympathizers here. The landowners had more in common with the Confederacy than the Union. But the librarian can tell you all about that. He'll probably load you up with all kinds of books." He wet his lips. "There's something else I wanted to talk to you about." He was hesitant to continue. "You didn't tell me about the light you saw the other night."

"No, I didn't think it was important," I said, shaking my head.

"If you see anything else, anything out of the ordinary, will you let me know?"

I shrugged. "Sure, but to be honest, I figured it was a car or truck on the road."

"I think it's a good thing we changed the locks." His tone was lighter. "I can tell you now that the locks were old. A nudge on one of those doors could have been enough to pop it open."

I thought back to the appearance of Daniel's first letter. I'd thought someone had broken into the Cottage and left it as a prank. It was a good thing I didn't know about the door locks.

"It's all taken care of now," he assured me. "You're safe. No one can get in."

Right. If you only knew.

He must have sensed my thought and looked over at me. "There's nothing to be afraid of."

"Thanks to you," I said quickly.

"And we have to let Mr. Saffire know that your driver didn't show up."

I listened to him with half an ear as I thought about how to handle the research into Daniel and Emma without revealing the truth. No ideas were popping up.

"Earth to Emma, are you still with me?" TJ called me back from my thoughts.

"Yes, that's a good idea," I said.

"Because it's important to stay on your weight loss program," he added.

"Yes, good idea. Wait, what?"

"Caught ya. You're a million miles away. That's okay. You've got a lot going on. I'll pick you up after your session and take you to the library. We might even find an ice cream cone along the way."

I couldn't help but smile. Then I groaned. "But first, I have to respond to my attorney's emails." I pulled out my phone and checked the bars. "At least I have service. The sooner I get this done…" Quickly, my eyes ran through his messages. More administrative stuff. I tapped out a quick response and put the phone away with a sigh. "Done."

"Good. Why don't we just enjoy the sights for a while? We don't have to talk. You can think your thoughts, okay?"

"Yes, thanks."

I wasn't sure what I was going to say to the reference librarian. I didn't want anyone to suspect anything. I made a mental note to look up information about the writing styles and writing instruments in the 1860s. The beautiful pen Uncle Jack had given me was used mostly to sign my name. I kept almost every note electronically now. It would be good to know how they wrote to one another in the Civil War era, in case I decided to assume the persona of Emma from long ago. What a strange thought. But oddly comfortable.

CHAPTER TEN

Farmer's Almanac: "Useful, with a pleasant degree of humor."

First issued in 1792 during George Washington's first term.

It seemed like hours before I escaped the torture chamber of physical therapy. I knew that I was being unfair. The therapists were only helping me, but why did making you better have to hurt so much? I scanned the parking lot looking for TJ, only to find his truck tucked into the only shady spot, but it was so far away. For someone else, it was only some quick steps. For me, it bordered on a never-ending trail of ouch. I tried to focus on him, rather than the hurt. He was reading a small magazine propped up on the steering wheel. When I was feet away from the truck, he noticed me and jumped out to open the passenger door.

"All done?" he asked, as he helped me up to wiggle into the seat.

"Yeah, finally." I tried hard to hide the face I knew I was making when my leg hurt.

When I was settled, he searched my face as if looking for some cosmic answer. I felt uncomfortable under his scrutiny.

"Are you okay?" he asked tentatively.

"Well, other than feeling like I've been hit by a truck *again*, yes, I'm fine."

He nodded, though I could tell he wasn't convinced. He closed my door and got into the truck. "I think you've earned that ice cream cone."

His thoughtfulness brought me some comfort. "Yay! Thank you for bringing me and waiting. I'm sorry it took so long and that I'm in such a bad mood."

"No problem. I'm glad you came in August. If you'd waited any longer, I would have been a ghost."

Strange, I thought, *that he would use that word.* I asked, "Why?"

"That's harvest time. I only eat, sleep and harvest for weeks. Right now, I have the time and I'm glad to help. Let's get you some ice cream."

It had been years since I'd been to a Dairy Queen. All their unusual concoctions on the menu were tempting, but I settled for a single scoop of chocolate with chocolate jimmies. With all the inactivity over the past months, excess calories were building up in critical areas. I didn't want to diet to wear the clothes in my closet once I got back on both feet. The jeans skirt and loose yoga pants I'd been living in hid a multitude of sins. But it was nice to sit in his truck and talk for a few minutes while we ate an icy cold bit of heaven.

"What were you reading when I came out of P.T.?"

He whipped out a slim magazine with an orange and green cover that I'd seen stuffed in the back pocket of his jeans. "It's the Farmers' Almanac. I was checking on the weather forecast for the upcoming weeks."

"Really?" *What a strange man.* "Wouldn't it be better to use a weather app and watch the radar?"

He held up his index finger to slow me down. "Don't dis the

Almanac. It's been right on the money with its winter forecasts. It's right more times than not."

I shook my head, not buying into his argument. "Sorry, I prefer technology like satellites."

"The Almanac has got weather forecasts and lots of good information." He flipped to a page and read. "Abraham Lincoln read the Farmers' Almanac."

"He didn't have a Smartphone and apps back then," I countered.

"He didn't use it for farming. He used it to win a murder trial. According to this article, he showed the jury that the moon was low in the sky on the night of the murder. There was no way the prosecution's chief witness could have seen the murder committed by the light of the moon. It's got lots of interesting factual tidbits like that."

"Speaking of facts, do you think we could go to the Maryland Room now before I collapse? The physical therapist wore me out."

Quickly, he started the engine and we were on our way. The library was a charming brick building with a landscaped courtyard at the entrance. I would have preferred the front door closer to the curb, but it was like an oasis in the middle of town. TJ escorted me through what he described as the newly renovated reading areas, offices, and stacks. It seemed very well stocked for a small-town library. I chastised myself for thinking like a big city girl. I didn't come to the Eastern Shore for big city living. This library had something very different to offer: historical information about Talbot County, where the Cottage, and Waterwood Plantation were located. Besides, if I were at the Central Philadelphia Library, I couldn't navigate its many floors and miles of walkways.

The thought of unraveling the mystery of Daniel and Emma put a smile on my face. Fortunately, it masked my surprise at seeing the woman at the librarian's desk. She was young and radiated energy. She wore jeans, but her outfit was more of a coordinated jeans pantsuit. The jacket was embroidered with lots of colorful flowers. Her hair and makeup were perfect for a fashion magazine photoshoot. The red-framed eyeglasses were the only thing that fit with the stereotype of a librarian. I shook off that old simplified and uncomplimentary image just in time to hide my confusion.

She looked up and smiled. "Hello, how may I help you … TJ!" She slipped off her glasses.

His eyes were wide with surprise. "Stephani?" Then he frowned in confusion. "What are you doing here?"

"I'm working here as an intern, thank you very much." She put her glasses on again with a little defiance.

"But I thought you were—"

"Doing hair?" She shook her head back and forth so her sleek cocoa brown hair swung gently in a perfect shape. "Oh no, I don't do that anymore."

TJ rubbed his chin. "But you were so good and—"

She cut him off again. "I wanted to do something worthwhile, so here I am. Her eyes flitted over to me and bore in.

"Hello, I'm Emma Chase. I just moved into my Uncle Jack's Cottage down in—"

"I know who you are." She flashed a million-watt smile. "News travels fast around here. Welcome to the Shore and to our library. What can I do to help you?" A quick glance at TJ seemed meant to dismiss him.

"I'm looking for information about the Cottage," I said quickly.

TJ touched my arm. "Are you all set?" I nodded. "Then I'll leave you ladies to it. I'll be back in about an hour."

Stephani pulled out a sturdy wooden chair at a large library table in the center of the room. "Why don't you sit down? Using crutches can be exhausting. We'll discuss your research plan."

I was grateful for her consideration and slid onto the chair while she got a pen and paper to take notes.

She asked, "Do you want to do a genealogical search of your uncle who left you the Cottage?"

"Ah, no, not exactly. I'd like to know about the land where the Cottage sits. It is surrounded by a place called Waterwood."

Stephani's pen stopped moving. "Waterwood?"

"Yes, is that…"

She rose from her chair and hustled to a tall filing cabinet in the corner. After a little searching, she returned with a thick manila folder. "Let's start with the file on Waterwood, a well-known and old property in Talbot County. You can use my pad, but next time you should bring your own."

"Oh dear, I appreciate that you found all this material, but I'm afraid I don't have time to page through it all. TJ will be back soon. As you can see, I'm not in the best shape, recuperating from an accident. I don't suppose…"

Slowly, she shook her head. "I'm afraid the file material can't leave this room. I'm sorry. If I could bend the rules, I would."

My face drooped from disappointment as I gazed at the file.

Quickly, she added, "We have a new machine that will allow you to scan any piece to an email and it's free."

I checked the antique Grandfather clock in the corner of the reference room. "I have a little time before TJ comes back to drive me home."

She helped me work through the file and found a few examples of letters written during the Civil War. Looking carefully at the handwriting, I got an idea. By the time TJ walked into the Maryland Room, copies of many documents were on their way to my email inbox.

"TJ, can you give us a few more minutes?" Stephani asked.

"Sure," TJ said, looking a little uncomfortable.

"Good, I'd like to give Emma a few books she might find interesting, books that circulate." She headed out of the room then turned back with the grace of a ballerina. "You do have a library card with us, don't you?"

Oh, how I hate red tape and bureaucracy.

I started to explain my situation when TJ interrupted. "Can you check them out on my card?" He asked, reaching for his wallet. "She's visiting. I'll make sure the books come back on time."

Stephani took his card with a slight smile. "Of course." She leaned closer to him. "It will be our little secret."

While we waited for the stylish librarian to return, I thanked TJ for ferrying me around and sharing his card.

He had a mischievous look on his face. "You looked surprised when I suggested you use my card."

"I did not."

He put his hands on his hips and said playfully, "I want you to know that this farmer/handyman uses the library a lot."

Stephani returned, bearing a plastic bag from a grocery store. "I made several selections for you based on your interests. I took the liberty of bagging them so you can keep everything together." She winked at TJ. "We wouldn't want anything to get lost."

TJ took the bag without a word.

I stood up on my crutches. "Thank you so much for your help."

"I hope you'll come back soon and tell me how you're doing with your research. I'm here most days. In the meantime, I'll see what else I can find." She turned to TJ. "And you can come back, too. It would be nice to see you again."

After we said good-bye and headed to the main door, I was bursting to ask how he knew the pretty librarian, but he deflected that topic.

"Why the sudden interest in our history?"

I pulled up sharply, almost teetering on my crutches, and had to think fast. "If I'm going to be living here, I thought I'd learn something about the area. It will add to the stories Uncle Jack used to tell me as a kid. That's all. What else do I have to do?"

TJ shrugged. "Oh, I don't know. You could work on your book?"

"Ideas are percolating. Besides, everyone knows how important research is to a writer. It triggers ideas, builds a storyline and the development of a character, you know, that kind of thing."

"So, you're writing about the Eastern Shore?" His interest in my book was getting irritating, especially since I had no clue about the story.

"Wouldn't you like to know?" I started propelling myself forward, hoping to put an end to the subject of our conversation.

He stood in place. "Yes, I would like to know."

Getting no response, he caught up with me and we walked to the truck where Ghost met us with one deep-throated bark. It made TJ smile, but it startled me so much that I wobbled dangerously on my crutches. TJ shot out a hand to steady me.

"Easy there." Concern colored his voice. "Guess you haven't spent a lot of time around dogs. Ghost was just saying hello, saying he is glad we're back."

I could only nod. I was worn out. My nerves were frazzled. Thinking about Daniel and reading about the times when he and Emma lived had taken a toll as well. I climbed into the truck, leaning hard on TJ's support. As I let out a long sigh, my ringing cell phone made me jump. My obnoxious attorney had shattered my moment of relaxation.

CHAPTER ELEVEN

"You have to write the book that wants to be written. And if the book will be too difficult for grownups, then you write if for children."

—Madeleine L'Engle

As TJ opened the driver's side door, I said, "I'm sorry, I have to answer this call while I have phone service."

He walked away to give me some privacy as I touched the screen of my phone. "Hello, Mr. Heinrick."

"Hello, Ms. Chase. I thought I would call and see how things are going for you."

I was so surprised by my attorney's polite attitude that I pulled the phone away from my ear to check the caller ID. Yes, it was him. Had he had a personality transplant?

Stop it! I ordered myself. *He's not supposed to be a friend. He needs to be tough, so I get the compensation I deserve. Be nice!*

"Thank you for asking, Mr. Heinrick. I'm doing quite well. And it is probably time for you to call me Emma. After all, you've seen my most intimate medical records." I suspected that I'd made the man blush.

He cleared his throat. "Well, I— Yes, I suppose I have. Are the physical therapy sessions working well for you?"

"Yes, sir. I feel stronger every day. The therapist said I am doing well."

But the recovery isn't fast enough for me.

"I'm glad, but there's no reason to rush things. Your return to normal activities should be tempered." He stopped and cleared his throat. "I want you to progress, of course! But..." His voice trailed off. I knew he was thinking about the case and the proposed settlement amount. "You're not planning on going back to work yet, are you?" A tinge of worry was in his voice.

"No, not at all. I'm still taking some painkillers that don't make me behave well for little children. Also, I don't have my strength back. It will be a while, I'm afraid."

He tried to hide his relief by clearing his throat. "Tell me, how are you spending your time? Resting all day, I suppose."

"No, I get out and about. I don't need a long afternoon nap anymore." I paused, feeling unsure if I should let him in on my secret. Then, I figured, he was part of my life, at least for the time being. It might even improve our interaction. "Mr. Heinrick, I decided to do something while I'm here that I've wanted to do for a very long time."

"And what is that, Emma?" He was tolerating me as an uncle humors a little girl. When I didn't answer immediately, he repeated, "Emma?"

"I'm going to write a book." There it was. I found myself holding my breath for his reaction.

"A book?" he burst out. "What kind of book?"

"A story for children."

"Oh, a book for children. That's all. You—"

"What do you mean, *that's all?*" My back straightened as my defenses went up.

"Well, I—"

"Writing a book for a child shouldn't be something slammed

together." I was climbing on my soapbox about something dear to my heart. "A children's book deserves the best effort of the writer and I…" I wanted to say something more about writing a book, one a child deserved.

"Yes, yes, I understand. But I wasn't talking about the quality of the book. I was thinking about money. You don't expect to make a lot of money from writing this book, so if you want to do it as a hobby, that's fine. It won't have a bearing on the case or the settlement amount."

I was right. His priority was money. There was no reason for him to see my lack of confidence in my writing skills. Let him make the case, get the settlement, and I'd say good-bye.

"Now, my dear Ms. Chase. You must consider that your brush with death and all the mind-altering drugs they've given you have taken a toll. Please consider. Sit back and read a book. Don't write one."

Bravo, Mr. Heinrick, I thought. *Your bucket of ice water certainly hit the mark.*

"Thank you for that thought. I will keep them in mind. And now, I'm sure you have important things to do. Thank you for calling. Good-bye."

I should have felt a certain level of satisfaction when I ended the call, but I didn't. He had stoked the flames of self-doubt I'd been battling. I promised myself that I wouldn't discuss my goal with a naysayer. I hoped I could put a copy of my book in his hands someday. Of course, to do that, I needed a story and that was eluding me.

I touched the horn to let TJ know I was finished with the call. He walked back to the truck and got in.

"Let me guess," he said, starting the engine. "That was your favorite attorney."

"How did you know?" I feigned surprise.

"Well, your clenched fist was a giveaway. Forget about that guy and let Mr. Saffire and me take care of things on this end for now."

Relieved, I leaned back in my seat. TJ might have put his finger on the reason why I had no patience with Mr. Heinrick. He was the active connection with the accident that had almost taken my life, caused daily pain, and changed the way I lived. No wonder he had become a target of my wrath, though he was a pompous…

I saw TJ's quick look of concern. "You look all done in."

I rolled my eyes. "Do you say such flattering things to all the girls?"

"No, I mean it. What with the move and physical therapy, you—"

I couldn't let him finish. There was one more thing I wanted to do before we leave the town center. "Could we please make one more stop? Please. I promise to stay in the truck. You could go in and purchase two little items for me."

He looked at me from the corner of his eye, filled with suspicion. "You don't need some girly-girl thing or…"

I stifled a giggle. "No, nothing like that." He breathed a little sigh of relief. "Stephani said there's a craft store by the Amish Market wherever that is. I want to get a calligraphy pen and a bottle of black ink."

His eyebrows shot up. "Are you taking up calligraphy now? You'll have internet access soon."

"No, it's nothing like that." I tried a sweet voice to persuade him. "I only want to try something."

He shook his head as he put the truck in gear. "I swear I'll never understand women," he muttered almost to himself. "She's exhausted, but wants to stop for a pen and some ink."

He might not have approved, but minutes later, he handed me a paper bag with the items I wanted in it. He reminded me in typical easy-going TJ-style that he'd promised to make my life on the Eastern Shore as easy as possible. And he did.

I laid my head back and watched the passing countryside, planning my next move with Daniel.

CHAPTER TWELVE

"The first use of a form of the word *witch* was in c. 890 in the *Laws of Alfred* and referred to a man who practices witchcraft or magic."

—*The Oxford English Dictionary*

Riding along in comfortable silence, we drove past sun-kissed fields of corn and dark green soybeans. The beginning of an idea—about the Civil War, the divided state of Maryland, and life on the plantation—started forming. It was no wonder that after so much enforced rest, my brain was ready, eager to tackle any kind of problem. I snatched a pen sitting in the center console and started making notes. Out of the corner of my eye, I caught TJ trying to steal a look at what I was writing. Not ready to share any information about Daniel, I tucked the paper into a book.

"Yes?" I asked, sounding like the teacher who'd caught a boy with his hand in the cookie jar.

"I was wondering what you're scribbling. Something for your book?"

"Yes, as a matter of fact, it is."

"That's good," he said with a look of pride on his face. "I guess it helped that we went to the library. Research must be important when you're new to novel writing."

I bristled a little. It had been years since anyone had said I was *new* at something. No, that wasn't exactly right. It had been years since I started doing something so new that I didn't feel qualified to tackle it. Words didn't scare me. My minor in college was English because I'd always dreamed of writing a book for children. And now was the time.

"You're doing that thing again. Does your neck or throat hurt?"

"What?" I looked down and saw that my fingers were touching the hollow of my neck right where my necklace should have been. "No, I feel fine. It's just..." A sigh bubbled up from my toes. "Six years ago, I taught my first kindergarten class. Some of the mothers knew it was a dream come true for me. At the end of the year, the children—and their mothers—gave me a necklace with the initial "C" pendant for my last name to commemorate the event. I wore it every day." My breath caught at the memory. "Sometime between the accident, flight to shock trauma, ICU, and surgeries, the necklace disappeared and I miss it." I took a deep breath. "I guess you think it's a little childish. After all, it's only a piece of jewelry."

"No way," TJ declared. "It celebrated a major accomplishment in your life. Knowing it was there must have reminded you of your strength and determination. That's what has gotten you to this point."

"And where am I? At Square One with both my writing and my walking." *How pathetic.*

He shook his head thoughtfully. "No, I wouldn't say that. You're probably at Square Two or Three with your walking. Getting set up with the new therapists was a big step... ah, no pun intended."

I laughed and felt grateful. Since the accident, I'd lost my sense of humor and fun. Almost constant pain and the difficulty of getting around could do that to a person.

"And what I said about being new to writing, I didn't mean to insult you. The fact that you've started the work, well, you should be proud of yourself. For what it's worth, I'm happy to support you."

"Is that why you told Catherine to invite me to her writing group?" I conjured up an evil smile.

He winced. "I was only trying to help. There are a lot of talented and experienced people here who had amazing careers before they moved to the Shore. Some of them are still doing surprising things."

"Do they have internet access?"

"Well, it's funny you should mention the internet," he said, eager to change the subject. "I checked with the telephone company and the installer may show up tomorrow afternoon."

"That's wonderful." I sat up at hearing the good news. The sudden movement tweaked my leg and sent pain shooting through my body.

"Are you okay?" Worried, he pulled to the shoulder and stopped. "What can I do?"

"Nothing, nothing at all. I'll take a pill when I get home. It's a good thing Maria had me take one this morning before we left. I have to be more diligent about the pill schedule."

"You're starting a lot of new things. Don't let it get you down. You're on the right track."

I covered my eyes, hoping I could hold back the tears. Then I remembered a conflict with the schedule. "I have another P.T. appointment tomorrow. We didn't do a full workout session today because they needed to do evaluations. How am I going to be there for the telephone installer?" Things were getting complicated again.

"No problem. That's why you have Maria. I'll let her know after I take you back to the Cottage."

"Thank you," I whispered as I leaned my head back and considered this farmer/ handyman/philosopher. "Do you think you might be able to take me tomorrow again?" One of the hardest things for me to do was to ask for help.

"Sure, I have to check out a few things, but I can do that on the way back if you don't mind a detour?"

"It's an early appointment." I decided to push my luck. "Think we could go by the library again, please?"

He looked over at me. His eyes crinkled as he smiled. "Is this what it's like spending time with a budding writer?"

I gave him a shrug with one shoulder. "I guess."

"It depends how early this early appointment is. Is it *your* early or *my* early?"

"What do you mean?" I was confused.

"On the farm, I'm up by five o'clock, maybe earlier. During harvest, I barely see my bed."

I clutched my throat as a joke. "Five o'clock? In the morning? No, we're not doing that. The appointment is definitely *my* early…8:30."

"Ha! Middle of the afternoon." We laughed easily together. "Don't worry, we'll work it out."

When Mr. Saffire hired TJ to fix the house, I wondered if he chose him because he'd fix me as well. I sighed, hoping I had the energy to deal with two new men in my life—TJ and Daniel.

Back at the Cottage, TJ waited until I was inside. It felt good to lock the door and let the Cottage wrap its comfort around me. After taking a pill, I went directly to the desk, hoping to find another letter from Daniel. In a way, I was relieved there was nothing there. I still hadn't decided how to proceed. The library books fit on one of the desk's shelves like they were meant to be there. They all looked intriguing, but I pulled the book about legendary lore. It felt good to nestle into Uncle Jack's recliner. In moments, I was asleep.

Hunger pangs woke me about sunset. One ice cream cone did not make a satisfying lunch. Groggy, I went to the kitchen, convinced that dinner would be peanut butter and jelly. How wrong I was. Maria had left a treasure map of small slips of paper identifying the foil-wrapped and glass-covered dishes in the fridge: *Meatloaf, mashed potatoes, peas, two crab cakes, green salad and dressing.* Pitchers of lemonade and sweet tea sat on the top shelf.

Bless you, Maria. You are an angel. I wish you'd included dessert.

I should never have underestimated her. A plate of beautiful chocolate brownies sat on the counter. While dinner heated up in the microwave, I nibbled on a small piece of brownie that brought back a sweet memory. Uncle Jack always said one should never take a chance and always eat dessert first. Especially if it was chocolate. We only did that when my mother was not around. She would have yelled at us. Once the microwave dinged, I sat down to a feast with the book about Shore folklore for company. It took only a moment to realize that this was the happiest, most content I'd felt in the months since the accident.

Making the arrangements to sublet my condo, packing up most of my things, and moving down to the Eastern Shore, doing those things wasn't easy, but, at this moment, I was certain it was worth the energy. It sounded trite, but I felt it was meant to be. Months earlier, when they loaded me into a medivac helicopter, I got a glimpse of the tangled mass of steel and chrome that was once my car. At that moment, a spark of spirituality flared inside me. I couldn't have survived that impact without divine intervention. I didn't credit any organized religion, but I knew it was something greater than me. I'd whispered a thank-you in the quiet of my heart. I still had that feeling.

Feeling grateful for the here and now, I didn't leave a crumb on my plate. Maria was a miracle in the kitchen. If I kept eating like this, I'd blow up like a blimp, but I didn't care. It felt so right to have one more brownie. I poured a tall glass of milk to go with it. The pages of the book flipped to another section that was about the creek outside my window. When I saw the chapter heading, I swept my eyes over every part of the kitchen. Why did the book fall open to that page? Was the spine cracked at that place or had a ghostly hand given it a little help? It wasn't a good idea to read about creepy goings-on after sundown while sitting in the Cottage all alone, but I was curious. I sank into the chair and began to read about Virtue Violl, the witch who once lived across the creek from the Cottage by the Lone Oak. It was tedious to read a story reproduced with old spellings, like an *f* for an *s,* but I tried.

In the year of Our Lord 1712, a woman named Virtue Violl of Talbot County lived on the Point of land at the far end of the landowner's property, well beyond the Lone Oak that stood alone, as if it had scared away all the other trees. The new landowner did not need it. He had acres and acres of good soil to till so that the crops would take care of his family and add silver to his purse. Using his spyglass, he could observe the place where the old woman lived.

It was not a house. It was a hovel with slanted walls that barely held up a dilapidated roof. A strange light often appeared at night, moving around the Point. People believed she was signaling the dead.

I soon found I didn't have the energy to concentrate. Skimming it, I learned that Virtue was arrested for being a witch.

I closed the book, hoping to contain the disturbing story between its covers. I didn't want to look out to the point across the creek where the woman once lived. Did the people who lived nearby blame every bad thing that happened on that old woman? I guess life would be so much easier if you could blame someone else, especially if you believed in witches and ghosts.

My smile faded. *Believed in ghosts.* Until a few days ago, I would have dismissed that notion out-of-hand. If I couldn't see it, feel it, touch it, it wasn't real to me.

Until Daniel. I could see, feel and read his words on paper.

My crutches thumped as I went to the writing den. I took the letters down from the cubbyhole and slid the blank sheet aside I'd put on top to hide the letters underneath. I slid first one blank sheet then another and another. Had I dreamed it all? Was Daniel a product of a drug-fueled imagination? I checked the front and back of each sheet again. Blank. I moved a sheet off the short stack from the cubbyhole. Blank. Blank again.

Then there was a page with the words, *Dear Emma,* written at the top.

I was so relieved that I fell into the large leather desk chair. I hadn't dreamed it. I wasn't losing my mind. Once my breathing returned to normal, I picked up the letter and began to read it again. But no! This wasn't the letter I'd found only yesterday morning when I'd met Daniel. It was the letter that had appeared this morning on the desk. I leafed through the other sheets quickly. No, the first letter was not there. I examined the inked lines of his most recent letter and they seemed slightly faded. Then I realized what was happening.

Daniel's words were evaporating.

I spread out the sheets on the large writing area of the desk. I ran my fingers over every one of them. The surfaces were all smooth.

If the pen didn't leave a scratch on the skin of the paper, I reasoned, *perhaps the ink has not disappeared completely. Maybe there might still be a ghost of the words left there.*

Methodically, I held up one piece of paper after another to the light of the lamp, hoping to see a trace of Daniel's writing. Page after page, there was nothing but an ocean of white. As I was about to lower the last sheet, I thought I saw ... something.

I scooted the chair closer and removed the lampshade. The light was blinding. Uncle Jack must have needed the wattage to see as his eyes grew tired. Squinting at the area close to the top, I could make out a broken line of curves, the curves that formed Daniel's first words to me.

I mouthed what words I could make out to help me memorize them. Using one of the pristine blank sheets, I scribbled down the words. Now, at least, I had the essence of his message.

With care, I captured them again on paper and dictated them into my phone's note app along with the words in the letter that had appeared that morning. There was no reason to take a chance of losing them, too.

Relieved, I fell back in the chair. It had been quite a day. Now, I had to use what energy I had left to take me upstairs to my journal and bed. As I was about to turn out the kitchen light, I glimpsed the point of land across the creek the witch had once called home. The old tree stood like a sentinel, its dark outline against the deepest blue of the moonlit sky. The moon wasn't full yet, but it would be soon. I always marveled at how many stars appeared in the Shore sky. The effects of moonlight were magical as well. I remembered the Farmers' Almanac listed the dates of the full moon. Maybe TJ would know which night would be best for moon-gazing. I smiled at the thought of making use of his small magazine then switched off the kitchen light.

In the darkness, something outside the window caught my eye. A flash of light. By the tree. Moving around. In search of something. Then it was gone.

CHAPTER THIRTEEN

"If you cannot write straight without lines, draw very faint lines with a soft pencil and afterwards erase them; or, better still, slip a heavily ruled piece of paper or cardboard under the paper, so that the lines will show through."

How to Write Letters
by Professor J. Willis Westlake, 1883

The past few days on the Eastern Shore helped me take a big step toward one of my goals: get off the prescriptions. After a day of activity, I was exhausted at bedtime. As long as I took the painkiller early in the evening, I could sleep soundly without a sedative. It was another small step toward getting back to normal. The sun woke me, its gentle rays creeping through the east window and across the ceiling. It was the same way I greeted the morning when I was a child. Once again, I sent a silent thank-you to Uncle Jack for leaving me the Cottage. I was up early enough to get ready for my P.T. appointment so I wouldn't look like a *schlub* this time.

As I was about to head down the stairs, my phone rang. What a surprise! I made sure I didn't move as I answered the call.

"Ms. Chase! Oh, thank heaven." Mr. Heinrick was gasping for air. "Are you all right?"

"Why yes, Mr. Heinrick. I'm fine." His urgency tickled my curiosity. "You don't sound well, I'm sorry to say."

He barked in my ear. "Ms. Chase, WHERE are you?"

Caught. I hadn't told him of my move to the Shore.

"I sent a messenger to your apartment," he sputtered. "There are papers that need your signature and do you know what he told me?" I decided to let him tell the story, hoping that he'd run out of angry steam. "Security allowed him to go to your door since my office has delivered papers to you before."

He knocked on the door and a foreign gentleman answered. He said you don't live there anymore. You don't live in your apartment anymore!" He took a deep breath and bellowed, "Ms. Chase, WHERE ARE YOU?"

In the sweetest voice I could muster, I began to explain. "Mr. Heinrick, I told you I inherited my Uncle Jack's Cottage. I came down to the Eastern Shore to take possession." Slowly, I described subletting my condo, arranging physical therapy sessions, and a mountain of other details. "You see, Mr. Heinrick, there is no reason to worry. I'm fine."

I could imagine his cheeks swelling with breath as he harrumphed.

"No reason to worry? Of course, there is reason to worry! My client disappeared. You could have been abducted for all I knew. You really should have notified me. I can't begin to detail all the ways this could affect your case if the other side gets wind of your jaunt out of the city." He let out a deep sigh. "But, as far as I know, it's our secret."

I wasn't sure how I felt about that. I wasn't doing anything wrong. No one could believe I was faking my medical situation.

Mr. Heinrick cleared his throat and spoke again in his most controlled voice. "Now, all you have to do is return to the city immediately and we'll say no more of this escapade."

"Um, I'm afraid that's not going to happen, Mr. Heinrick, at least not for another six months."

"WHAT?"

"Perhaps you didn't hear me. I've sublet my condo. I'll be spending the next six months here at the Cottage. And before you get yourself all upset again, there's nothing we can do about it. I arranged it this way for a reason. So I couldn't go home."

"The reason for your eccentric behavior eludes me."

"My behavior isn't eccentric," I said with growing indignation. "I'm doing what is right for me. The doctor approved it, so here I am."

I heard his quiet groan of submission. "Well, if you insist, I suppose there's nothing I can do to persuade you to—"

"I'm afraid there's nothing you can say or do. Cell phone coverage is spotty in this area, so I'm having a special line installed in the house. Once I have better service, I'll be able to respond to your calls and emails promptly. I think you'll find I'll be a very cooperative client."

He didn't give up easily. "But you won't come back to the city?"

"No, I'll be here on the Maryland Eastern Shore."

He sighed again. "Very well. But there is one thing you must do. Not for me, but for yourself. You must keep alert to any strangers. Note if anyone seems to be taking an unusual interest in your activities. If that is the case, you must let me know immediately. *Immediately*, do you understand?"

I wondered if the man repeated himself like this to a jury. If he did, would they be as annoyed as I was?

"I don't understand," I said.

"It's quite simple. If the defense knows you're there, it may send spies to watch you. I don't want anything to undermine this case."

"Spies? I'm not faking anything. Mr. Heinrick—"

"Oh, do not poo-poo the idea. If our positions were reversed, I would do the same thing. They want to make sure you were truly hurt and not lying about your injuries."

I was aghast. "All anyone has to do is look at my chart, X-rays, and scans to see—"

"I'm not going to debate legal maneuvers with you. Be aware of the people around you. If anything suspicious happens, promise me that you'll notify me immediately. Promise."

Now, it was my turn to sigh. "Yes, Mr. Heinrick, I promise."

"Very good. I'll have my secretary contact you for an address to send these papers. I assume you get mail wherever you are?"

I wanted to prick his supercilious bubble. "Yes, we have all the modern conveniences here, like electricity, running water, indoor plumbing—"

"All except reliable phone and internet service."

I had to end this call before I exploded. "I'll give you the address now." There was a little arrogance in my voice.

He dismissed the idea. "No, I'll have my secretary take the call."

I gave the information to the poor woman who worked for him. The man was so frustrating. Always telling me what I could and could not do … and when. I lumped him with all the bossy doctors and nurses. Yes, they were helping me, but I was so tired of people controlling me. I felt sure that if I'd told him I was coming to the Eastern Shore, he would have forbidden my move. I couldn't let that happen. I wanted, no, needed to be here.

Calmer, I put the phone safely in my pocket and made it down the steps without too much pain. I wished I could look forward to finding another letter from Daniel, but I'd been too tired to write to him the night before. It probably was proper etiquette in the 1860s to wait for a response before one wrote again. Nevertheless, a wave of disappointment washed over me as I hiked up my crutches and headed to the kitchen for breakfast.

At the doorway to the writing den, I stole a peek at the desk where the other letters had appeared. A short note was there.

Dear Emma,

Forgive me for writing so soon and showing how anxious I am to hear from you again. I only wanted you to know that you are in my every thought.

Yours with great esteem,

Daniel

I snapped a picture of the note and scribbled down a quick copy of the letter in case it started to fade before I got back from the P.T. appointment. Safely tucked away with the other letters and copies in the cubbyhole, I smiled as I hurried as fast as I dared to be ready for my driver.

On the road, we passed a large field of short green plants. "Do you know what they're growing there?" At heart, I was still a city girl. Like most people, the only crop I could recognize in the field was corn.

"Those are soybeans."

"Does that land belong to Waterwood?"

He turned quickly and gave me a strange look. "That's a curious question."

"I'm learning a bit about Waterwood from the papers I'm reading at the library. It's natural to wonder about the land surrounding the Cottage. I'll read more about it today if you can take me to the library after P.T.?" A feeling of almost desperation surged inside me. It had been a long time since something had sparked my interest like this.

TJ stared at the road for a minute. "I don't know why it's so important, but yes, you can research to your heart's content for about an hour. On the way back, I need to check on something. It won't take long, okay?"

"That sounds only fair," I said with a smile. This man was comfortable, easy, not complicated like so many men I'd met since my divorce. We drove along the main route to Easton in relaxed silence until I uttered the obligatory groan as he stopped at the door for P.T. – Pain Today.

The happy therapists worked my body. The only thing that stifled the groans was the thought of going to the library. There was another reward. They gave me permission to begin to use my leg, but it was going to take concentration and patience to master this next step in my healing. After the session, I moved slowly, deliberately, across the sidewalk to meet him as he drove up. He jumped out, came to open the passenger door, and folded his arms across his chest. "Look at you. You've graduated. Well done!" Ghost barked his approval, too.

My face felt warm. I bit my lip to push down the tears that threatened to erupt. Tears, not from frustration, but tears of pride and relief. Maybe the leg would function again. Maybe I'd walk normally again.

He opened my door. "Okay, let's get this champion into her chariot and away from this painful place." He winked. And I smiled.

We stopped for a quick lunch, but I turned down the offer of another ice cream cone. If I kept using ice cream as an antidote for frustration and celebration, my leg wouldn't have a chance of carrying the additional weight that was reappearing at an alarming rate.

At the library, I made my way to the Maryland Room all alone, feeling independent. Stephani sat at the librarian's desk, her glasses on top of her head holding back her shiny dark hair. She wore a turquoise blue summer sweater set that brought out her blue eyes.

"Emma," she exclaimed. "How nice to see you again." She pulled out a chair at an empty table. "Why don't you sit right here? I have a short stack of things for you. It will only take a moment for me to get them."

I pulled out a notebook in anticipation of what she would bring, like a little girl waiting for milk and cookies after school. Only this was better. I reached over to a library computer and typed in a few keywords for a search. The results were helpful. I had time to make a few quick notes.

"Oh, you found something already." Stephani reappeared with her arms full.

I closed the cover of my notebook. The last thing I wanted the girl to see were my notes about how to deal with a ghost.

"There's a lot of material here." She sat down across the table from me. "Will you be working for the rest of the day?"

I shook my head. She slid the pile to her side. "Let's see if I can make it easier for you. Tell me where you are in your research so I can pull out things in a logical order?" She put her arms around the stack as if protecting it from me.

We talked about what I'd found so far about the Cottage and my interest in the Civil War period. That point made her pause for a moment. Her manner seemed strange. Then, throwing off her hesitancy to let me see the papers in the stack, she jumped right in with enthusiasm. She laid papers, files, and pamphlets in front of me with comments about what I might find in each. Family members often spent countless hours doing genealogical research then donated the results to the Maryland Room. There was a page written in Old English with the modern translation typed below. There were old and modern maps. Maybe I'd misjudged this summer intern who showed real love for the research process.

I sat back in the chair and said, "You've been very helpful. I appreciate all you've done." The clock chimed the hour. "I have to leave, but there's one more thing. I've been reading about a witch – though probably just an old woman – by the name of Virtue Violl and another woman named Katie Cobin."

Stephani stiffened. "Why do you want to know about her?"

I fumbled for a response while trying to figure out why she had become almost hostile. "Curiosity. Do you have anything about her?"

Stephani continued to look at me like I had some oatmeal leftover from breakfast stuck on my lip. Then her face lit up. "Maryland isn't a state known for its witches. There are only five recorded stories in the whole state." Her voice climbed higher with her excitement. "But it's not about witches. It's about people maligning women because they're different. That's what we're talking about here, isn't it?" She took a much-needed breath and waited for my answer to her question.

"Ah, I suppose so," I answered, not sure how to respond to this burst of enthusiasm. "I'm interested in the people who lived around the Cottage. I don't care if they were witches."

"Well, it should be part of your consideration. After all, as professional women today, we owe a debt of gratitude to them for standing up for themselves and their beliefs," then she added, "and having the courage to live on their own." She stood as if to honor the idea and took in a deep breath and let it out slowly.

Under control again, she continued. "I'm afraid I don't have anything about Katie Cobin in the materials. I can take a quick look in the files, but didn't you say you had to leave soon?"

I swung my eyes around to the clock dial. "You're right. TJ is waiting for me." I gestured at my leg. "I can't drive yet," I said with a weak smile.

"Oh, he should have come in." She gathered up the copies she'd made for me. "I'll carry these out for you. As we walked outside, she said. "Maybe I could do some research for you during my shift this afternoon. I won't be busy today since the weather is so beautiful."

"That would be very kind of you. I'm not sure when I'll be back. Could you write down the references so I could look them up the next time I come?"

"I have a better idea." She gave me another bright smile. "I don't live far from you. I could make copies of anything I find and bring them by the Cottage for you."

"You know where I live?" I was uncomfortable.

"Of course, everyone knows where Jack's Cottage is." Her voice became softer. "I didn't know him, I mean, as a friend, but I know he was very nice. I'm so sorry for your loss."

Her sincerity touched me. "Thank you. That's kind."

"What do you say?" Her blue eyes danced. "Shall I do the research and bring you what I find?"

"Well, if it's not too much trouble."

"That's what we do here on the Shore."

TJ saw us emerge from the building. He rushed over, took the materials from Stephani, and, without pausing, sprinted back to the truck.

I was a little surprised by his behavior and tried to cover for him. "Thank you so much for your help today and well, everything."

"I didn't do much. I'm interested in her, in them, the witches, too." She paused and straightened her back in a more formal stance. "It's my pleasure. I'll see you soon."

CHAPTER FOURTEEN

"We have heard this morning that Thomas Lloyd's wellhouse was burned by lightning during the storm last night." August 3, 1864

—The Willis Family Journals 1847-1951
Edited and Annotated by James Dawson

Settled in the truck, TJ asked, "Are you still okay about making a detour on our way home?" He asked. "Or are you hurting?"

Even though I felt the effects of the therapy session, I wasn't going to give in to the pain. I checked the time. I still had more than an hour to wait until I could take the next painkiller. A distraction would be good.

"I had a good session in the reference room again. Stephani found some good references and filled in a few details. Local knowledge is always valuable."

TJ stared through the windshield, suddenly intent on the road ahead.

I was curious why he seemed to shut down. "How do you know her?"

"It's a small place. People know people." And that was supposed to close the discussion.

I shifted my gaze through the windshield to look down the road like he did. She seemed a little young to be his girlfriend, but these days, one never knew. "Who is she?" I asked.

He didn't say anything.

"An old flame?" I suggested. "Or maybe your current girlfriend?"

Still no response. I turned toward TJ. His finely chiseled face in profile didn't have the raw ruggedness of a life dedicated to working the land. There was more here than I first imagined.

A man with layers. How unusual. I was intrigued.

What would I find if I peeled them back? But who am I kidding? This man won't let just anyone into the private areas of his life. He had to live with the whims of nature on the farms. He'd try to control what he could.

I dropped my hands in my lap, declaring the end of my guessing game. "Whoever *she* is, Stephani was very nice to me today. I appreciated her help and the research she's doing for me. That's all I care about."

TJ seemed ready to move on as well. "At least your timing was good." He pointed off to the northwest. "It looks like we dodged a storm. See the line of dark clouds? They're heavy with rain. We could use some, but I think the harvest will be okay, might even be a little late this year."

I powered my window down and took a deep breath through my nose. "Oh yes, I can smell the rain."

"Not bad, for a city girl," he said with a touch of admiration in his voice. "Hear the rumble?"

I listened hard and heard a roll of thunder in the distance. "Are you sure it's not coming this way?"

He pointed at the tall pines. "Look at the tops of the trees. They show the wind is blowing away from us. Still, we have to be careful with a thunderstorm. The Weather Service is always warning that lightning can strike the ground from as far away as fifteen miles from the center of the storm."

A shudder ran through me. "That's scary."

"Yes, it is. It all comes down to respecting Mother Nature. She always has a surprise waiting for us. We have to anticipate and be aware."

"And not do anything stupid," I added.

He chuckled. "I think that's what I said."

It was my turn to laugh as he turned on a flattened grassy area leading into a cornfield.

"We're going to stop here for a few minutes, okay?"

"Sure, fine," I said, looking around, trying to figure out what interested him here and coming up without a clue.

I released my seat belt and moved into a more comfortable position. Ghost followed him as he got out of the truck. The dog was so quiet that I kept forgetting he was riding along with us in the back seat of the cab. TJ leaned over to inspect the cornstalks. The plants were drying out with their leaves turning brown at the bottom.

I heard a rustling sound and looked around. TJ had disappeared. Without moving my aching leg too much, I tried to spot him, but he was nowhere in sight. I called out, but there was no answer.

Abandoned in a cornfield, now that's novel, I thought.

All the talk about the surprises Mother Nature dishes out made me uneasy. Or maybe I was tired. Whatever the reason, I knew I'd feel better when TJ reappeared. I twisted around a bit and peered out the back window to the main road. In the distance, something caught my eye.

"Oh!" I jumped when he opened the door. "Ow!"

Ghost jumped to his place in the back and leaned his head toward me.

"Are you okay?" TJ asked, his voice full of concern.

I was embarrassed that almost everything I did showed how vulnerable I was. "Yes, I'm sorry. I'm fine. Just tired, I guess."

He put the truck in gear and started backing out to the shoulder of the road.

"It looks like someone's having a barbeque nearby and the grill has gotten out of control a little."

"A barbeque? Where?" He touched the brakes and looked around.

I pointed back through the rear window. "Over there, toward the storm clouds. Do you see it?"

He stabbed the accelerator and swung the truck toward it. "That's smoke."

"Yes, that's what I said," I stammered, surprised by his extreme reaction. "Somebody must be—"

"That's not a barbeque! That's one of Johnny's fields! It's on fire."

CHAPTER FIFTEEN

"About nine O. C. last night we discovered a fire at Doctor Matthews. I immediately took the hands and ran over. We succeeded in the saving three chests of Carpenter tools, but very little other properties. All his farm buildings were burned down together with his crop of wheat, eating corn, farming implements, my treasure and deliveries, all his wool and about $200 worth of materials versus new building." August 1, 1864

—The Willis Family Journals 1847-1951
Edited and Annotated by James Dawson

With tires spinning, we took off down the road toward the smoke. I braced myself as we sped around corners. Finally, he pulled over by a field where the smoke was getting thick. For a better view, he jumped up on the truck, uttered an oath, and yanked his cell phone out of his shirt pocket.

"I hope I've got cell service out here." He punched three numbers and mumbled, "Come on! Come on!" Then in full voice, he said, "Yes! Get me Fire. There's a fire in Johnny Sutherland's cornfield on…"

The details blended into the background as I watched the smoke growing thicker and spreading over the field. I wondered how a person calls for an emergency response to a cornfield. Does it have an address like a house? How did TJ know this was Johnny's field? There was so much to learn about living in the country.

The excitement and anxiety of finding a fire in a field were infectious. It wasn't about a whimsical curl of smoke from a barbecue. Orange flames were starting to lick the tops of the cornstalks. Black smoke that rose from the center of the field was getting thicker. To me, wildfires happened out West. The East Coast always seemed too built up, too urban, for this kind of thing to happen.

"TJ, look!" I pointed toward the flames that were no longer licking the plants. They were consuming them.

"Yes, I see it." He jumped back in the driver's seat and drove the truck down the road so we were upwind and pulled over on the shoulder.

"We'll be okay here for a bit." He patted my hand to comfort me and maybe to reassure himself.

We sat in silent fascination, watching the flames spread from the middle of the field. Smoke billowed and darkened the area. The fire department wouldn't need an address. The smoke would lead them right to the fire.

"The closest fire station is St. Michaels." Anxiety made TJ's voice raspy. "I hope they're not out on another call. They need to get here now. It will take Easton longer to respond."

At first, the siren wail was faint, like something imagined, conjured up from a real desire for the trucks to come. It grew louder as the fire started to growl.

"They're coming! I can hear the sirens." And the single sound became sirens from more than one emergency vehicle. My relief was so intense, a tear leaked out of my eye and ran down my cheek.

As the sirens grew louder, I noticed that I was rubbing the thigh of my right leg. Not to relieve pain, because it didn't hurt, at least not any more than usual. It was a nervous movement, my hand moving back and forth. Back and forth. As the sirens got closer, the motion got faster and the pressure on my leg grew. I froze.

Oh no! It was happening.

A flashback. The fire, the danger, triggered it. Post-Traumatic Stress had kicked in. The therapist, the one for my head, had warned me about it. Knowing what was happening didn't make it any less scary.

I didn't remember anything of the accident—from the moment of impact to the moment I woke up blinded by red, white and blue lights, strapped to a gurney, drowning in pain—my brain harbored the memory. A trigger might be seeing a car accident or a disabled vehicle off to the side of the road. Or hearing sirens.

I was reacting to the sirens. The therapist told me what to do, how to hold on to what was happening in the present. Somehow, I forced myself to stop rubbing my leg. I leaned back to get more comfortable. Then I closed my eyes and started to breathe. Deeply. Slowly. I concentrated on the air, drawing it in, blowing it out. I felt my muscles begin to release their tight grip. The sirens were louder. People were coming to handle the danger. I didn't have to do anything. When the bright red, shiny trucks pulled up, their emergency lights flashing, all the activity distracted me from my buried memories.

The trucks stopped on the road bordering the field, leaving an opening as a gateway into the field. A bull of a truck roared down the road, turned to the gateway, and plowed into the cornfield. Its high bumper smashed cornstalks as the truck moved relentlessly toward the fire. A light mist settled on the windshield. An emergency crew was firing a hefty stream of water around the flames to create a soggy barrier. It wasn't long before the roiling smoke seemed to ease.

TJ came over and leaned against his open door. He shot me a

look filled with questions. Instead, I asked him what was happening.

"That's a brush truck," he explained. "They'll drive in a circle around the fire, knocking down plants and laying a blanket of water. That will help keep the flames from spreading." He hiked himself up on the truck's running board, wet his finger then held it high above his head. "But the wind's picking up. They need to hurry to focus in on the flames and knock it all out."

We watched and waited, along with others standing next to their trucks parked along the road. So many people had been drawn to the field by the smoke and the radio calls. An emergency radio crackled and a crew by a pumper truck moved around to prepare for action. The massive brush truck lumbered out of the field and took on another load of water so it could go back to work.

The adrenaline rush of the first discovery of the fire was bleeding off. I began to think about getting home.

TJ took off his cap and smoothed his hair back. "I think it's going to be all right. They're getting it under control. These guys train for this kind of thing."

"Guys?" I pointed to a woman, as thin as a wisp in a turnout coat that almost engulfed her.

TJ nodded. "Point taken, but I bet she'd think it was a compliment to be called *one of the guys*."

He was probably right. But something was wrong. I hadn't known him very long, but I half expected him to have a snappy comeback about the whole female-in-a-male-dominated-job thing. Something was bothering him, so I waited quietly to find out what it was.

He took off his cap again and wiped the sweat off his forehead with the back of his hand. He raised his chin. "The wind is freshening, probably from that thunderstorm. It's changing direction, too." He checked the shape of his hat's brim. "It will be okay if they can knock it down," he said more to himself than to me. "There's something about this field…" He whacked his hat against his arm, then put it on again and pulled it down tight.

"But I'll be darned if I can remember." He leaned against the door and crossed his arms while he watched the action in the field.

A truck flew up the road and careened to the gateway into the field, fishtailing and gouging tracks in the soil. He stopped and a man got out yelling and waving his arms. He ran to a knot of firefighters.

TJ straightened up. "That's Johnny. This is his field. Something's wrong." He unfolded his arms. "That's it! The shed in those trees. It's got chemicals in it." TJ ran toward the firefighters.

I couldn't hear what Johnny was saying, but it didn't look good. His arms flew around. He pointed to the trees and back to the fire in the middle of the cornfield and back again. The firefighters' heads swiveled around as they followed his gestures until everyone's attention settled on a place at the far side of the field.

The firefighting unit scrambled in controlled chaos. Three men hustled together to consult. Someone picked up a microphone. Radios crackled. Crew members, wearing heavy turnout coats and protective helmets, scrambled back to their trucks. One truck stayed in place, ready to replenish the brush truck with gallons of water. Others jockeyed around in a coordinated maneuver to move toward the trees where Johnny was pointing.

I was so distracted by all the activity that I didn't see a puff of thick smoke until it engulfed the truck. In the backseat, Ghost coughed and sneezed. The wind had changed. I reached over and flipped the ignition key to *Accessory*. I wanted to close the windows, but Ghost kept poking his head outside and straining for air. I didn't want to strangle him with the power window. I tried to talk to him, but he ignored me. Then I remembered one of TJ's commands.

In a stern voice, I gave him an order. "Come. Now."

Surprised, he swung his head in my direction and moved toward me. I reached over the driver's seat and hit the control buttons to close all the windows. Then I shut off the outside circulation and turned up the air-conditioning. At least we could breathe while we waited. Ghost left big nose prints on the window glass as he followed TJ's movements outside.

In the field, smoke was churning up in clouds again. Flames blazed above the stalks, heading toward the road. Toward us.

A firefighter got TJ's attention, pointed to the woods then to the road. His message was clear. *Get out!* In a second, TJ started running toward me. I pulled my seatbelt, ready. He leaped into his seat, released the brake, and we took off at breakneck speed.

"What's wrong? Where are we going?" I asked as we charged down the road.

He coughed some smoke out of his lungs. His face was wet with flecks of ash caught in beads of sweat. His hazel-green eyes flashed with urgency. "We're getting away, as far away as possible."

"What happened?" I looked in the big outside rearview mirror but couldn't see anything but smoke rising from the field we'd just left.

He coughed again. "You saw the madman in the truck?" I nodded. "That was Johnny. He farms that field. He told the firefighters about a small building on the far edge that he uses for storage."

"Are they scrambling to protect the building?"

"They are scrambling," TJ said in a grave tone, "to protect all of us. There's ammonium nitrate stored inside that building. It's fertilizer used on the farm."

I thought of the bright blue liquid fertilizer I used on my houseplants when I remembered to feed them. Then my brain started to make connections. *Fertilizer. Farm fertilizer.* My throat tightened. "No, you don't mean…like Oklahoma City?"

TJ nodded his head slowly.

Oklahoma City. Bomb.

He took a deep breath. "Yes, if the flames reach that building…all that will be left is a deep crater."

I looked in the rearview mirror again, but couldn't tell what was happening.

"They told us to get out," he explained. "They'll evacuate anybody else close by,"

"Are they evacuating, too?"

A sad smile appeared on his face. "Of course not. Their job is to run toward the danger, not away from it. They'll get in there and, I suspect, water down the building to keep it from heating up or igniting from the sparks flying around. And they'll keep working to put out the fire in the field."

TJ turned the wheel, pulled over to the shoulder, and stopped. Fire truck after fire truck screamed toward us, lights and sirens flaring. The noise was piercing. I crouched in my seat and covered my ears. In a moment, TJ touched my arm and I realized they were gone.

"Didn't I tell you? Always racing toward the danger." He glanced up the road. "Here comes another one."

I covered my ears again and watched an ambulance streak by.

"Does that mean someone's hurt?" I asked, my voice quaking.

"No. These crews live the motto, *Be prepared...* just in case." He checked the road in both directions and pulled out.

"Don't you need to stay?" I asked.

"No. These people know what they're doing. They don't need a novice getting in the way, no matter how good my intentions might be."

"Will they be okay? I mean, with the chemicals and everything, things could get out of hand..." I didn't want to think about the possibilities.

"No, everything will be fine." He paused for a moment, thinking, then added. "Unless, of course, we hear a big boom." He glanced my way. "Hey, don't worry about it. I heard them calling in an additional alarm. These aren't city boys. They deal with farms and farm chemicals all the time. Don't worry."

He looked at me again, a little longer this time. "You're pale, Emma."

"Probably because I'm late for my pain pill, I'm hurting, but not much." The last thing I wanted him to know about was the PTSD attack. These last hours of being treated like a normal human being were exquisite.

"What do you say I take you home?" he said.

I nodded and started the slow breathing exercise again so the flashbacks and all didn't start again.

As we rolled along, past field after field, I began to wonder. "TJ, whatever made you go over to those fields? I mean, they're not on our way home."

"It's all part of my job."

"As a handyman?" I was confused.

"No, I only worked as a handyman for Jack." He winked at me. "I do custom planting and harvesting. Johnny is one of my clients."

"Custom? How does that work? I thought a farmer planted the seeds and harvested the crop." I felt like a real city girl.

"You're right, in theory. When you're farming hundreds of acres, you need big machines to do those things efficiently. Not everybody can afford or wants to spend the money on the combines and all. It's expensive. That's where I come in. I have the equipment and experience. They pay me to work in their fields and get the job done, whatever the season. My crew and I will start harvesting around the 15th of September if all goes the way I expect weather-wise."

Things were starting to fall into place. "Is that why you read the *Farmers' Almanac?*"

"One reason. It's right more often than those slick *meteorologists* with the big hair and heavy makeup on TV. And there's lots of useful information and ads in there, too."

Now that I thought about it, all the clues were there at the beginning. "So, you work for the farmers and take care of me?"

He shrugged. "Pretty much, when I'm not taking care of my own fields."

"Where are your fields?" I asked.

"I rent certain fields around the county from landowners who don't want to farm them. That's in addition to farming my own."

"And where are your fields?"

"All around you and the Cottage."

My jaw dropped. "You own Waterwood?"

He checked his rearview mirror and seemed to concentrate on

his driving as we made our way down the empty road. Quietly, he answered. "Yes, what's left of it."

"What do you mean, what's left of it?"

"In its glory days," he explained. "It was one of the largest plantations in the county, one of the largest on the Eastern Shore."

I stared out the windshield, trying to process this new information.

"Don't misunderstand," he continued. "*Land rich* doesn't mean wealthy. There are lots of expenses – taxes, upkeep. The thought of heating the house in the winter staggers the mind."

"You live in the main house?"

He sighed. "Yes, but it isn't as grand as it once was." He gestured with a nod of his head. "Almost home." And he clicked the turn signal for the road to the Cottage. I looked at the fields and thought about this man and his connection to Waterwood. And Daniel?

He interrupted my thoughts with instructions. "Don't forget to take your pain pill when you get inside. There's no way you're backing out of the meeting tomorrow night."

"What meeting?" I was hoping he'd forgotten.

"The meeting of the writing group. Catherine said she'd pick you up at six. I'll give you a ride home afterward. Take a nap before if you can." Suddenly, he held up a hand in submission. "Look, it's what you said you wanted. You want to write. Catherine says you need support. I don't know anything about books, except how to read them. The only thing I can do is to get you with people who can help you. I only meant…"

"I got it. But that's tomorrow. I have a lot of reading to do today." And I added in the quiet of my mind, *the first thing I have to do is read about how to deal with a ghost.*

CHAPTER SIXTEEN

"Before the development of the fountain pen by Waterman & Co. after the Civil War, a person using a dip pen needed a traveler, a small, portable inkwell that kept the ink secure. The tiny traveler came in different shapes, such as an acorn, ladies hat box, or leather-covered case and was a source of personal expression."

— Member of the International Society of Inkwell Collectors

At home, after a quick snack to put something in my stomach, I popped the pain pill and sat, waiting for it to kick in. The smart thing to do would be to take a nap, but the adrenaline was still pumping from the field fire. And Daniel was overdue for a response. It wouldn't be smart to rile him.

I made my way into the writing den, moving slowly to learn how to negotiate the Cottage with both legs and the crutches. It made things better, but it was still awkward. Relieved, I plopped into the chair at the desk. If I sat still and rested my leg, it was almost as good as taking a nap, right?

I wanted to prepare to write an appropriate letter to Daniel. I pulled out the research pages about writing instruments used during the Civil War. I set aside the last letter from Daniel along with copies from the Maryland Room to use as an example of the handwriting from that period. Preparations to write the actual letter were cumbersome. I needed paper, pens, a bottle of ink and a rocker blotter for the wet ink. Fortunately, the desk had lots of cubbyholes and niches to organize things. It wasn't as convenient as using the internet and typing out an email, but it certainly got me in the mood.

I opened the ink bottle without mishap and dipped the pen into it. It wasn't as classy as using an antique inkwell, but it worked as long as the nib didn't go too deep into the bottle and drench the paper with wet ink blobs. It took some trial and error to get the pen and ink right.

Then it was time to test my penmanship. I sent out a silent thank you to my elementary school teacher who had patiently drilled us in the art of cursive handwriting. The flowing style was rapidly becoming a lost art. Many schools didn't even bother teaching it to today's students. They even print their signatures. I'd read the reports in the news about the demise of cursive handwriting, but the ramifications didn't hit home until I took on my first student teacher. I wrote a note and handed it to a student to give to her. Moments later, she was back asking me to decipher it. I thought she couldn't read my handwriting, but that wasn't it. She couldn't read the words at all. I'd written using cursive. From then on, I had to print every note for her.

My normal handwriting wasn't fancy or flowery. During the Civil War, people took their time forming words on a piece of paper, especially capitalized letters. Some were ornate, even in a simple letter from a Union soldier to his wife.

I spent some time practicing so I didn't speckle the paper with ink droplets. Slowly, I moved the nib across the paper more evenly. Then I made a sample alphabet of the capital letters to use for reference. The other impressive thing about handwritten documents from that time was how straight each line was. They had an eye for keeping the words lined up evenly.

The content of a letter was vital to people of that era. It was their primary source of news. But the presentation mattered, too. I made a note to find some lined paper to slip underneath the blank page to give myself a fighting chance of writing a respectable letter.

Finally, I was ready to write to Daniel, but what was I going to say? It would be better to draft the contents, make any corrections, and copy it using the dip pen and ink. It was a natural point to take a break. And a perfect time to sit on the patio.

I felt a bit guilty. The thought of writing a 19th-century letter had driven away any thoughts about the firefighters. I hadn't heard a boom, so they must have handled the situation successfully, just as TJ said they would. I picked up the stack of library materials and stopped in the kitchen for a cool drink before delving into the dos and don'ts of dealing with a ghost.

It took some work and innovative thinking to get everything out to the patio, but it was worth it. The air was clear and the humidity was low, a rarity in August in this region. I felt like I was falling into a trance as I gazed at the water. The tide was coming in so all the mud that could get smelly in the summer heat was covered. The breeze tickled the green leaves that would soon be turning into a colorful show of reds and golds. It was there, across the creek, that a creepy old woman had once lived. A witch, it was declared. She was the target of the local people's anger, grief and frustration when things happened that they couldn't understand. In the 1700s, it must have been easier to blame the strange old woman for things like the appearance of disease, sudden loss of a child, or the destruction of a homestead. I thought it was curious that the landowner didn't move Virtue Violl off his property. Why would he allow a witch to live so close to his family? I'd have to ask TJ if she was one of his ancestors.

The Lone Oak now soared about eighty feet into the clear blue sky. It wasn't tall and skinny. It was full and well-shaped. Its branches beckoned to be climbed. I knew the view would be phenomenal. Not for me. I had work to do. I put my leg up in a comfortable position and began to make notes from the articles I'd printed at the library:

When dealing with a ghost, relax!

That's easy to say on a bright, sunny day, I thought. I wasn't proud of how I'd panicked when I'd found Daniel's first letter on the desk. It was a natural response for a woman used to living alone in a major city with more than one deadbolt lock on her door.

A ghost feeds off fear. Daniel must have binged that first morning.

I loved the next line: **Remember the ghost is probably like you, only dead.**

It's often best to leave a ghost alone. Think of it as a quirky house guest. That might work if the ghost wasn't writing you letters and waiting eagerly for a response.

Ask the spirit to leave. Hmmm, too late for that one.

Keep a record of everything, sightings, feelings, strange occurrences. Well, I'm trying to do that, but the content of the letters keeps disappearing. At least, my copies were holding up. I made a mental note to type everything into a document on the computer. Or would that allow Daniel to haunt my computer? The thought of Daniel fooling around with all my lesson plans saved in memory made me uneasy. I made a mental note to keep Daniel and my computer separate.

Bless your home. Use anything from a vial of holy water to special prayers by clergy to a full-blown exorcism. I decided it might be better to skip this option for now. Daniel seemed like a sensitive man. I didn't want to think how he would react if he was forcibly separated from the woman he thought was *his* Emma. Plus, I was not comfortable with the idea of telling anybody about the ghost, at least not yet. Maybe never.

Invite a paranormal group to do an investigation. If I didn't want to tell a priest or minister about the ghost, let alone TJ, why would I ask ghost hunters who lug around weird equipment in the glow of a green light to invade the Cottage? No, this wasn't an option either.

Another article had other recommendations:

Ring a bell in each corner of each room to break up the

negative energy.   I didn't think Daniel was a source of negative energy, but I circled this suggestion. It would be easy to do, just in case.

Burn sage and allow the smoke to waft through the house. I knew many cultures use sage as a purifying agent. This wasn't an option right now. I'd had enough smoke for one day.

I looked in the direction of the field that had caught fire. There was no smoke in sight. The firefighters were probably back at their station houses eating chili and Johnny was on the phone with his insurance company about a claim.

Something, out of the corner of my eye, snagged my attention. When I turned my head to look, there was nothing there. It must have been the bushes moving in the breeze. Only the air was still. All this reading about ghosts must have set me on edge. I wondered if the painkiller was making me hallucinate. It might be time to cut it back. I scribbled a note to check with the doctor's office.

I shuffled my research papers and found a small book stuffed in there. It covered the folklore of the Eastern Shore. There was a statement from an issue of "McBride's Magazine" published in 1886. It said that Virtue Violl was not the only witch who had lived on the Point. I scanned the article. Another woman had settled on the same piece of land. Katie Cobin was lonely, deformed, ugly, and wretchedly poor. People claimed that she terrorized both adults and children. Many wore charms to protect themselves against her spells. After she disappeared, they reported that a gauzy specter lit by an eerie light wandered around the old Lone Oak.

I was overdosing on the stories of the supernatural. There were a lot of suggested remedies, but not one for a lonely, lovesick ghost. I put the book aside and caught myself staring at the Point. Why had the Lone Oak drawn two women there to live out their wretched lives. Were they witches? Probably not, but still… What was it that drew them to that place?

I took a long drink of lemonade to center myself in the here and now. Of course, an unexplained light in the middle of the night was upsetting. In today's world, it was probably a flashlight. Centuries ago, women might have wanted privacy. But to do what? I trembled for a moment as the face of the detective flashed in my mind's eye. The other night, someone had wanted privacy to bash a boy's face in with a shovel.

I leafed through some more articles about dealing with ghosts. Some of the self-proclaimed spiritual experts wrote about the constant battle between heaven and hell, dark angels and ... the list of eerie entities was a long one.

Okay, that's enough. I was frightening myself. I didn't need to do that. It would be best to finish looking at all this material and get on with things. All this talk about the supernatural was enough to make me think I was hearing things and seeing things that weren't there. Some of the advice and recommendations made me laugh out loud.

A rustling sound behind me made me jump.

A woman asked, "What's so funny?"

CHAPTER SEVENTEEN

"It is a great violation of propriety to send an awkward, careless, badly written letter, as it is to appear in a company of refined people, with swaggering gait, soiled linen, and unkempt hair."

—How to Write Letters
by Professor J. Willis Westlake, 1883

My breathing stopped. My stomach clenched. My hands curled into fists. PTSD, again. I didn't begin to calm down until my brain registered the fact that I recognized the voice. it was Stephani from the library who had asked the question.

She rushed to my chair. "I'm sorry. Are you all right? I scared you." Her words of concern tumbled out like a waterfall.

I took a sip of my lemonade and was embarrassed to see the glass shaking in my hand. I sucked in a deep breath and insisted in a thready voice, "Don't be silly. I'm fine."

"I'm so sorry," she repeated, as she sank into a patio chair and looked like a lost puppy. "But I did scare you,"

"Well, maybe a little." As casually as I could, I turned over the pages about dealing with ghosts so she wouldn't see them. "I haven't adapted to being in the country yet. Still on my guard as one must be in the big city." My laugh sounded forced.

She leaned forward in her chair and pushed her red-framed glasses up her nose. "I did knock on the door several times," she assured me. "Knowing that you can't drive, I thought I'd check out here." She cast her eyes over the water view and sighed. "If I lived here, this is where I'd be on a day like today."

"And here you are." I liked the girl and appreciated the company, but I would have preferred to be alone, to recover after such a fright.

"Yes, here I am." She reached into a huge purse, the kind that is so popular with everyone but me. I didn't have enough stuff that I wanted to lug around with me all the time. Women I knew always claimed it was a fashion statement. I believed it was a conspiracy of orthopedists who specialized in back and shoulder ailments to drum up business.

"I brought the materials as promised," she said. "I was able to find a few things, but – well, you'll see when you go through it." She gave me a tentative smile.

I took the papers and added them to the pile of reference materials. "Thank you so much for doing this work."

Her smile relaxed into a genuine one. "It's my pleasure. I'm glad to help. Work like this gives me more experience and that's what counts in my internship."

"I appreciate you bringing the papers all this way," I added.

"I don't live far from here. My family has owned land close by for hundreds of years. We don't have what they once had, but my mom still has a house with a few acres." She picked up her purse. "Speaking of my mom, I should be going. If there's anything else I can do to help you, I hope you'll let me know. Oh!" She put the purse back on the table and dug around inside for what seemed like several minutes.

Proudly, she pulled something out and handed me the

librarian's business cards with her name and phone number written on the back. "If you need anything, you can contact me directly."

"As a matter of fact, there is something. I don't know what your schedule is, but if you're running back and forth to Easton, you may be able to help me out."

"Sure, what do you need?"

"I have regular appointments for physical therapy sessions and I need a driver. Do you think you might be interested?" I'd imposed enough on TJ's time. Plus, Stephani and I could spend the time in the car talking about local history.

"Sure, I could do that if we can mesh our schedules," she said.

"I'll pay you, of course."

She almost giggled. "If you can cover my gas, that would be great."

"I think I might be able to do better than that." I held up the card she'd given me. "Why don't I call you and we can compare notes? I might even be able to change my schedule of appointments to coincide with your schedule."

She had a dazzling smile. "That sounds great." She swung the purse strap on her shoulder. The weight seemed to throw her off balance for a moment. "Is there anything else?"

"As a matter of fact, there is." I shuffled through the papers that had hidden the small book. "There's an article in this book about a woman who once lived on the Point over there."

"Oh, you mean Virtue Violl," Stephani put her big purse down on the table again. "Everybody around here knows about her. They say that her ghost walks some nights when there is a full moon." She held up her hands and shook them as she made scary noises. "I hope you don't believe in that kind of thing."

"No, it's not about Virtue. This woman lived over there almost a hundred years after Virtue." I picked up the book and opened it to the bookmark. "Here it is. Her name was Katie Cobin." When I looked up, Stephani's face had gone so pale that she looked like she was carved out of marble. "Stephani?"

She took in a sudden breath. "Y-yes, why do you want to know about her? It's only hocus-pocus."

"I know, but it's part of the history or folklore that touches the Cottage. Do you think you can find me more information about Katie? It says…" I checked the page again. "Yes, here it is. There's a brief mention that her ghost still walks 'for a reason.' Do you know what that reason is?"

"No." Her voice was thin enough to fit through a straw.

"Well, maybe your research will tell us something," I suggested. Stephani still stood like a statue. "It's worth a try or maybe we could ask the reference librarian when he comes back from his conference."

A hitch of breath came out of her mouth. And I felt guilty. "Don't worry, your reputation as a research intern is safe with me." It was good to see a young person dedicated to her job.

"Oh, okay. Thanks." Stephani moved her head so her dark hair swung back and forth. "I'll see what I can do." she said as she left, taking the brightness of the day with her.

I settled back in the chair and looked around. As a child, I'd loved watching the world from this spot. It gave me a wide view of the creek, the Lone Oak, and more. Nothing had really changed. The creek still ran with the tidal shifts. The Lone Oak was a bit taller, but today, the vista was flat. I only saw the brittle brown edges of the normally bright pink petals of the massive Crepe Myrtle bushes. The fiery red maple leaves looked rusty without the sun's rays shining down on them. A gray-white cloud cover had sucked the sparkle out of everything. The scene fit my mood. Bored and boring. With nothing to really engage my mind, thoughts I had been pushing away overtook me.

I loved being a kindergarten teacher and I missed my little students. I think my career choice was fed by my experiences with Uncle Jack. Yes, he was a beloved uncle, but so much more. I admired him. He was always there to guide and protect me. He always encouraged me to try new things, expand my horizons. I wanted to be like him, for other children. To do for them what he had done for me. Now that my life had changed, I finally admitted I still needed Uncle Jack. But I had to face it. He was gone. Tears prick my eyes.

"Are you okay, lady?" a rough male voice asked.

Three young men had slipped around the far corner of the Cottage and taken up positions on the edge of the patio, the tallest one in front. All my protective city instincts kicked in. Reaching for the phone, I said in the most menacing voice I could muster, "Get out! I'm calling the police."

The tall one held up his hands in surrender. "Stephani would tell you there's no need for that. I guess we just missed my big sister."

Big sister? As those words sunk into my brain, I started breathing again. If he was Stephani's brother, he was probably all right. I never would have guessed the young man was related to Stephani. His hair was muddy blonde compared to her luxurious chocolate brown. He had an impressive unibrow, but her eyebrows were gently shaped. His head was long and narrow with a squared-off chin compared to her delicate heart-shaped face. And his smile was puny.

"I'm Josh. I thought I'd come by to be neighborly," he said as he looked around, taking in the crutches. He stepped forward and extended his hand. "And I wanted to express my condolences."

I hesitated then shook hands. "Thank you."

Then the young man held his hands together at his waist and gently nodded like a priest. "Mr. Jack was a good man."

I wanted to think he was sincere, but something felt off. Or maybe it was the painkiller. I mentally shook myself and touched the note to call the doctor's office about the pills. They might be skewing my thinking.

Josh continued. "Let me introduce my associates." He opened his arms to include the two boys who had appeared with him.

"This is Justin. We call him the Tin Man." The short, lanky boy had narrow hips that barely held up his jeans. His straight blonde hair was parted in the middle and combed down over his ears with short pieces like bangs brushed to the sides. He moved up and glanced at Josh. As if he'd received permission, he stepped forward and shook my hand.

"Nice to meet you, ma'am." Then he moved back and stood behind Josh's right shoulder.

The third young man seemed nervous about being left out so, he stepped up. "Hello, I'm Edward Ray."

Josh shot him a look of disapproval, complete with narrowed eyes and a slight shake of his head. "Yes, he is the newest addition to our little group. We call him Toad."

"Toad?" The name escaped my lips in surprise. It wasn't an appropriate nickname for a boy with clear skin, curly dark brown hair, a bright grin, and deep dimples. I thought it was a more appropriate nickname for Josh whose body shape was square. It must be a teenage male dynamic to give the best looking one in the group an ugly name.

"Yes, ma'am," he said proudly. "It's a nickname." Toad scurried back to his position behind Josh and Tin Man.

"That's our posse," Josh said, almost formally. "We welcome you to the area. If there's anything we can do to make your life easier..." He gestured to the crutches. "All you have to do is let me know. We can be helpful." He gave me a smile that dripped with sugary sweetness.

The patio door banged open and Maria, my housekeeper, marched outside. "I think you should leave Miss Emma alone and leave," she announced. "Now."

"Of course. It was nice to meet you." His words were polite, but his eyes were hard as he looked at the woman who had interrupted his visit.

"You might phone first before you just pop in," I called out as Josh led the group away, hoping to draw some boundaries.

I barely caught what Maria mumbled under her breath. "Or don't come at all." I was about to quiz her when she launched into one of her monologues of run-on sentences.

"I was beginning to think someone had kidnapped you. I looked all over the Cottage, downstairs, of course, and even upstairs, not that you would go upstairs in the middle of the day, but one never knows what someone is going to do." She took a deep breath. "When I saw those boys here..." Her mouth tightened. "I wanted to grab a rolling pin and chase them away." She caught my glance at her empty hands. "I didn't know if you had one. Instead of wasting time looking for it, I figured I could …" Her mouth tenses. Then, with renewed energy, she went on, "I'm here because TJ warned me that the telephone company called him to say that the installer was coming today and that I should be here to let him in, so you weren't disturbed, in case you were napping on the sofa or something."

After my brain waded through all those words, I sat up in my chair in excited anticipation. "He's coming to install the internet connection?"

"And the phone, yes," she added. "He drove up behind me."

Thrilled with the idea of being connected to the world again, I reached for my crutches. "At last."

"Don't you trouble yourself. Leave the poor man to do his job because it's getting late. You want him to finish today." She looked down and shook her head decisively. "No, a job half-done is not a job finished."

To me, her logic was baffling. With a little shake of my head, I said, "No, I should—"

"Stay right where you are. I'll bring you a snack like they do in England. Oh, what do they call it…?" Her drone drifted away as she went inside.

I was almost afraid to move without Maria's permission. A chilling thought crossed my mind: she might take away my crutches if I don't behave. I leaned back in my chair and a smile grew on my face. This was turning into a Very Good Day. First, I made it to the P.T. appointment without hysteria and won the right to use both legs to walk. Progress. Definitely progress.

The visit to the library had turned up some fascinating research. Seeing the field fire—well, maybe that wasn't so good for the landowner, but I had to admit it was exciting. The memory of the lights and sirens and the reaction they triggered in me darkened my mood. But I reminded myself, I handled the flashback without too much trouble. And I had found myself a driver so I didn't have to rely so much on TJ, the mystery man. Also, Stephani showed promise as a researcher.

I put my hand on the growing stack of research materials and smiled. Yes, I was getting a lot of information. Then, like a trickle of cold water turns into a gushing torrent, a lack of confidence took over my being.

And what was I going to do with it all?

CHAPTER EIGHTEEN

"The task of a writer consists of being able to make something out of an idea."

— *Thomas Mann*

N*ow, what?* Yes, that question was haunting me. *What was I going to do with all my free time?*

I'd made the move from Philadelphia. I was settled at the Cottage. My medical condition was improving. Support services were in place. Now, I should focus my efforts on writing a book. I had lots of information and stories, but I didn't want to write my first book about witches. The kids might like it, but stories about witches and ghosts always scared me as a child.

If I were honest with myself, the story of Daniel and Emma had captured my imagination as I was piecing it together. But a picture book about a young couple in love who'd lived at Waterwood so long ago? I laughed out loud thinking about the "I'm gonna vomit" look on the boys' faces and the girls' moon-y expressions. The young lovers' story was for adults. What did I know about writing for adults? The thought almost made me break out in a cold sweat. I worked with little ones. I understood little ones. Not love.

I thought I'd found my forever love in high school. Our hopes, our dreams, our plans meshed. Our relationship even survived four years of college. He majored in pre-med. I studied elementary education with a concentration on kindergarten. Right after graduation, we married in what I thought was a storybook wedding. Armed with my teaching certification, I got a job in the same city as his medical school. We planned to start our family when he knew where he'd do his internship. Everything was set. What I didn't see coming was the fact that I wasn't the only woman in his life. I was his ticket to becoming a doctor while he chased after everything in scrubs. How could a woman who'd locked away feelings of betrayal and rejection write about true love? I'd packed away my dreams of love and family so I could get up every morning. I gave what love I had to the kids. I touched the place where I'd once worn my necklace and smiled. My kids.

No, I needed to find a story for a picture book for my kids. The clock was ticking. Information resources were in place now with the support of Stephani, my researcher, and the soon-to-be installed internet connection. I needed an idea. TJ was right. I hated to admit the support of other writers was important, especially to a newbie like me. And my first writing group meeting was tomorrow night. They'd want to know what I was working on. It was only natural. I wished I could answer one question: *What are you writing about?*

Maria flew through the door with a tray of goodies and more commentary. "I have a surprise for you and you're going to love it so much."

Behind her stood a man in jeans and a plaid shirt with a belt of tools hanging at his waist. In one smooth motion, Maria offered him the plate of cookies. While munching, he made sure I could connect to the internet.

"Well," he declared. "We know that works and—"

A sound of a ringing telephone came from inside the house.

"And we know the phone works, too." He smiled. "Even though I'd already checked that."

I signed all the paperwork and insisted the man take a handful of cookies with him while Maria waited with the cordless receiver. It was supposed to be only for emergencies and to piggyback with the internet connection.

"It's your sister." She hustled over and handed me the phone before I could wave her off. Well, I guess even good days must have a dip or two to make us appreciate them.

I plastered a smile on my face and lifted the phone. "Hello, sister."

"Oh, Emma, thank goodness! I haven't heard from you. Why haven't you called? So many horrible things kept popping up in my imagination. I thought I was going to have to come down there myself to protect my sanity." She sighed. "How's my little sister?"

When I realized my sister and Maria had something in common, I had to smother a giggle. They both could spew out a flood of words in a single breath.

She barely paused. "How are you doing? All moved in? And I have wonderful news. I think I can come down in two weeks. Still have a few things to work out, but I have to make sure you're okay. Mother would never—"

"Caroline!" I said and winced because it was a bad idea to yell at my big sister. Her tears would flow for the smallest reason. I should be polite. After all, she was the only close relative I had left. I didn't want to think about Uncle Jack right now or my sister would notice and bombard me with calls, questions, and eventually, a visit.

"Caroline," I repeated in a gentler voice. "It's wonderful that you care so much. You don't need to worry about me. I'm fine. I'm making spectacular progress." Silently, I gave thanks that I didn't have to lie about my progress. "I think the worst is over. I only need to rest and do my exercises."

Like fuel tossed on a fire, she pounced. "Are you doing your exercises? Is there someone there making sure you do? Would a personal trainer help?"

I squeezed my eyes shut and bit my lip to keep myself from screeching at her. After taking a deep breath, I calmly responded. "I'm surrounded by good people who are helping and encouraging me. One highly-motivated individual is keeping me focused."

I swear she never took a breath. "Really? Who? Did you meet someone? Tell me—"

"Caroline, it's me. There's no one on the planet more motivated to get back to normal than me. Now, you'll have to trust me. I'm doing well and getting stronger every day."

Silence on the line. Uh oh, was she cooking up some other scheme to complicate my life?

"Well, if you're sure," she said reluctantly.

I almost gasped in surprise. Quietly, I said, "Yes, dear, I'm sure."

"I don't want anything else bad to happen to my little sister." Her motherly voice could suck the air out of a conversation.

"I appreciate that. You need to take care of yourself and—"

"But I'm okay. Todd watches out for me and the girls. You don't have anyone," she whined as if it was my fault.

Ah, the pity was about to flood the line as usual and I'd had enough of it, going back years. "Oh, Caroline. I have to go. The telephone man needs to finish up the job," I said quickly.

"But—"

"Give my love to everybody. I'll talk to you soon. Thanks for calling. Bye." I clicked the Off button and put the phone down with a sigh. That might have been my first call from my sister on the newly installed line, but it wouldn't be the last. I made a mental note to get a new phone with a clear caller-ID display.

I gathered the research papers and notes into a stack. I couldn't absorb one more thing. This had been an exhausting day. Maria, with her uncanny sense of knowing when she was needed, appeared with a fresh dish of cookies.

"Thank you, but no. I don't need any more cookies. If you

leave them here, I'll eat them all." I began to pull the crutches into position when Maria put her hand on my arm.

"You won't need these right yet and the cookies aren't for you. Sit down. You have visitors."

I stayed in the chair and had the weird feeling that her uncanny abilities had stretched to forecasting the future. My eyes followed her as she pulled out two chairs and dusted them off.

"I'll get some fresh lemonade and glasses," she announced as she headed back to the kitchen.

Sitting alone at the table, it felt like someone had thrown a party and I was the first guest to show up. TJ came around the corner, followed by the police officer in uniform.

"Outside, enjoying some fresh air?" said the officer. "That's good, that's good." His words were friendly, but something in his manner sounded my warning bell. This wasn't a social call. There was trouble and it had just arrived on my patio.

"Afternoon, ma'am. I'm Officer Conklin. We met yesterday. Detective Craig Mason is in charge of the investigation and asked me to come by to see you."

"Craig called me," TJ explained. "He wanted to come by the Cottage earlier to give you some information but got caught up in things."

Now, all my warning systems were active and my protective screens were coming online. I wanted to appear calm or else TJ would become a suffocating worrywart. "Of course, why don't you both sit down? Maria is bringing some—"

"Fresh lemonade for two hardworking men." She completed my sentence as she put down a tray with four glasses filled with ice and a round pitcher like the Kool-Aid commercials. Once she made sure we had everything we could want, she pulled out another chair and sat down. I almost asked her to go back to the kitchen, but if the subject was safety—if there was a lunatic running around and swinging a shovel in people's faces—she had a right to know. We all turned our attention to the officer.

When he realized we were waiting, he popped the rest of a cookie in his mouth, took a quick sip to wash it down, and cleared his throat. "Yes, well, I'm afraid the news isn't good. Detective Mason is investigating the incident over at the Lone Oak Tree, right over there. Following up on an anonymous tip, a young man was found at the foot of the tree, grievously injured."

The sociable smile melted off TJ's face. "Yes, we know. It was Kid Billy." TJ's body stiffened. "What's happened?" His Southern lilt was back. It seemed to show up when something upset him.

The officer's eyes swept back and forth, watching us closely for any reactions as he delivered his news in a monotone. "The young man died. He died early this morning from wounds inflicted over there." He jerked his head toward the Lone Oak.

TJ leaned forward, his face scrunched up in disbelief. "Wait, what? Kid Billy is dead?"

The officer watched us carefully. "Yes, sir."

My body sagged as the air went out of me. The next moment was quiet as the news sunk in. Then the questions came fast and furiously as my eyes strayed across the creek.

I'd seen the lights that first night. Unless the witches of the Point were walking with lanterns, I'd seen the flashlight carried by the killer. My stomach clenched. What if I'd paid attention? What if I'd called the police? Would the boy still be alive? Was I partially responsible? I stared across the creek.

"Emma?" TJ's voice penetrated my thoughts.

"Yes? Sorry, what?"

"The officer wants to confirm when you saw the lights before you went to bed."

I nodded. "Of course. I saw the lights the night before you found the body."

The officer looked at me with his eyes narrowed. "Miss Chase, did you call the tip line?"

A little laugh escaped my lips. "If I told you, it wouldn't be anonymous, would it?" I didn't give him time to respond. "Just to be clear, I did not call your tip line. I couldn't. I didn't have phone service until a few minutes ago." I turned to TJ. "By the way, thank you for making that happen."

TJ nodded in acknowledgment.

I directed my attention back to the young officer. "I'm curious. What time did the anonymous call come in?"

He checked his notebook. "The log showed the call came in at 3:34 AM."

"The person who called must have been there when the boy was attacked," I said. "Nobody would have been passing by at that hour. And if the caller knew what happened, he could have called for an ambulance, don't you think?"

"Yes, ma'am, I do. I was sent to the scene before dawn. Once the sun came up, we could see everything. It was bad. Blood everywhere." He shrugged his shoulders. "It makes sense. The Kid was hit in the head more than once. Head wounds bleed like crazy, even if the attack isn't fatal. The Kid would have bled out right there under the tree if we hadn't gotten the call. Even so, the ambulance guys had a hard time getting him stabilized before they could transport him."

The officer seemed to relish the opportunity to give us a full report with more detail than we needed. The PTSD therapist had said that it was a common coping mechanism for people to do that as they processed a traumatic situation.

"Yes, blood everywhere," he continued. His eyes shifted off to the side, not seeing us but the scene. "And there were ruts. Deep ruts, like from big truck tires." He shook his head once. "Couldn't get any casts of tire treads. The place was too torn up. Drivers must have peeled outta there in a panic once they saw the Kid wasn't getting up." He glanced at the Lone Oak and shook his head again.

His description made things fall into place in my mind. "Well, that goes to show that the person who called your tip line must have been terrified. Probably had taken part in the attack in some way and felt guilty afterward. You should talk to--oh, what do they call it on the TV crime shows--yes, you should talk to the victim's associates."

"Yes, ma'am. We're doing that," confirmed the officer. His eyes focused on TJ. "Was he a friend of yours, sir?"

"Whoa, slow down. I've seen him hanging around the streets

of St. Michaels. That's all. Talk to his associates. Believe me, he was no friend of mine." TJ leaned forward. "Still, he didn't deserve to be attacked...or killed. I feel sorry for his family."

"Yes, sir. He was only 17 years old. According to his dad, he'd had a job with an auto repair shop in Easton. He went on and on about how he loved cars and trucks and could keep anything running on the road. It's a shame. He was getting his life straight." The young officer got up and adjusted his belt holding pounds of gear, including his gun.

"I'll be going." He dug into his shirt pocket and gave each of us a business card. "If you think of anything else, be sure to give us a call."

"I'll walk the officer to his car," TJ said.

TJ was back in a moment and fell into a chair. "That was horrible. But you had a good idea of how to handle the investigation." He leaned back and folded his hands behind his head. "You're a natural at this. Are you going to write a mystery story?"

This is what it felt like to be blindsided. How did the conversation go from murder to my book?

TJ was waiting for an answer, but I was tongue-tied. Me, who had counseled distraught or irate parents, addressed PTA meetings, faced down a school principal about a budget decision. Now, my mouth wouldn't work. I was losing my grip. I couldn't dismiss this man because he was taking an interest in what I was doing. I couldn't admit that I had no ideas for my children's book. I couldn't tell him that the only writing I was doing was correspondence with a ghost.

In a panic, I said, "You can't ask a writer about a book that's still in development."

TJ put his hands flat down on the tabletop and pushed himself up so that he stood his full six feet plus. "Well, if you don't want to tell me about the book, that's fine. When you meet with your new writing group tomorrow night, you'll probably have to tell them something. I hope you have a good story for them."

I groaned as I turned away so he couldn't see the wave of panic that went through me. Then I realized he was playing with me. Two could play the same game. I turned back to him. "That's right, the meeting of writers is tomorrow night. Tell you what, I'll go willingly if we can go on a field trip in the morning."

"What did you have in mind?" A trace of suspicion showed on his face.

"I'd like to take a walk. My physical therapist said exercise is good, but she suggested that I still needed someone with me, just in case." I sighed. "It's so awkward and frustrating to think I need a caretaker."

"Not to worry," TJ said. "I'd be happy to walk you around the house or down the driveway anytime."

"Could we go to Waterwood tomorrow?"

TJ started shaking his head almost immediately. "No, no, no. I'm not taking you up to the main house. There's no way I'm ready for visitors."

"No, not the house," I said quickly. "I want to go to the family cemetery." I don't think he could have looked more surprised if I'd slapped him. "I feel a connection with Waterwood. After all, the Cottage is surrounded by the original plantation. Did you know there are some references to Waterwood in the papers pulled for me in the Maryland Room? It would be interesting to see if anyone I've read about is buried there. I'm curious, that's all. But if you don't want to…"

He took off his ball cap and ran his fingers through his hair. It looks soft and thick, gently streaked by the sun. Then he hid it underneath the cap again. "Well, I don't understand why you want to go there, but I have time tomorrow morning. Yes, I'll take you." He glanced down at my leg. "Do you think you can manage it?" He asked with a tinge of hesitation. "I try to keep the grass mowed."

"I'll be fine," I assured him.

"Okay, I'll pick you up at nine." As he walked away from the patio, he added, "And don't forget to lock all the doors and windows, at least until they catch the bad guy."

The bad guy. I was so preoccupied with Daniel that I kept

forgetting about the attack on the young man. My poor brain was having trouble managing the pills, doing exercises, and now, protecting myself.

I was tired, but it was too early to go to bed. There was one more thing that could distract me. I could write a letter to Daniel.

CHAPTER NINETEEN

"There is a bill before the Texas State Legislature that states that if a husband is in the U.S. army or navy, the wife has ample grounds for divorce."

—*Baltimore Sun* Newspaper, January 31, 1862

After dinner, I went into the writing den and made myself comfortable at the desk. I took out my calligraphy pen with the metal nib and reached for the bottle of black ink. I remembered how difficult it was to control the amount of ink on the pen point. Uncle Jack had bought an inkwell at an auction once. I ran my eyes over the many shelves of books and knick-knacks. Finally, I spotted it in a dusty corner.

The small crystal inkwell sat on a square bronze base decorated with an owl's face on each corner. Uncle Jack said he liked it because the owl was a symbol of wisdom. A person had to be smart if one was going to write with pen and ink in an old-fashioned way. That's the challenge I faced. This was my chance to build my connection with Daniel and to find out more. I suspected that if I didn't write this letter, I would always regret it.

I opened the bottle of ink and, with a steady hand, poured a quantity into the inkwell and set it back on its base. I pulled a sheet of paper, dipped the pen, and began to write.

My Dear Sir,

I never meant to give you the impression that I wanted you to leave my life forever. Pray, tell me what has transpired during this time of your silence. I truly want to know.

Yours most sincerely,
Emma

I laid the pen down and moved the inkwell to the side. I gently blew on the words so that the ink would dry. Then I remembered the rocker blotter tucked away in a cubbyhole. Our ancestors had the time and ingenuity to develop useful tools to help with everyday tasks. Why blow on wet ink when there was another way? Of course, I preferred the efficiency of emailing and texting, but writing a letter the old-fashioned way was, I don't know, elegant.

I'd made my decision. I set the finished letter in the center of the writing surface of the desk. I went to the door and turned out the light.

Before climbing the stairs to bed, I looked across the creek to the Lone Oak. No lights were waving around there tonight. All was quiet on that mysterious piece of land that was once home to two old women believed to be witches. Now, the local lore could add the mystery of how a young man had lost his life there. The thought sent me around the house to recheck the locks and close the curtains then I'd tackle the stairs.

The next morning, I found that once again I had forgotten to close the drapes in the upstairs bedroom as the warm rays of the rising sun caressed my face. I dressed quickly in a pair of comfortable jeans and a light pullover sweater of deep rose and went downstairs. Long pants were good for traipsing around an old family cemetery. One never knew if the mosquitoes were hungry or a tick was waiting to chomp down on bare skin. I'd learned my lesson as a child visiting the Cottage.

I smiled when I got to the bottom of the stairs. The thought of finding a letter from Daniel on the desk didn't scare me anymore. Now that I'd decided to build the connection, I wanted to see what my ghost had written to me overnight. And I wasn't disappointed.

On the desk, in flowing script, was his response.

My Dear Emma,

I was relieved to receive your letter. When it did not arrive immediately, my concern grew, but my patience was rewarded. Thank you so much for your caring and constancy.

I deeply regret that I did not say a proper goodbye to you before your father and I left Waterwood. It gave me great pain to ride away without telling you of our departure.

I waited by the Lone Oak tree for as long as I could. If I may be so bold, I wanted you to know that I carried you with me in my heart. But it was not to be. I kept telling myself that you were detained for a good reason. As we rode away, I told myself over and over again that your absence was not because you didn't care.

I am sure that your father's decision to leave seemed sudden. It was not. Over the many weeks before that fateful day of our departure, your father weighed the arguments about the declaration of allegiance surrounding the War Between the States. As you know, I spent my days with him as he walked the land, attending to his many daily responsibilities. I spent hours listening to him speak aloud of the many things said by each side of the debate, those favoring the North and those feeling strong ties with the South.

When he first expressed their arguments, I thought he was talking to me, trying to make me understand the divisions facing our state of Maryland. I soon learned I was wrong. He was trying to better understand the situation himself. He was facing a great decision that would affect the future of Waterwood and his dear Emma. Little did I know that this decision would affect my life as well.

For a while, the disagreements between the Union representatives and Southern sympathizers were far away. Then the situation changed and tensions moved across the Chesapeake Bay and into Talbot County and our very own town of Easton. Federal troops came from Baltimore and seized ammunition, muskets, cannons, and sabers from the Easton Armory. Those armaments had been stored there since the War of 1812. That act of seizure made our citizens realize that the government believed that we would storm the building, commit thievery and use the arms against our fellow Americans. Many found that idea abhorrent.

Could they imagine an even more offensive act was about to be perpetrated by soldiers from Baltimore under orders of the government? I think not.

When the Union soldiers came to Easton, dragged a judge from the bench, and arrested him, it was a source of upheaval.

Your father was greatly agitated. That was the moment that he felt the federal government had gone too far. He knew it was time to make a stand.

He reflected on both sides of each argument. In the meantime, he had to be careful to avoid confrontation. Do you remember the time he took away your peppermint stick? People were calling it secessionist candy. It was striped red and white and didn't have any blue representing the federal government. He thought it was trivial, but he didn't want trouble.

Though he was a citizen of the great state of Maryland, a state that remained in the Union, he felt his ties were stronger to the Southern cause. He believed your mother would have supported him in this decision if she were still alive. She may have joined the ladies of other Eastern Shore plantations and made faces at the federal soldiers on the street. Many local residents would not walk under the Stars 'n Stripes flag hung over the sidewalk on Washington Street.

Once your father made his decision to support the South, he ordered provisions and made equipage ready. Everyone quietly worked to prepare provisions for the Confederate army and the supplies needed.

I was honored and humbled when he asked me to accompany him, to tend to his needs on this trek. He declared that we had to make haste and depart as soon as humanly possible. He was fearful that the men of the town committed to the Union would try to stop him. We needed to slip away without detection. He hoped to return soon to prepare another shipment of supplies without anyone the wiser.

As I made final preparations, my heart ached to talk to you, even if it was only for a moment. I looked everywhere. You were not to be found. When I saw Joshua in the stables, I asked him to deliver a message asking you to meet me at the Lone Oak, our tree.

My father was sworn to secrecy by your father. He beseeched my father to protect Waterwood and the most precious one in his life. You, dear Emma, his daughter. It gave me great pride when my father gave his blessing to my upcoming travels. I too begged him to care for and protect you.

The time was nigh for us to leave. I went to the Lone Oak and waited in vain for you to come. As your father decreed, we rode away as the last rays of the sun disappeared. I kept looking over my shoulder, hoping to catch a glimpse of you one last time. It was not to be. The lands of Waterwood faded in the gathering dusk. Would I ever cast my eyes on them again?

Emma, I hope you will accept this explanation of what happened and truly believe that my heart stayed with you and Waterwood on that day and every day thereafter.

Ever Your Servant,
Daniel

Tears prickled my eyes as I laid the letter down and looked out the window to the great tree across the creek. It must have been agony for Daniel to ride away, to do his loyal duty without saying goodbye to Emma. Not knowing why she didn't come must have troubled him.

Then I wondered about this other person named Joshua. Why had he failed in his mission to deliver the message from Daniel? Was he a rival for Emma's affections? Did he resent Daniel because he was the son of a plantation manager? Or was he a slave who refused to take orders from the young man?

I gazed at the Lone Oak, its large leaves fluttering in the breeze. It must have been growing on that spot for more than 150 years if it was their meeting place in the 1860s. A smile crept over my lips as I thought about Emma and Daniel spending time under that tree, a special place for two childhood friends who grew to be grownup lovers. Had they carved their initials in its bark? I promised myself that when I could walk without any assistance, I would look for myself.

With a start, I realized I hadn't copied Daniel's latest letter. I didn't want it to fade away before I captured his words. Quickly, I took a picture with my phone then typed the words into Daniel's computer file.

CHAPTER TWENTY

"Flower, Bird, Wind, Moon."

—*Japanese Proverb, meaning Experience the beauties of nature and learn about yourself.*

True to his word, TJ pulled up in front of the Cottage at nine o'clock. I settled into the passenger seat, eager for our expedition to the Waterwood cemetery. I wasn't sure how I would feel seeing a stone marker with Daniel's name on it, but it was something I needed to do. We drove down the long gravel driveway from the Cottage to the main road and turned left.

Soon, we made another left onto a small gravel road crowded by towering stalks of corn, their green leaves drying golden brown in the sun. They blocked the view of everything around us except the sky. It felt like we were driving down Alice's rabbit hole.

TJ followed the curving road until we reached the far end of the fields when he turned onto a large, mowed area of grass and parked in the shade of a gnarled, old tree.

A tall red brick wall with bright white mortar enclosed the

gathering of stones marking the graves of people associated with Waterwood. An intricate iron gate blocked the entrance. TJ unlocked it and it swung open easily on its hinges. As we walked inside, it might've been my imagination, but it felt uniquely quiet in this place.

"This cemetery has been here since the beginning of Waterwood," TJ said in a hushed voice. He must have felt the peace and reverence as I did. "The plantation dates back to the time before the Revolutionary War."

He pointed to a grave marker in the shape of an obelisk that must have been fifteen feet tall. Its white marble was blinding in the sunshine. "And that's where they buried the man who started Waterwood. He was a crusty old captain who made his fortune on the high seas. The king gave him this land for services rendered. Of course, the original land-grant was for many more acres than we have today. Over the centuries, the land has been subdivided for the many sons and daughters of the family. And whenever they needed money, they sold off some acres. It wasn't unusual, but I wish that they had been able to hold it all together."

TJ and I meandered between the markers. They were all in good condition, a sign of TJ's tender care. The earliest stones were about four feet in height, except for the captain's grand marker, of course. There were many, too many, small white stones marking the graves of infants and young children. It seemed that around the early 1800s, the convention for grave markers shifted to large stone slabs. I eyed the names chiseled there, hoping to find Daniel's name quickly.

"What are you looking for?" asked TJ. "Someone in particular?"

I was hoping to find the grave without concocting an excuse for TJ. I had to think fast. "I'm amazed to see the names of some people I've been reading about."

He nodded. I was relieved that he accepted my explanation. He walked slowly between the graves, reading off the names.

"Let's see, there's John Dorset and Elizabeth Dorset." He stopped by one marker and looked down. "And here's…" He stopped then quickly turned to another collection of markers. "Over here—"

"Wait, who is buried there?" I maneuvered around so I could see the name for myself and when I read it, I froze. It read, Emma. Just Emma. It was unsettling to see my name carved on a gravestone, especially after barely cheating death only months earlier. No wonder TJ tried to distract me. I too wanted to look away, but I forced myself to read the rest of the words marking her grave. Below her name were the words *Wife of Joshua*. I checked the dates. They were in the right period. Was this Daniel's Emma? The part of me where I'd buried my romantic notions long ago fluttered awake. I didn't want to know that she had married someone named Joshua.

Was it the same Joshua who was supposed to deliver Daniel's message? Was he the reason Emma didn't meet Daniel at the Lone Oak the night he left Waterwood with her father? Did Joshua fail Daniel so he could win Emma's hand in marriage? I swayed with the thought.

TJ rushed over and gripped my arm to steady me. "Are you okay?" His face filled with concern. "We'd better go. This is too much."

I took a deep breath and stood straighter. I had to maintain my newly won independence. "No, no, I'm all right. I think it was the surprise of seeing my name like that. I'm okay now."

"Are you sure?" I nodded and he too looked at the gravestone. "Oh, you were looking at *her* marker. Emma of Waterwood. She seems to have a strange effect on people."

"What do you mean?" I wanted to know.

"Some people say that she is restless. Some have reported that they've seen her walking along the shore near your property line." Quickly, he added, "But I don't believe any of it."

I knew Daniel was eager to connect, but why was Emma agitated? "It says that she was the wife of Joshua. Do you know that name?"

"He married into the family. Emma was the daughter of the plantation owner back then. My aunt did some genealogical work on the family tree and, if I remember correctly, Joshua was the son of another local landowner. That marriage complicated the lines of inheritance regarding the Waterwood lands. I don't remember the details. If you're truly interested, I could check the library at the house and see what is there."

"Oh yes, that would be wonderful."

"I'll let you know what I find." TJ pulled his keys out of his jeans pocket.

I didn't want to leave. Not yet. "Before we go," I said quickly. "Could you see if there is another name in the cemetery? Is there a Daniel here?"

TJ gave me a puzzled look then made his way around the stones, checking the names. "Who is this Daniel? Do you have a last name?"

"Oh, I came across some of his letters in my research." It wasn't a lie. I wasn't doing all my research in the Maryland Room at the library. I hoped TJ wouldn't ask for specifics.

"No, I don't see that name anywhere." He was standing in a grassy area without any markers. There were two small tree stumps cut close to the ground. "I have no idea who is buried over here."

"But wouldn't the church have burial records?"

"This is a private family cemetery. The records were kept by the family. Somebody misplaced them."

"Maybe nobody is buried there," I said, hoping to hide my disappointment.

"I think the area inside the wall is pretty full. The modern graves are outside the wall. Some of my ancestors don't have markers."

"Why not?"

"It was once considered bad luck to place a gravestone for someone dearly departed, even if it was for a member of the family."

"Why? Wasn't it a sign of respect to mark someone's grave?" I asked.

He shook his head. "There was an old superstition that if you placed a gravestone for someone, you would be the next to die."

"That's creepy."

"Well, if you can't have superstitions in a graveyard, where can you have them?" He pointed to the old tree stumps. "I guess these might be a sign of another old tradition of burying a person with something like a walnut in his mouth in the hope that a tree would grow to mark the person's final resting place naturally. I guess these trees didn't last."

That story made me shiver. I felt the first twinges of PTSD starting. I had come too close to needing a grave marker. "I think you're right. I think it's time to go."

As we made our way back to the truck, I thanked TJ for bringing me to his family cemetery but said no more. I had come in search of Daniel and found a troubling mystery.

As we drove up to the Cottage, TJ cleared his throat as if he had something to say but was reluctant to say it. "Ah, is it possible for you to reschedule your P.T. appointment for tomorrow morning? Something has come up and I won't be able to drive you until after lunch."

"That's okay, I have someone else I can call. I don't think it will be a problem." I hid my smile of pride that I was taking another small step to controlling my life.

He frowned. "Who is that?"

"Stephani. Remember I met her at the library?" *Of course, he did*, I thought as I remembered his reaction at seeing her. "She said if I ever needed a ride, I should let her know. If it's a problem, I'll reschedule the appointment. It's not a problem. Thanks again for bringing me to your family's cemetery today. It was interesting in more ways than one." I flashed him a big smile.

"You're welcome."

When we arrived back at the Cottage, I remembered something. "You will let me know if you find any information about Emma or Joshua at your house?"

"I don't understand why you're so interested, but I'll take a look tonight."

I watched him drive off and turned to work my way

inside. *Slow and steady. Slow and steady,* I murmured to myself when the front door burst open and Maria welcomed me home.

"Hello! I was worried when I didn't find you here when I came. I looked all over the Cottage, on the patio, everywhere! Then I figured that you must be at your physical therapy appointment or out with Mr. TJ. I've been getting my work done." She took a breath in relief. "But I must say, I was really glad to see you getting out of his truck."

I knew it was important for Maria to think I was getting stronger or I'd have someone else trying to baby me. It felt so good to sit down at the kitchen table. I would never admit that the trip to the cemetery was more demanding than a P.T. appointment, but it had been worth it. Maria fussed around the kitchen and I enjoyed a wonderful lunch on the patio that helped rebuild my strength. I don't know where Mr. Saffire found her, but she was a gem.

Maria slid the patio door open and came out, holding a tall, chilled glass of milky liquid. "I brought you something special because I know how much you like coffee, but it's too humid to have hot coffee in this afternoon heat, so I thought I'd bring you a surprise."

She put the glass down on the table in front of me, beads of condensation running down the side. It was a magnificent glass of iced coffee.

"Wonderful!" I took a sip and relished the taste. "It's perfect, just the way I like it. Thank you, Maria."

"You're welcome. Think of it as a celebration of your accomplishment."

"My accomplishment?"

"Sure, you're making good progress. When I first saw you, you could barely get around. Now, you're using both legs. Before you know it, you'll be walking without any help and even driving again."

When I realized what a full recovery would mean, I reeled. I didn't want to drive again, not ever, now that I knew what could happen. It was hard enough to get into a car to be driven someplace, let alone get behind the wheel.

Maria must have noticed my reaction. "Of course, we don't have to think about that right now. You still have a long way to go and I certainly don't need to talk myself out of a job."

She turned to look out at the water, land, and sky. "This is such a beautiful spot. If I lived here, I'd probably sit outside on this patio to watch the landscape change with the seasons. It's all happening right in front of us."

"I agree with you," I said. "Even when I was a child, Uncle Jack and I would sit out here for hours and just watch. A blue heron lived around here for a couple of years. He acted as if he owned the Cottage. I spent so much time watching him, I even gave him a name, Ernie," I said, smiling at the memory.

"Was he a nice bird?" She asked.

"No, not really. If I went down to the water while he was looking for dinner, he would squawk at me to go away. It was worse than the sound of fingernails dragged down a blackboard. I'd watch him watching the water. He would stand so still his blue feathers would ruffle in the breeze. The fish must have thought he was part of the sky or a plant until he would strike. Then, of course, it was too late."

Maria sighed and looked up at the immense dome of blue sky above. "I like the geese. Most people don't." She shrugged. "They can be nasty birds when they're riled up. They have a strong sense of family. They mate for life, watch out for their young and fly in a V formation. Many spend the winter here on the Shore, always calling out to make sure everybody knows where everybody is. Used to be that way with families, but now the kids can't wait to go off to school, get jobs someplace else, travel who knows where, doing who knows what. It's enough to put you in your grave before your time."

She started collecting my dirty lunch dishes. "Have you ever seen the Monarchs?"

"No, I think I was back in school when the butterflies flew south for the winter."

"It's an incredible sight. At first, you're alone. Then one bright orange butterfly settles on a nearby bush. The next minute, there are hundreds of them. I read they fly all the way from southern Canada, which is a place I've never visited, to central Mexico, which is another place I've never been and have no interest in going. I hate crossing the Chesapeake Bay Bridge, let alone traveling all the way up to Canada. I wonder if it bothers them to drink the water in Mexico."

I had to start coughing to stifle my laughter. This woman, so conscientious about her responsibilities, said some of the funniest things. I had to listen carefully to her ramblings because somewhere in there, I would find a nugget.

Maria went inside to finish her work, leaving me alone with my thoughts. What was I going to tell the writing group? TJ was right. They would expect me to introduce myself, talk about my writing accomplishments, and give them an idea of what I was writing. My only writing accomplishments were notes to parents and student progress sheets. Maybe I was approaching this the wrong way. Maria brought me some paper, the cordless phone, and a sheet of orange origami paper before she left for the day. First, I smoothed out the sheet of orange paper, thinking about the ancient Japanese art form called origami: *ori-* to fold and *gami-* paper. An origami shape must be made without cutting, pasting, or marking the paper. A simple concept that takes a lifetime to master.

To begin, I had to select a shape. Crane? Butterfly? No, I thought a fish was more appropriate. It needs courage and determination to swim upstream, the same dedication I needed to tackle my goal of writing a book.

Why can't I be content with rehab and recovery? I sighed. *Because that's not the way I am.* I scooted my chair closer to the table and started folding. The minutes flew by and my confused thoughts settled. I put the little orange fish on the table. It worked its magic. Whenever I was in the classroom and got the urge to fold, it was a sign that things were not going well. Creating a shape allowed me to catch my breath and entertain the kids at the same time.

Now, the little orange fish got me in the mood to think about the book. Would the kids enjoy another book about the Civil War? I was about to start a list of other ideas when the phone rang.

"Hello, my dear Ms. Chase."

I was so surprised by my attorney's polite attitude that it took me a moment to respond. "Mr. Heinrick?"

"Why yes, of course. I thought I would call and see how things were going for you?"

"I'm still making progress. I want to use a cane, but the therapist said I wasn't ready."

"No, no, you must take your time," he insisted.

"I will. Believe me, this therapist will make sure I don't reinjure myself. But I do feel stronger every day."

"No need to rush," he stressed. "I hope you're resting all day, every day."

I swear the man wanted to put me on a glass shelf. "No, I've been going to P.T., of course, but I'm doing some research at the library and—"

He cut me off. "You're not wasting your time trying to write that book you mentioned, are you?"

"Well, I—"

"Oh, my dear Ms. Chase. You have much to do to recover from your brush with death and all the mind-altering drugs. Relax and don't worry about a thing. If all goes as I plan, you won't have to worry about a thing. And with that, I must wish you a good day. I have some other calls to make."

With hands clenched, I was determined to do things my way, I focused on something else I had to do before the meeting. I needed to write a response to Daniel's letter. I knew I wouldn't have the energy to write it when I got home. I gathered up my things, including my little orange fish, and went inside.

CHAPTER TWENTY-ONE

"Focus more on your desire than on your doubt and the dream will take care of itself."

---*Mark Twain*

I took out Daniel's letter that I had found on my desk this morning to read the words as he's written them even though they were already fading away. I knew I had the content saved on my computer and in my photo gallery, but there was something about seeing the words he had formed with his pen.

I had to pause for a moment and give my mind and emotions a little shake. Daniel was becoming very real to me. I had to remember that this was an unearthly presence.

Daniel wasn't alive, not anymore. He was lying in a grave somewhere. I wished he had been buried in the family cemetery. It would've helped somehow to see his name carved in stone in the place he loved so much. Where was the body of this man?

I sat quietly and let his words echo in my mind as I reread the story of long ago. Certain lines touched me:

I wanted you to know that I carried you with me in my heart. But it was not to be. The words brought a tear to my eye. I could do nothing to change the past. I could only offer a little comfort. I made a note to do just that. I read more of his letter.

When the Union soldiers came to Easton, dragged a judge from the bench, and arrested him, it was a source of upheaval. I wanted to find out more about this incident and made a note for my next visit to the library.

Do you remember the time he took away your peppermint stick? Yes, I couldn't ignore this reference.

He believed your mother would have supported him in this decision. I'd acknowledge this line, too.

I was honored and humbled when he asked me to accompany him. Daniel deserved my recognition of his loyalty.

My recognition? Oh, dear. I'm getting very involved. It was time to write my response. I took a fresh piece of paper, opened the inkwell, dipped my pen, and wrote to my ghostly correspondent.

My Dear Daniel,

I too was troubled that we could not say goodbye before you left with my father. Sometimes, the good Lord declares that certain things are not to be.

I thank you for offering this correspondence about my dear father and the dilemma he faced. I knew that something was troubling him, but he spoke almost nothing about it to me.

I too remember the moment he took away my peppermint stick. It was fraught with tension. I remember the quiet mumblings about the confrontation in Easton with the soldiers and how it upset my father deeply.

I am comforted that you traveled at my father's side. I can think of no one else I would want with him.

I too feel the absence of my mother most keenly. If only she were here to support him and, if I may say, me.

You are kind to consider my sensibilities, but I beg that you do not withhold any details –great or small –about the thoughts and musings of my father.

Please, I pray, continue the story of your journey after you left Waterwood. The more I know, the more I will understand. The more I understand, I hope, the greater peace I will feel in my heart.

If I may be honest, this sentiment is true about my father and about you. Please, if you feel so disposed, share your thoughts with me as you have so many times before. I await your next letter.

Most gratefully and faithfully yours,

Emma

After I blotted the ink and gave it a few minutes to dry, I tucked the letter away in the cubbyhole. I would put it out before I went to bed after the writers meeting.

A glance at my watch made it clear that I had to get going if I was going to take a short nap, dress, and be ready for Catherine when she came to pick me up. I started the slow ascent to the second floor, not sure if I wanted to take a hot shower or a short nap. I suspected that a tall glass of scotch might be a better way to prepare for the evening's activities.

As I walked past a mirror in my bedroom, I almost gagged at what I saw. Me... with a messy braid and cockeyed bangs. I wasn't fit to be seen by anyone, let alone a group of observant writers. I grabbed a pair of scissors and headed to the bathroom. I straightened my bangs and shortened my braid. It wasn't perfect, but it had to be better than it was.

Now, I was running late. It took me a long time to decide what to wear to a meeting of writers. I bypassed a pantsuit, too formal. I decided against jeans, too casual. Maybe if I dressed the part, I'd feel more like a writer so I pulled out a black maxi skirt with a black sleeveless top and a funky pair of earrings. Yes, it was a creative type looking at me from the mirror. I was proud of myself that I got downstairs as Catherine drove up in her oyster white Jaguar. She was dressed in a soft, flowing white silk dress that almost matched her car. She seemed to favor the frozen shades of an ice princess.

I forced an excited smile on my face and made my way down the steps. The walker was inside, leaning against the foyer wall. I held an old cane from the closet firmly in my hand.

"Oh, Emma," Catherine called out. "I'm so glad you're coming tonight. Every writers group can benefit from fresh blood, especially ours."

She didn't smile.

I had to ask, "I hope you don't mean that literally?"

Her laughter rang out. "You're so funny. I just know we're

going to be great friends." And we were off. She didn't even wait until we were on the main road before she started probing.

"You know, TJ didn't tell me very much about you. Why don't you use this time to tell me about yourself?"

I didn't think I'd have to face this question until we got to the meeting, but it would be good practice. "Well, I majored in elementary education in college and have a minor in English. I teach kindergarten now."

"OH! You must be sick all the time!" She swiveled her head toward me. "You aren't carrying germs now, are you?"

"Catherine, keep your eyes on the road." I chuckled to hide my fear. "No, I haven't been in the classroom for a long time."

"Oh, sorry. One can never be too careful as one gets older."

"Now, it's your turn," I said. "Tell me about yourself."

"Well, I'm working on a memoir. I come from a very interesting family."

I hoped she couldn't see me rolling my eyes in the growing darkness as we flew down the road with the waters of the Chesapeake Bay off to our right. The sun almost touched the horizon. It wouldn't be long before night would fall well before dinner time. The August humidity and high temperatures were still with us, but fall was not far away.

Thankfully, she soon clicked the turn signal and we drove onto a gravel driveway marked only by a split rail fence. It was one of many roads that branched off the main roads and led into woods or cornfields. Often, these drives did not lead to farmhouses, but to beautiful homes especially ones with spectacular views of the water. The meeting place for the writers group did not disappoint.

Even though the house was new construction, it incorporated design elements of a Victorian home plus the ambiance of large, brightly lit windows and a huge wraparound porch. Catherine pulled up in a parking area where her Jaguar fit right in with the BMWs and Mercedes-Benzes.

It was slow going for me to make it up the front steps. I wasn't adept at using the old cane. Halfway up the front steps, I chided myself for letting my pride and vanity overwhelm my need for support.

Finally, at the front door, Catherine hit the doorbell and walked right in. I followed her into a two-story-high entryway. I caught glimpses of modern furnishings rather than antiques. The hand of a talented interior designer was evident. Catherine continued down the hall to the kitchen that overlooked the water. There, a flood of recessed lighting revealed a collection of women talking and munching away.

Catherine clapped her hands. "Hello, everybody! Let me introduce Emma Chase, our newest member."

The five women felt like a mob as they surrounded me to shake my hand, pat my arm and introduce themselves. I didn't catch any of their names in the confusion.

Catherine clapped her hands again. "Okay, girls, let's give the woman some room to breathe. Denise, why don't we let Emma sit there then we can all introduce ourselves?"

With a meek smile, Denise floated off a high barstool at the island counter. She had a petite, willowy body that reminded me of a pixie, but instead of being pert, she was so shy, she seemed to sink into herself. Denise drifted over to stand at the shoulder and one step behind a woman who towered over everyone else by height and sheer will. I estimated she was about 5'11" with ramrod straight posture that made her look taller. Was that a natural position or was she wearing a brace?

"That is a good idea," the tall woman declared. "We will make our introductions as a group so Emma only has to tell us about herself once." The woman smiled, but her black eyes focused on me, full of judgment. "I'm Gretchen Fleischer." Her long bangs hid her eyebrows and just touched her large, stark white glasses. "Welcome to my home." She paused.

And I responded dutifully, "And a beautiful home it is. Thank you so much for the invitation." Suddenly, I felt like I was attending one of my mother's club meetings of Mainline Philadelphia where everyone wore a conservative A-line dress and a strand of pearls and knew her place.

A middle-aged woman in an olive-green midi skirt and matching short sleeve sweater set that did nothing for her sallow complexion stepped forward. She was so overweight that her boobs blended in with her tummy so her silhouette was flat. "I thought the hostess was supposed to go last, Gretchen, but you know best." She turned to me and announced. "My name is Zelda. I won't tell you my last name. It's too long. You'll never remember it." The sentences came out like a bird pecking at the ground. "I hope you fit into our group."

What a strange thing to say. The group went right on with their introductions.

"Hello, my name is Maureen." This tall woman was an ocean of calm, in sharp contrast to the pecky Zelda. Maureen's silver hair was pulled back in a no-nonsense ponytail at the nape of her neck. She was wearing shoes that I didn't see very often on the Shore: two-inch heels. They were a statement that she still opted for looks over comfort. She turned towards the woman standing behind the statuesque Gretchen. "Let's not forget Denise."

"Oh, um, I'm Denise Walters." Everything about the woman who'd given me her seat blended together. Her strawberry blonde hair with a hint of red hung straight around her pale face. She had a dusting of small freckles across her nose and under her watery blue eyes. "Um, welcome to our group." Her soft voice would be blown away by a gentle puff of wind. Having introduced herself, she stepped back behind Gretchen, fading away.

"I'm delighted to welcome a new member to our group," Maureen said, filling the awkward silence. "I'm looking forward to hearing about what you're working on."

Gretchen rushed towards me. "Oh, we will talk about that after we eat. Now, Emma, tell me, do you prefer red or white wine?"

And the bustling around the kitchen began. Serving dishes, plates, and utensils appeared. I felt like I had to apologize. "I'm sorry, I didn't realize we were going to have dinner. I should've brought a dish."

Gretchen chuckled. "Oh no, that is not necessary. I love

cooking and entertaining. When I am executing a menu, I shuffle my husband off to another part of our house. He does not care. He knows there is a tray of wonderful dishes coming his way." She glanced down for a moment then raised her laser-sharp eyes at me. "Are you married, Emma?" Her lips pulled tight in a challenge.

I shook my head.

"I see," she said and I felt like I'd just been slid into a certain category. Gretchen continued quickly to cover that moment. "Preparing dinner for our writing group each month is a wonderful excuse to play with new recipes."

"It's fun for her, but not so good for our hips," Zelda remarked. Everybody laughed. Gretchen blinked twice while maintaining her plastered smile. It was with a sigh of relief that we sat around the oval table of rich mahogany in the dining room and enjoyed a gourmet feast.

CHAPTER TWENTY-TWO

"I love deadlines. I like the whooshing sound they make as they fly by."

— *Douglas Adams*

At the end of the truly gourmet meal, cups of fragrant coffee were handed around, along with some chocolate cookies. With a brush of a hand over her bangs, Gretchen settled herself at the head of the table again. "All right then, shall we start the meeting? Maureen, why don't you begin?"

"Gretchen, as you know, I…"

I tried to concentrate on what each woman was saying as we went around the table but was soon overwhelmed by too much information: where each one had moved from, where they were living now, their marital status, what they were writing, and what they hope to do with a manuscript once it was done. Watching and listening, I understood a bit more about my Uncle Jack. Whenever I visited him here on the Eastern Shore, we spent most of our time at the Cottage with brief trips to the post office, the stores in Easton, or cruises on the water in one of his little boats. He wasn't involved in the local social scene. Now, I knew why. These ladies, especially the single ones, would have hunted him down like a bloodhound. I shook off this thought so I wouldn't burst out laughing.

Catherine, sitting primly next to me, was finishing up her comments. "Emma, I'm making really good progress on my story about my mother and father when I was a little girl." She tittered. "That's all I'll say right now, so I won't ruin it for you when you read it."

I can't wait, glad that she couldn't hear my sarcastic thought. My hope of finding a friend here was fading.

"And now, why don't you tell everyone about yourself, Emma," Gretchen said.

Catherine took over. "Emma is a working girl from Philadelphia." She made me sound like a prostitute. Then things got worse. "She is a kindergarten teacher," she said with a … was it a sneer?

The older women—Gretchen and Catherine—moved back in their chairs. Were they germophobes? Denise and Zelda both glanced down at the papers in front of them. I figured they'd lost interest in me. Only Maureen kept her attention on me.

Catherine wasn't done. "She almost killed herself in a terrible car crash. As you can see, she survived, but she's dealing with a serious injury to her leg." She turned to me. "It's the right one, isn't it?"

This ice queen had certainly done her homework. She didn't get all this information from me. *Just wait until I see TJ!*

Catherine droned on. "She's doing her rehabilitation here and is living in the Cottage she inherited from her Uncle Jack and she's going to start her first book." She turned to me with a smile as genuine as a piece of plastic. "Isn't that right, Emma dear? Why don't you tell us what your novel is about?"

My worst fear was now a reality. I, the hotshot teacher who wasn't afraid to face a sobbing five-year-old, was caught flat-footed. Time to be straight with these people who I'd probably never see again. "I hope to write a children's book, maybe a picture book. I don't have a story yet, but I might do something about the Civil War."

I thought of that old cliché: you could hear a pin drop. But the rugs were too plush.

Finally, shy Denise piped up in the awkward silence. "That's different." Her voice was thin like a delicate strand of thread. "I'm thinking of trying something in the romance genre."

"Oh, Denise," Gretchen declared. "I don't think it is the type of story you should even consider doing." Gretchen made her pronouncement without looking at the small woman who sank back in her chair. "You're better off sticking to poetry,"

Taking charge, Maureen put her elbows on the table and leaned forward. "Emma, have you studied the accepted framework of a picture book?"

I almost laughed with relief. "Not exactly, but I've read a lot of them."

"You should become acquainted with it first, then think about the characters in the story."

Gretchen cleared her throat to draw everyone's attention. "Emma, I'm not sure this group can be any help," she said, dismissing my interest in books for children. "But you're welcome to participate in one of our writing exercises."

She passed sheets of blank paper around to everyone with a flourish. I could feel a tightness starting in my chest. Oh, how I wished I had a car outside and could escape. Of course, that would mean I'd have to drive and I'm not sure which activity scared me more right now.

The ladies sitting around the table went through their writing rituals. One concentrated on selecting the appropriate pen from a fat pouch while another opted for a pencil. One meticulously put a lined piece of paper underneath the blank sheet so the words would be straight while another one closed her eyes for a Zen moment. Zelda dug deep into her colorful tote, pulled out a tiny doll that looked like a Smurf with ratty purple hair, and put it next to her paper. I wanted to ask if that was her muse, but I didn't dare. Optimistic Denise asked for a second piece of paper in case she hit her stride.

Catherine seated on the other side of me mumbled, "or gets wordy as usual."

"The exercise this evening," Gretchen proclaimed, "is to spend fifteen minutes creating a no-good, very-bad antagonist. Because, as I always say, if you don't have an exceptional antagonist, you don't have a story. Ready? I'm timing you. Begin now."

I stared at the blank page, rolling my favorite pen between my fingers. I thought of some of my favorite stories for children. They didn't have dark, complicated antagonists. The Brothers Grimm themselves would have fit in well with this group.

"Fair warning," Gretchen proclaimed. "One minute."

The doorbell rang and Gretchen sang out, "Come in."

TJ walked into the dining room and took a small step back when faced with all the admiring ladies. I don't think I was ever so relieved to see anyone in my life. "I'm here to pick up Emma," he said. "but I see I'm early. I'll wait outside in my truck."

He turned to leave, but I wasn't going to let him go. "NO!" The ladies all stared at me. "No," I repeated calmly. "I mean, it's been a long evening for me, and I think it would be good for me to go now. You know, with my leg and all." It was the first time that I had used my physical condition as an excuse, but there was never a better time to start.

The ladies got up to walk me to the door so they could talk to TJ. While they were fussing and tittering about my handsome chauffeur, Maureen shook my hand, slipping me a small piece of paper. When she gave me a gentle hug, she whispered, "That's my phone number. If you want to talk about writing, give me a call. I'll come to you."

As we walked out the door, the ladies called out, "See you next month and bring your good-looking driver."

CHAPTER TWENTY-THREE

"At risk of sounding foully pompous I think that writers' groups are probably very useful at the beginning of a writing career."

—Bernard Cornwell

Once TJ and I had escaped to the porch, he shot me a look of disbelief. "A cane? When did you graduate to a cane?"

"Not now." I caught his arm and leaned on the handrail. "Get me out of here."

Once in the truck and heading down the main road, TJ said, "Now, are you going to tell me—"

I interrupted quickly. "How wonderful your idea was to go to this writers group? Absolutely not! It was the worst evening I've spent since I went on a blind date in high school."

He looked at me as if I'd lost my mind. "No, that's not fair," I said softly. "The idea of going to a writers group was a good one. It's just that this one was horrible. I've read that a good writers group is supposed to support you in whatever you want to write and will make thoughtful, constructive suggestions. That is vital.

Writing is hard, especially for someone just starting. Having the right kind of support can make all the difference."

I grunted as I remembered their reaction to my teaching career and my kids. "The only thing these ladies are interested in is a good glass of wine, dinner, and an opportunity to snipe at each other. No, change that. I must admit the dinner was fabulous. Gretchen is a great cook, but I have no idea what kind of a writer she is. Nobody brought anything to critique." I threw my hands up in the air and let them fall in my lap.

"Okay, now that you've had your rant, do you feel better?" he asked.

I didn't want to admit it, but I did feel better.

"Maybe this group wasn't a good fit for you," he continued. "I'll keep my ears open to find another one in the area."

I almost blurted out, NO! But I locked my lips tight. Why couldn't he just do handyman things? He was only trying to help. If he found another group, I didn't have to go.

I settled back in my seat. "Thank you. And thank you for coming to get me tonight. I'm sure you have other things you and Ghost would rather be doing."

He smiled as he glanced my way. "No problem, we're glad to do it, especially while I have the time. A few weeks down the road, I'll be working all hours with the harvest and won't have time for anything until it gets cold." He smiled at me again.

"What, what is it?" I ran my fingers over my lips. "Do I have something on my face?"

He chuckled. "No, I like seeing you like this. Not so uptight. Maybe you're getting more comfortable with my driving."

"I – I'm comfortable." I could hear the lie behind my words. I hoped he couldn't.

"In the beginning, you were tense. You watched how I did everything. You must have almost bitten your tongue off to keep from telling me what to do."

"I did not. I think you're a fine driver."

"And the other day?" he asked. "Are you gonna tell me that you weren't nervous?"

Driving made me nervous, period. It didn't matter who was behind the wheel. I was used to being independent. Now, I was at everyone's mercy. I could feel resentment bubbling up and tried to tamp it down. Why was he pushing this point?

"All right, I'll admit I was a little nervous, but—"

"A little?!"

That did it. I erupted. "OKAY! I was a nervous wreck. Those ladies back there think it must be terrific to be driven around by a stunningly handsome chauffeur. No, don't get any ideas. I'm just voicing what they were saying. I don't even want to think about what was going through their minds."

"Emma, maybe—"

"I don't need to be treated that way. There's nothing to envy about my situation." I stared out the windshield, my eyes boring holes into the darkness. "I don't need people in my life who think they know everything about everything. Why should I want to spend time with a simpering group of wannabees out here, so far from civilization?" I shifted my gaze to the passenger window. There wasn't anything to see in the dark, only the reflection of my face staring back at me.

I straightened up. "No, coming here was a mistake. I thought I could do it without Uncle Jack, but I was wrong. I need to go home, home to Philadelphia."

TJ cleared his throat. "That's going to be tricky since you won't have a home to go to for another few months."

I'd forgotten that a stranger was living in my apartment. I peeked at TJ out of the corner of my eye. If he showed any sign that this was funny, I didn't know what I would do. But he looked straight at the road, his face not betraying whatever he was thinking.

"I-I can, I-I have…" I stopped. I was stuttering. I began again. "I can stay with friends. I can go to a hotel if I have to."

He shot me a look of surprise. "For months?!"

"Eyes on the road, please. One bad accident in my life is enough."

He shifted his eyes back to the road. "But you're comfortable here."

I folded my arms and didn't answer. There was no way I would let his down-home logic crack my resolve.

He ignored my defiance. "Seems to me you should stay where you feel settled. After all, you'll have to deal with the same thing in Philadelphia that you're facing here. Won't do any good to run away."

I turned my head slowly to look at him. "What? That makes no sense."

"Yes, it does," he insisted. "There are mirrors in Philly, too. Maybe it's time for you to face yourself and accept who you are."

My breath caught before the words came out in a flood. "Your arrogance knows no bounds. Who do you think you are?" It was time for me to set this man straight. "I'll tell you who you are." I turned toward him as far as the seat belt would allow. "You're just a man with a big education who has come to this community, ready to tell people what they should do and how. Sure, you probably know plants and soil, but that doesn't make you an expert about people. You have big equipment—combines and planters and who knows what else. You roll over other people's land, believing you're doing some good. Well, let me tell you that being hired to spread seeds or harvest crops doesn't allow you to roll over people's lives." I shifted around and folded my arms. "You have no right and no say in my life."

Ghost growled as TJ steered to the side of the road and slammed the truck's brakes. We sat staring silently out the window. I tried to catch my breath. Part of me cringed as I waited for the explosion. He'd probably call Mr. Saffire tomorrow and quit. I'd gone too far, but I didn't care.

TJ shifted the truck into park and looked at me. His hazel-green eyes drilled straight into mine and quietly said, "You want to know what I think? I think the way you get over your fear of driving, maybe the way to get you over your fear of anything, is to get mad, really mad. If that helps, get good and mad. Doesn't matter to me."

I looked down at my hands clenched in my lap but didn't say a word.

After a few moments, he drew in a deep breath and said quietly, "You're right." He gave a curt nod and repeated, "You're right. I'll take you home."

We rode the rest of the way home in stony silence, the kind that makes you want to shiver from the cold. TJ stopped the truck at the front steps of the Cottage. I gathered my things and put my hand on the door handle.

"Wait, Emma, let me—" he said, as he launched himself out of the cab.

"I don't need to wait for anyone," I called out after him. "I can take care of myself." I opened the door, took out the cane, and slid from the seat.

"I guess you'll have to, now that Jack is gone," he breathed. He raced up the steps, unlocked the front door, and came back to me.

"What are you doing?" I asked. It seemed everything he did irritated me. "You don't have to walk me to the door. We're not on a date."

"No, we're not," he said. "I thought I might help you up the steps and hold the storm door open while you made your way inside. This isn't Philadelphia, you know. I was raised a Southern gentleman and you're trying to navigate with just a cane."

I bit out the words as I reached for the railing. "Well, fine. You can stand there and watch me do this by myself."

It took everything I had to pull myself up each one of those steps. Pain was shooting down my leg and up my back. I worked hard to keep my face blank. My anger flared as I realized he was right. I needed help. But I wasn't going to ask for it.

I cleared my throat, hoping my voice would sound normal. "I guess I should thank you for bringing me home. You spared me from spending one more minute with that awful woman."

"Awful woman? Who are you talking about?" TJ asked, sounding a little defensive.

"Why, Catherine, of course. She never stopped talking. And

her gossipy comments. She should be a reporter for some celebrity magazine."

At the top of the steps, I dropped my cane. I didn't know whether to scream or cry when he picked it up and held it out to me. I wanted to stomp inside, slam the door, and lock out the whole world. Instead, I grabbed it and struggled the last few feet to the door.

"Thank you again for your help," I managed to say through clenched teeth. I felt like a bomb was about to go off inside me. The man was only trying to help. Only I didn't want his help. I didn't want anybody's help.

He must have sensed that I was about to snap and took a quick step back. "Good night, Emma." He turned and danced down the steps back to his truck.

I should have let it go, but I couldn't. I called after him. "One more thing, TJ."

He turned. "Yes, ma'am?"

"Don't go making decisions for me ever again."

"Excuse me?" He sounded lost.

"You heard me. Don't ask someone to come by to say hello. Don't sign me up for any groups. Don't do anything without asking." I could hear the acid in my voice, could almost taste the bile in my mouth. "Especially some two-bit writing group." His silent surprise allowed me to continue. "You're not the boss of me, TJ. Nobody is. I'm the boss, only me. My ex-husband couldn't control me and neither can you. Not you. Not those women. Not the doctors and all their minions." I was screaming. "You don't get to decide anything for me."

Proud of my declaration of freedom, I turned quickly, too quickly, and went down hard.

CHAPTER TWENTY-FOUR

"If you looked in the dictionary this morning for the definition of the word *hubris: excessive pride or self-confidence,* you would find my picture."

—*Emma's Journal*

I lay sprawled on the floor like a broken doll. White-hot pain flashed from my hip to my foot. Pain shot up my back. The throw rug for muddy feet by the door was my downfall. Above all, the humiliation was too much to bear. Tears burst through and wouldn't stop. I don't know how long I lay there soaking my top, the rug, and the floor with my tears.

When the sobbing slowed, a handful of white tissues appeared in front of my face. TJ hadn't left. He hadn't run away. He'd gone to find the tissue box and came back to wait until I was ready to use them. He didn't say, *poor baby.* He gave me room to find my own way. I was grateful. And a little guilty. I hadn't been the nicest person.

I'd been taking out my frustration on other people since I'd arrived on the Eastern Shore. I didn't do that when I was in Philadelphia because, I now realized, I hadn't spent much time with people. Oh, I had friends. They'd come to the hospital and rehab, but I think they were relieved when I went home. They could focus on their own lives again. They teased me about watching daytime talk shows, reading, and eating bonbons. But this man who I'd verbally beaten black and blue handed me tissues without a word, and waited.

I wiped my face and blew my nose. I used some of the tissues to soak up the droplets on the wooden floor. His empty hand reappeared and he took the soggy mess. It was time to get up. But I was afraid to move. I'd fallen a couple of times before, but this was the worst of all.

Had I sprained my leg? What if I'd broken it? Fear engulfed me. Would I ever get better? Would I always be a cripple? Did I need an ambulance? What if the doctors wanted me in the hospital again? What if they need to operate?

My eyes grew hot. Tears prickled my lids. Going to the hospital might lead to the worst operation of all: amputation. I couldn't go back to the hospital. If I started crying again, I was afraid I would never stop. I wanted to stay on the floor forever, but that couldn't happen. I had to know what I'd done to myself. I had to move. If I could do that, maybe, just maybe I could get up.

The handle of my cane appeared by my side. TJ had retrieved it and was holding it out to me. The anger surged again and I batted it away. "No!"

"Then, let me help you," he said softly.

I felt his hands touch me. "Don't!"

He snatched them away. "What can I do?"

"Leave me alone!" I bit my lip to force the tears and the angry words away. "Go away. I need to do this myself." My arrogance had caused this fall. It was my fault. It was up to me to fix it.

"Sorry, can't do that. My job here isn't done until you're up and off the floor. Now, tell me what you want me to do." It was a statement spoken calmly and matter-of-factly. The only thing that gave away his deep concern was his heavy southern accent which only appeared when he was stressed or upset.

"Nothing! I don't want you to do anything." I hadn't a clue what to do. Uncle Jack would have known how to take care of me. He could always tell if all I needed was a kiss, band-aid, and a get-on-with-it-girl for a skinned knee or a mad dash to the hospital when I'd fallen out of an apple tree and fractured my arm. But he was gone. I was on my own. I could imagine him shaking his head at me. I'd been making bad choices and now I'd caused this fall. I did this. Now, I have to fix it. "Leave me alone!"

"'Fraid I can't do that, Miss Emma." His boots moved by me and up two steps of the stairway.

When I looked up, he was sitting there with arms crossed over his chest, looking at me, waiting.

"I told you to leave," I tried to make it sound like a demand, but it came out like a whine.

"Nope, that's not what you said. You told me to leave you alone." His tone was empty of emotion. I had nothing to push against. If he wanted to play semantics, so could I. "All right. Let me be clear. Go Away! Go Home!"

"As I said, I'm afraid I can't do that," he stated flatly.

Okay, I'd play his silly game. I was beginning to feel optimistic. The stabs of pain were easing. Maybe I would be okay. If I could lay here until my body was ready to cooperate, I might get out of this situation with some shred of dignity.

With an equal lack of emotion, I asked, "Why can't you just go away?"

"I told you. I come from an old Southern family and my mama raised her son to be a Southern gentleman, or at least she tried. She wouldn't think much of me if I walked away, leaving a lady on the floor, now, would she?"

I heaved a sigh. "You aren't going to leave, are you?'

"No, ma'am."

"Even if I promise I'll be fine?" I said, with a last shred of hope.

161

"No, ma'am. I'm going nowhere until I *know* you're fine, or at least as fine as you can be tonight."

"Fine. Suit yourself." The words squeezed out between my clenched teeth. I looked around and carefully placed my hands to give myself the most leverage and began to move.

"Whoa there," he said, reaching for me. "Before you start flailing around, don't you think we should consider the possibility that you did some real damage? Maybe we should call an ambulance so the experts can move you without hurting your body?"

I looked up and wanted to stare holes into his head. Barely restraining my anger, I declared, "After what I've been through, I know what real damage feels like. Been there, done that." I rubbed my leg gingerly. "I've only pulled some muscles that are still recovering from being immobilized in the cast. Nothing more."

"Well then, go ahead and get up," he said with a trace of a self-satisfied smile.

I repositioned my hands and started to tense my shoulder and arm muscles to pull myself up then I relaxed. His words about doing more damage were echoing in my mind. Plus, I knew what kind of pain would strike when I put those muscles to work. I was about to ask for his help when he opened his mouth and re-ignited my independent spirit.

"Give up yet?" he asked.

I looked at him quickly, searching for even the smallest hint of a smirk on his face. I thought I saw a ghost of one, but now it was gone.

"Never!" I bellowed.

"Okay, Tiger! What I meant to say was, are you ready to accept my offer of assistance so you can get up on your own, that is if you're sure we don't need medical help?"

"I'm sure." I hoped I was right. "What I'm not sure about is what accepting your assistance is going to cost me."

He shook his head in exasperation. "You don't give up, do you? Just let me help you. Please."

The ticking of Uncle Jack's grandfather clock filled the house.

It was time to admit that I needed help. It was one more thing in a long list of things that was hard for me to do. "Okay, you can help me, but only this one time."

"That's fair," he said as he got up and positioned himself behind me. "Just this once."

"What are you doing back there? I can't see you."

"Tell me if I hurt you." He slipped his hands under my arms and I was up on my feet in one smooth, stable motion.

I wasn't actually on my feet since they barely touched the floor as he carried me to the living room sofa in front of the fireplace. Ever so gently, he placed me on the cushions in the corner to give me some support.

"How did you know how to do that? You're better than the orderlies in the hospital."

"Hours of practice for my place with the emergency services. Now, are you okay for the moment?"

"Yeah," I said, surprised that I was.

"Okay, I'll be right back." He was on his way to the kitchen when he called out, "Where are your pain pills?"

Within fifteen minutes, I was ensconced in front of a glowing fire, snuggled down with blankets and pillows from my bed and pills in my body.

"I hope you don't mind that I pulled a beer for myself. Jack always kept a supply in the fridge on the porch." He popped the top with a gush.

"You're making yourself comfortable? I'm okay now, and yes, I'll admit it, thanks to you. You don't have to stay."

"Yes, I do, until those pills kick in and I know you're okay."

I'd learned my lesson. It would do no good to argue so I shut up and watched the fire until my eyes drooped.

CHAPTER TWENTY-FIVE

"We (writers) have to continually be jumping off cliffs and developing our wings on the way down."

— *Kurt Vonnegut*

I thought I'd closed my eyes for only a minute, but when I opened them, sunlight streamed through the windows. I hid my face in the pillow, but even that small movement was a mistake. My muscles were reminding me of the fall I'd taken the night before and making me pay for my arrogant decision to use the cane. I needed a pain pill and I needed it now. I had to get to the kitchen. When I tried to sit up, waves of excruciating pain roared up and down my leg. The rest of my body shivered. I collapsed on the sofa again. Slowly, the rich aroma of freshly brewed coffee penetrated my pain-addled brain. I heard footsteps. I couldn't protect myself from a flea. Trying to be brave, I pried open one eyelid.

"She's alive." TJ walked in carrying two steaming mugs. "I

thought the smell of coffee might wake you up." He put a mug down on the coffee table for me.

I wanted to reach for it, but there was no way. "I feel awful." I sounded pathetic.

"I'm sure you do."

I wanted to cry. Being in the hospital certainly had the advantage of a nurse with medicine just a button away. Humiliation only added to the pain. I didn't want a lecture about my screwball attempt to rush my recovery. I had no choice. I needed the pills. He must have read my mind. He left the room and when he came back, he put the painkiller bottle on the table.

"Can you take them with coffee or do you want a glass of water?" he asked.

"Water would be great."

Had he come by to check on me this morning or stayed all night? He delivered a glass of water and helped me move into a sitting position.

I plastered a fake grin with clenched teeth on my face. "Thank you."

"I brought you some toast. It's not a good idea to take pills on an empty stomach."

I smiled at him with real gratitude. "That's a good idea. I think I need to take two pills this morning."

He took a step toward me. "I thought you were down to one..." His voice trailed off. "Okay, you know what's best."

He shook two pills out of the bottle and I downed them with the entire glass of water. He stoked the fire and we watched the flames in comfortable silence while I nibbled the toast and sipped coffee.

Finally, when the stabbing pain subsided to an impressive ache, I felt I could breathe and talk normally again. I knew it was time to say something.

I took a deep breath and began. "About last night, TJ. I was—"

He cut me off. "Emma, you don't have to say a thing. Any

normal person meeting new people would want to look her best, not leaning on old crutches. I get it."

I sat up a little straighter. "Yes, but I—"

He overrode me again. "How you handle your rehabilitation is up to you. I'm not the one you have to convince. It's okay. Are you starting to feel any better now?" He asked with a strong dose of compassion.

"Yes, thank you."

"I'm glad you're all right," he said. "You don't think you did any real damage, do you?"

I glanced away. "I really won't know until I get up. The pain is down to a dull roar now and it doesn't feel like anything's seriously wrong. If it's okay with you, I'd like to sit here for a while."

"That's a good idea. Rest is what you need."

"You know," I began tentatively. "What I did last night was not crazy,"

He shot me a look of total disbelief.

"How am I supposed to find out if I don't push the limit?" My argument sounded weak even to my ears. One glance at the expression on his face proved it wasn't flying with him either. "Okay, I pushed the limit," I said in a soft voice. "I don't want to quarrel with you. TJ, I'm sorry. What I did was wrong. I'm not as strong as I thought. I'm grateful you were here to help me last night and this morning."

"Well, if that was an apology, it's accepted and you're welcome. One other thing, you might think about canceling your P.T. appointment for today and take it easy unless..." he added quickly. "You want them to check out your leg."

"No, I don't think that's necessary, but I'll talk with them. Maybe you could give me the phone before you leave. You do have to leave, don't you?"

He nodded slowly. "Yes, I do. I have a couple of appointments this morning. Maria is due a little later so she can help you."

"That's fine." I held out my empty mug. "As long as I can get a refill before you go."

He responded with a big grin and was off.

I heard him rummaging around in the kitchen, but I didn't care. The full dose of painkillers had lifted me onto a soft cloud. I put my head back to enjoy the relief.

I must have drifted off again, because the next thing I knew, there was a tray sitting on the table next to me, filled with plates of scrambled eggs, Canadian bacon, fresh toast with orange marmalade, and another mug of coffee. My mouth started to water. I didn't realize how hungry I was. While reaching for the fork, I stopped when I noticed the other thing sitting on the tray. It was a crudely shaped daisy with petals made of clay, painted pink and white, stuck on a toothpick firmly planted in a tiny flowerpot. I couldn't stop the tears filling my eyes as a memory came flooding back.

TJ came over and knelt next to me, his face filled with worry. "Hey, hey. I didn't mean to make you cry. Of course, my cooking isn't the greatest, but you haven't even tasted it. No fair crying till you give my breakfast a chance."

When he didn't get a laugh in response, he dropped the comedy and rubbed my arm gently. "Is the pain bad? I can call the doctor or an ambulance. Tell me what to do," he suggested with a deepening Southern accent that showed his concern.

I bit my lip, trying to get control again. I felt terrible letting my grief for Uncle Jack bubble to the surface in front of TJ.

I caught him looking at the tray intently then he snapped his fingers. "I get it! You don't like the flower. My mother always says a breakfast tray is better with a flower. I didn't want to waste time looking for a fresh one while the eggs got cold. I found this one in a cupboard. But really, Emma, I think crying about it is a bit extreme."

TJ had the perfect antidote for my tears: laughter.

I burbled my response. "No, no, the flower is perfect. When I was little, I made it for Uncle Jack. He loved daisies. I wanted him to have one every morning, even in the winter."

He nodded slowly and looked away. I had to remember that I wasn't the only one who had lost a special friend.

Quickly, I added, "I'm so glad you put it on the tray. It brought back a wonderful memory. Thank you."

He cleared his throat and said in a husky voice, "Maybe I should quit while I'm ahead and take the tray away before you try the eggs and bacon."

I made a grab for the tray. "Don't you dare," I said emphatically. "This is my breakfast and nobody is taking it away, not even you, sir!"

He stood up and saluted. "Yes, ma'am!"

He looked at his watch. "If you're okay, I need to get moving. I have just enough time to get back to my house to shower and change."

Suddenly, it hit me. "You were here all night?"

He shrugged. "I wanted to make sure you were okay. It seemed like the right thing to do."

I covered my face with my hands in embarrassment. "I am so sorry. I never meant to impose on you like that."

"Well, what do you say we make sure it doesn't happen again?" He moved crutches and a walker within my reach. "I found it in the coat closet. Maybe it will give you more support until you feel ready to go back to the crutches." I started to say something, but he wouldn't let me. "You'll be doing it for my sake, not yours." He pointed at the deep ruby red upholstered club chair. "That chair from your apartment looks good, but it's not that comfortable for sleeping."

I laughed. My emotions were riding a roller coaster. "Okay, I promise." I held up my hand. "I'll be a good girl. At least until you come back." I giggled. It felt good to laugh.

TJ settled me in with a thermos of coffee, the telephone, my laptop, and a couple of library research books. I wanted to ask him to look for a letter from Daniel, but I wasn't ready to field any questions about Daniel's identity or the nature of our correspondence.

"Maybe you can do some writing this morning," TJ said as he went to the door. "Maria will be here soon. I'll check on you later to see how you're doing."

I wanted to see if Daniel had written overnight, but I wasn't ready to tempt fate by trying to walk. The fall had frightened me right down to my core. No, I'd wait until Maria arrived. It would be safer to have someone in the house.

Someone, not just Daniel.

Soon, Maria was bustling around, peppering me with questions about why I was ensconced on the sofa. Finally, she gave up. She was fussing around enough already. After another round of pills, I felt strong enough to sneak down the hall to retrieve the latest letter from Daniel and a piece of origami paper, in case I needed to consider things. Back in the living room, I found a fresh mug of hot coffee. Maria was an angel. I settled back to read Daniel's letter.

Dear Emma,

I do not wish to distress you with the specific events that caused your father's anguish. You must know that he did not leave the hearth he shared with you with a clear conscience. He said it was a matter of principle. I hope that this is sufficient to salve the sadness I know you must feel at the absence of your father.

I have something to ask you that I hope does not offend you. Is it possible that you might think of me as more than your Dear Sir? I know my silence has brought you pain. I would not have wanted that in the whole world.

I hope you know that the situation was out of my control. If you will forgive the silence, might you consider calling me again by my Christian name?

If I see the words, Dear Daniel, at the opening of your next letter, great calm will settle on my troubled heart. If it is beyond your ability to write those words, I will understand. Our connection through these letters shall be enough.

Please forgive my rudeness and insensitivity. All I have talked about is myself.

How are you? If you have a need, know that your possessions are safe and ready for your use. Where there are money and valuables, it is possible to buy safety and freedom. The secret is safe with us. We would never reveal the location to others of that which can keep you safe.

Please tell me how you fare.

Yours most sincerely,
Daniel

I wished I'd had the foresight to bring the inkwell, my steel-nib pen, and paper with me into the living room. How romantic it would be to sit in front of the fireplace and write a response to Daniel's letter. Perhaps it's what his Emma would have done.

"Miss Emma…" Maria's sudden appearance startled me. "Oh, I'm so sorry. I didn't mean to surprise you. I thought you'd hear me coming down the hallway. My husband says I sound like an elephant when I walk around the house. You must be thinking deep thoughts."

I tried to disguise the fact that Daniel's letter that had fluttered to the floor.

She walked around the sofa and gave me a funny look. "Are you sure you're all right?"

She was a little too inquisitive. If I didn't get her out of the living room, she would bug me about the letter. "I was doing some research. Did you need something?"

Maria pursed her lips. "I guess you writers have to do some strange things to get inspired."

"Yes, we do. Is there something I can do for you before I go back to work?"

"I wanted to let you know that your dinner is in the kitchen. You only have to heat it. I made it super simple for you tonight. Be sure to take it slow so we don't have any more mishaps." She smiled at me and walked out of the room with a wave goodbye.

How did she know? I'd have to remember it wasn't so easy hiding things from Maria.

I waited until I heard the door close and her car engine start. Convinced I wouldn't be disturbed, I made my way back to the writing den and composed my response to Daniel.

Dear Daniel,

Thank you for inquiring after my health and well-being. I am comfortable and safe here at Waterwood, where I have always been and always hope to be. But I am sad to report that I am lonely and fearful for the well-being of those I care about.

No news increases my worry.

Please, I pray, tell me what happened after you left Waterwood with my father. The news of your expedition cannot be worse than not knowing.

Yours with great esteem,

Emma

While waiting for the ink to dry, I thought about the two men who'd left the one place they loved, heading into the horrors of war. With the benefit of history's hindsight, I knew that more than 620,000 men died in the Civil War, along with more than one million casualties. From my reading, I'd learned that bullets and bayonets were not the only dangers that took men's lives. Disease struck a brutal blow. Men marched shoulder to shoulder and slept in unventilated tents. Their camps were breeding grounds for germs they could not fight. I resolved to look for the grave of Emma's father if I visited the Waterwood cemetery again.

I remembered the gravestone carved with the name Emma. My name. Somehow, I had lived through that horrendous collision and I felt a responsibility not to waste a day wallowing in self-pity. But I kept postponing things. I told myself I couldn't do anything until I got out of the hospital, then I had to wait until I was released from the rehab facility. Now, I was carrying around not just a bum leg, but guilt. Sitting here in Uncle Jack's Cottage staring out the window at the beautiful landscape was a waste of time. It helped that I'd declared I wanted to write a children's book. The only problem was I didn't know quite how to go about it. And, of course, I needed a story.

Thankful that I had a piece of origami paper, I prepared to fold. This time I knew which shape I needed: A Llama. It was not an animal associated with Japan but had become a symbol of persistence in a difficult situation and hard work. Examining my little llama, I realized I needed more practice. It had a lot in common with my project. If I was going to publish a book, I was going to have to study and get to work.

During this lecture to myself, I heard the crunch of tires on the gravel driveway. It didn't sound like TJ's truck. I craned my neck to see a car pulling up. I scrambled to stand up as best I could when I recognized the woman getting out of the car. What perfect timing. It was Maureen, the woman in the writing group, who had offered to help.

CHAPTER TWENTY-SIX

"Start writing, no matter what. The water does not flow until the faucet is turned on."

—*Louis L'Amour*

When the doorbell rang, I called out. "I'm coming!" hoping she'd hear me. I finally made it to the front door and yanked it open as she was getting into her car.

"Hello! I'm here!" I called out, waving madly.

"I didn't think anyone was home," she said as she closed her car door and made her way back to the front steps. "I hope you don't mind that I didn't wait for you to call me, that I came by unannounced."

We settled in the living room. "I'm so glad you're here. I have a suspicion you might be able to help me."

She smiled. "I suspect I may be able to do that."

I glanced down and saw my mug half full of coffee and realized with a start that I wasn't a good hostess. "I'm so sorry. I should offer you something to drink."

She laughed. "You mean you're going to make fresh coffee and bake some cookies?" Her face fell when she saw the walker.

"Weren't you using a cane last night?"

I nodded. "Yes, my arrogant self was using a cane last night. When I got home, reality reminded me that I wasn't ready. Please don't ask for details. They're ugly."

She stood up. "What if I find the kitchen and see if there is any coffee left? One cup for me and a refill for you?"

"That would be terrific." Maureen made everything feel calm and natural.

It wasn't long before she returned and we settled in for a chat. Only, I had no idea what to say. It turned out I was worrying for nothing.

She folded her hands in her lap, her fingertips were elegantly manicured. The only telltale signs of age were little wrinkles at her wrists and crinkly lines at the corners of her blue eyes which sparkled with mischief.

"I am here today at the behest of your new writers group," she began formally. "The members have decided that you need help fighting your writer's block."

"My what? I don't have writer's block. I haven't even started writing yet so how could I have writer's block." I was spouting a weak position. "Forgive me, but who do these women think they are? Have any of them published, I mean with a real publishing house? I don't think so." I knew my reaction was extreme, but I couldn't stop. "Who do they think they are, talking about me behind my back? They're nothing but a group of old biddies who have nothing else to do than sit around, drink wine, and criticize other people. If they spent half as much time—"

Maureen held up her hands for me to stop. And when I did, she spoke in a soft voice. "I'm not going to waste time trying to change your mind. They do have a point, though a small one," she added quickly when she saw that I was about to argue with her. "I have more background than they do. I can tell that you are dealing with a bit of a block."

In deference to her polite attitude, I chose to drop the rant and speak in a civil tone. "Well, if I have writer's block, I'll fight my way through it, the same way I fought my way through things at the hospital and in rehab. After what I've been through, nothing is going to keep me down."

Maureen sat quietly and listened. "That's fine. I understand you've faced some difficult challenges recently. Probably, it was the sheer force of will that has gotten you to this point."

I relaxed and leaned back against the cushion. I felt confident I knew myself pretty well. That's why her next words took me by surprise.

"But you might try a different tack with writing. Why should you use your energy fighting through a block, when all you need to do is go around it and keep working?" She shrugged. "It's so much easier that way."

My jaw dropped. "You never hear of people going around writer's block. You always hear how they fight it valiantly or drown in a bottle of scotch."

Maureen laughed as she folded her hands in her lap again. "Sadly, that's what too many creative people do."

I cocked my head to the side and began to wonder about this elegant woman sitting in my living room. "Maureen, how do you know so much about the creative process?"

She took a deep breath. "I've spent my life with creative people, just like you. They had hopes, dreams, and visions of success. They put in a lot of hard work to learn their particular craft. And many relied on me for guidance and support." She looked down at her hands again. "I spent a lot of years guiding and nurturing a creative department of a major New York ad agency."

Again, I was surprised and impressed. I realized this woman had broken ground or destroyed glass ceilings for the women of my generation. "That was very unusual back then. I mean..."

Maureen laughed and waved my gaffe away. "Don't worry. I know I'm old. As they say, those were the days. I loved every minute of it. It was so much fun to work with such talented people and to *manage* the stuffed shirts, except I think today you call them suits."

I nodded with a smile. "What did you do?"

*"I play*ed with them." She sat up straighter in her chair. "Look at me. I'm almost 5'10" tall. That was considered very tall for a woman back then. Did I slouch? Did I try to hide my height? Absolutely not! I always wore high heels so that I could look them straight in the eye or even tower over some of them." She cocked her head and looked off to the side, remembering. "There I was in my three-inch heels, watching them squirm as I stood next to them before a meeting or at a reception. It was one of my secret weapons to get us on a more even playing field."

We broke out laughing.

"I know what you mean," I said. "I naturally tower over the kids, but it works when I have to deal with parents and administrators." I gently rubbed my leg. "Do you have any other secret weapons?"

A smile like the Cheshire cat spread across Maureen's face. "Maybe. Maybe I'll share a few as we get to know each other. Thank you for reminding me about those years at the agency. We were one of THE best, at least according to our Wall of Shame."

"Wall of Shame?" I asked.

"At least that's what I called it. We had shelves that ran from floor to ceiling and along more than one wall."

"For what?"

"Our awards," she said softly.

"And you called it a Wall of Shame?"

She shrugged. "Maybe it was more of a Wall of Embarrassment, because the industry, our very talented peers, thought our work was terrific. I got the idea of calling it that because one of the kids, for some reason, I always thought of the young staffers as kids, said that when he was little, his mother said he should be ashamed of himself for being so much better than the other kids in sports. She wanted him to *play nice*, not beat them all the time. We didn't play nice. We knocked the competition on its ass and gobbled up their clients. It was fun. So, dear Emma, keep working on something, anything creative, but do something every day. Every Day! You have to prime the pump. Then you have to keep working. Then you'll have a different problem."

"And what will that be?" I asked, intrigued.

"When the ideas and the words start flowing, you have to keep up!"

We laughed together again.

"I wish I had that problem of keeping up. I don't know where to start and I'm getting frustrated."

"Then let me give you one more morsel of advice. Stories are about people so, that's where you should start. Think about the hero of your story, even a children's picture book. Then you have to do something even more important."

She smoothed her gray silk slacks with the palm of her hand. That subtle gesture made it easier to listen to her wisdom. I felt like I was sitting at the knee of a mentor.

Maureen began to share. "This is probably one of the most important bits of advice about writing a story that you will ever hear. I know that sounds pompous, but it's true. Once you have a basic idea of the hero or heroine, work on your antagonist, the bad guy. But it doesn't have to be a person. For a children's book, it could be a *serious challenge* faced by the hero." She took a deep breath and took out her keys. "I think that might be enough for you to chew on for one day. I know you're convalescing and I fear I've worn you out with all this conversation." She stood up. "We'll talk again if you'd like."

"I'd like that, but you don't have to leave." I wanted her to stay. I felt nurtured by her compassion and kindness, not pity. She wasn't trying to control me like my sister. She wasn't ordering me to *just sit*, like my lawyer. Maureen was calm and supportive. All attributes I needed and appreciated right now. But she was determined not to wear me out and moved slowly towards the front door.

I reached for my walker.

"No, don't get up. Let me leave you with one more thought. If you try, you may succeed. If you do nothing, you are guaranteed to fail." She patted me on the shoulder. "I'll let myself out. Use your strength for something worthwhile. Your story."

"Now that you found your way here, don't be a stranger," I

said the same way my mother always did. It felt right. She had given me an exceptional gift.

For the first time, I felt empowered to write.

CHAPTER TWENTY-SEVEN

"[Oration, public speeches, reports are written as if] a thousand eyes are peering over the writer's shoulder and scrutinizing every word; while letters are written when the mind as it were in dressing-gown and slippers—free, natural, active, perfectly at home."

How to Write Letters
by Professor J. Willis Westlake, 1883

After Maureen left, I dove back into research materials collected from the library and found that Katie Cobin had earned a mention in the history books.

There was never a proper recording of the death of Virtue Violl. About seventy-five years later, when an old woman appeared on the Point, living by herself, in the same place as Virtue, the local people were sure that the witch had returned. When the new resident appeared in town, people shied away from her in fear that she would cast a hex on them. The men believed their women were being silly but kept their distance from her as well.

One day, Katie went to town and walked down the main street. People stood back to let her pass. But on this day, a little boy was curious. He broke away from his mother and ran up to Katie. His mother was horrified, but not brave enough to draw her son away. The townspeople watched in fear as the old woman knelt down to talk to the little boy. No one was close enough to hear what they said.

Then Katie reached into the pocket of her tattered dress, pulled out something in her fist, and gave it to the boy. He smiled and rushed back to his mother. She was angry. The boy had disobeyed her. She grabbed him by the wrist, forced him to open his hand and found a small stone there. The mother examined it closely. Its white surface was smooth and round. There was nothing special about the stone until the sunlight touched it. It sparkled.

Everyone in the crowd was amazed. The mother was terrified. She grabbed the sparkling stone and raised her hand high in the air to cast it away. Katie cried out for the mother to stop. Then she pointed at the mother and back to the boy. The message was clear: that stone was a gift from me to him. It is not yours to throw away. Slowly, the mother lowered her hand and returned the stone to the boy's hand. He quickly put it in his pocket and dashed off to play with his friends.

Later, other mothers challenged her for not throwing away the stone and protecting her boy. In self-defense, she claimed that the old hag used unseen powers to force her to put the stone back into her son's hand. People accepted her story, but they became leery of being too friendly with that family. The boy carried the stone in his pocket until his dying day.

Hearing the crunch of the driveway gravel brought me back to the present. It was proving better than a doorbell. I thought TJ had arrived, but one of those fun Jeeps that belonged on the beach had parked and Stephani had climbed out. Oh no! She had come to give me a ride to my physical therapy appointment, the one I'd canceled earlier that morning.

This isn't a good way to start a new relationship, I thought as I pulled the walker into position so I could go and meet her. I apologized for bringing her over unnecessarily. She was a little peeved. I couldn't blame her.

"You see, I fell last night and hurt my leg again," I explained. "I thought it was better if I stayed quiet today to rest the muscles. I canceled the appointment early this morning and completely forgot to call you. I'm so sorry."

Her lips grew thin as she evaluated my story. I suspected somebody in her life lied to her regularly. Finally, concern overcame suspicion.

"Are you okay?" Stephani asked. "I can understand that you would forget to call me if you were hurting and taking strong painkillers. It's not a bother, really."

"I'll be happy to pay for your time," I said as I started to look around for my purse.

"No, no, that's okay. Stopping here didn't take me out of my way." She looked around and her interest was piqued by the open books and notes spread over the coffee table and sofa. "Are you doing more research for your book?"

"I've been following up on some things about the area's history and Waterwood Plantation. Would you like to sit down and talk a little?"

"Yes, I have time before I have to get to the library," she said as she slung that huge purse off her shoulder.

"I'm glad, because I came across a story, an old legend really, that I wanted to ask you about." I told Stephani about the tale of Katie Cobin. She listened intently and took in all the information like a black hole without giving me a hint of a reaction.

I pointed out the window and said, "And to think the women lived right across the creek by the old tree...if it did happen at all."

She glanced out the window and then back at me. "You never know what to believe when you hear those old stories. In the early days, before there were bank vaults in this area, farmers and landowners would bury their valuables somewhere on their property for safekeeping when they traveled away from home for an extended time." She got up and walked to the window, her eyes firmly set on the Lone Oak. "There are stories about people dying while they were away and before they could tell anybody exactly where the fortune was buried. But can we believe everything we read?"

I too gazed out the window at the tree. "Probably not, but there is something intriguing about the stories of these two women and that tree. I wonder how it ended up on that point of land. Did somebody plant it, somebody connected to the Waterwood plantation?"

I caught a fleeting glimpse of Stephani raising her chin and looking down her nose at me. "You're not from around here, are you?" Then that look of contempt was gone.

The question threw me. She was accenting the difference between locals and people who came here from the Western Shore of the Chesapeake Bay. For some, that difference was a wide gulf.

"No, I didn't grow up here," I said carefully, "but I spent my summers with my Uncle Jack until I went to college."

"But you grew up in a city on the Western Shore." Her voice was flat.

"Yes, why?"

She chuckled. "It shows that you're not a country girl. That tree probably wasn't planted by a person. A bird might've picked up the seed someplace and dropped it there one way or another. That's the way Mother Nature does her landscaping. That old tree has been around for centuries, I bet," she declared. "It's seen a lot of happenings."

"Do you think it was there during the Civil War?" I was testing her.

"I'm sure it was."

"What about the Revolutionary War? Do you think it might've been a Liberty Tree? It might have been a secret meeting place. Seeing it out all alone fires up my imagination. It's certainly a great place for a lover's rendezvous. Do you think there are any initials carved into its bark?" I was on a roll. "With all the talk about witches living there, I wonder if satanic worship ceremonies were ever held under its branches?"

Stephani smiled at me. "Would you like to go over there and take a look for yourself?"

I gazed out the window again. "I'd love to, but there's no way."

"Why?"

I tapped the walker. "That tree is a long way from the road. I don't think I could navigate the ground, especially after last night."

"We could go in my Jeep. It can go just about anywhere. We could drive into the field and take a spin around the Lone Oak and come back. It'll only take a few minutes." She made it sound so simple.

Hoping I wasn't being foolish, I reached for my crutches. "Let's go."

I took the front steps slowly and was encouraged by how well I was doing. Then I had to get up into her vehicle. It would be at home on any beach but climbing aboard was going to be a challenge. She found an old cinderblock around the corner of the house and placed it as a stepping stone for me. After some tugging and wiggling around, I settled into the passenger seat and attached the seatbelt. I was unnerved there was no real door between me and the roadway. I clenched my teeth and focused forward. Stephani jumped in and we were off. I held on and silently coached myself to stay calm.

When we rumbled into the field, I held with both hands as we bounced around. Being under the Lone Oak was even more impressive than seeing it from the Cottage. Its trunk was massive. The limbs and branches spread out creating a safe place, a shelter for anyone who needed it. Its autumn leaves were beginning to show a tinge of red and orange, the comforting colors of a warm fire.

Looking across the creek gave me a new perspective of Uncle Jack's Cottage. Its many windows facing the water sparkled in the sunlight. Its cedar shingles had long ago weathered to a silvery gray. The stark white trim outlined the place that I now called home. I'd forgotten the gentle feeling of home the house always gave me when I saw it from this side, from the water. I never had the time to feel this way when driving up to the Cottage, first with my mother, then on my own. But I was always distracted by the excitement of seeing Uncle Jack to notice the effect the

Cottage had on me. On this side of the creek, I could truly enjoy it.

My eyes traveled along the far shoreline to a small cabin, now leaning hard to the left. It was situated in a tiny cove surrounded by reeds and fall foliage. Uncle Jack had kept a rickety old rowboat there for me, safe only to float on that little finger of water. I would drag the boat down to the shoreline so it barely floated then I'd lay down in it, and read while listening to the water gently lap against the sides. Oh, there were other places I could curl up and read, probably more comfortably, but this spot was special. I was surrounded by all the elements—nature, water, sky, birds, butterflies—that made the Shore magical.

Stephani jolted me back to the present. "What do you think?"

"About?" I asked.

"What happened here," she said as she drove slowly around the tree.

I tamped down my panic. Did she know about Daniel and Emma?

She continued as we jostled along. "You know, the murder and all."

She avoided as many of the holes as she could. Holes that the police said were dug the night of the attack. Were we destroying the crime scene? A quick scan of the area showed there was no crime scene tape. The investigators must have finished their work here. We bounced over exposed roots as Stephani drove to the base of the tree. It felt like we were stepping on its toes. As much as I wanted to find a heart and initials carved into the bark, there was no trace of any man-made mark there. Daniel and his Emma had met at this old tree more than 160 years earlier. Even if he had used his knife to make a mark, the tree would've reclaimed its skin by now.

"You look sad? Are you disappointed?" asked Stephani.

"What? Oh, no. I was thinking…"

"If you were thinking about treasure, you should share your ideas with me. We could compare notes." She laughed lightly. "I don't believe anything is here, but it's fun to think about."

"Somebody thinks there is treasure here." I pointed at the ground. "Check out all the places the police tried to fill in the holes."

"Have you talked to the police? What did they say?" Stephani wanted to know.

Fascination with crime wasn't my thing. Normal life was daunting enough. But I humored her. "The detective said some people were out here digging these holes looking—"

"For treasure?" Stephani asked eagerly.

"Well, he didn't say specifically that they were looking for treasure, but they were looking for something."

"What else did he say, the detective, I mean?"

"He thinks a fight broke out for some reason. Somebody swung a shovel and a young guy was hit in the face."

"And…?"

"And he died. Now, it's a murder investigation."

I twisted in my seat so I could get a better look at Stephani. "You don't know anything about it, do you?" I asked slowly.

"Me? Why would I?"

I shrugged to ease the sudden tension I felt in the air. "I don't know. You live close. Maybe you knew the boy who died?" *Maybe your brother knows something.* But I kept that thought to myself.

"I don't know anything. I think what happened is horrible," she said with a shudder. Stephani ran her hands up and down her arms as if to warm them. "It's creepy that those old women lived here. Do you think they knew about a treasure?"

"If they did, I think they would have dug it up and lived better lives."

"Well, if you have any other thoughts about finding treasure, you will let me know, won't you? Because it sure doesn't look like those people found anything, but trouble."

She looked at her watch. "I'm afraid I have to get going. I don't want to be late. Do you mind if I take you home now?"

"Ready." We rode back to the Cottage in silence, which left me alone with my thoughts.

Later, sitting cozy in my writing den, I couldn't stop staring at the Lone Oak across the creek. I was almost sorry that I'd let Stephani take me over there to look around. Seeing evidence of treasure hunting and violence unnerved me. I preferred my romantic vision of Emma standing by the tree in a long flowing gown, watching Daniel in his wool shirt and trousers carve their initials into the bark.

Wanting, no, needing to reconnect with the young lovers, I opened the yellow file folder containing Daniel's original letters. There would only be blank pages that had once held his beautifully flowing script. I was about to reach into the drawer where I kept the jump drive backup when I saw there was writing on the top page of the stack of paper. A new letter from Daniel had appeared while I was exploring the field and Lone Oak with Stephani.

I settled myself into the large leather chair and read.

Dear Emma,

I perceive that you truly wish to know about our travels. I have never been able to deny you and shall not begin now.

When we turned our horses away from Waterwood, it was the hardest thing I have ever done. I believe the same was true for your father. Our hearts, our lives, even our blood were part of the land there. Politics and a sense of doing what was right drove him toward the Confederacy. It was my duty to accompany him.

While we rode, your father was lost in quiet contemplation. When he did speak aloud, I was not sure if he was speaking to me or arguing with himself.

It was obvious that he was a man caught in a private conflict. He began by reviewing the reasons why he had walked away from the warm comfort of his home, friends, and, above all, the love of his daughter. You were very much on his mind. He talked about the mess of divided loyalties on the Shore. He could not resolve why people would not be considerate of the positions and concerns of their friends and neighbors. The people of the Shore worked shoulder to shoulder over the years, wrestling sustenance from the land, battling the elements, and celebrating the triumphs together.

The federal arguments had swept us all into the maelstrom. It was confusing, agitating, distressing. For some reason, people couldn't step away from the political arguments and maintain their friendships. He could not countenance people putting so much energy into hatred and violence, instead of working hard for a compromise that would benefit all.

I listened carefully to all he said. I too could not understand why these things were happening. Even though the arguments did not directly affect me as the young son of a plantation manager, out of loyalty to your father, to Waterwood, and to you, I followed him South.

The memory of those hours and each step southward continues to give me grievous pain. I know I did the right thing by riding with him, but my heart begged me to turn around and gallop, not walk, back to Waterwood and you.

Forgive me, dear Emma, I must pause in my letter writing now. My hand shakes from the memory and from the cold that is seeping into my body. My eyes grow full of tears so that the words swim before me. I pray you will allow me to rest and gather my emotions so that I may continue my report to you about our adventure South.

With great constancy and affection,
Daniel

My hands shook too as I held his letter. In the history lessons about the Civil War, I had read as a child, they emphasized the enthusiastic way Southern gentlemen rode off to war. I guess the wrenching decision to go was not discussed. Now, I could better understand why Emma might not have met Daniel at the Lone Oak. It would have been hard enough to say goodbye to her father. To say goodbye to the man she loved might have been more than she could bear.

I looked out the window as the wind picked up and moved the leafy boughs in a slow, sorrowful dance. Each branch looked heavy as it nestled against others, content to stay close and just exist. That's what grief felt like to me. Often, I wanted to sit, just sit, and not move. Too often. But like the wind forced the branches to move, life and Daniel's words roused me. I needed to quickly capture Daniel's words in electronic forms before they faded away. I did not want to lose this letter.

Once I had saved Daniel's letter on the computer and my gallery, I slipped it into the file where I knew his words would slowly fade away. He'd left me hanging at the end of his letter without finishing the story. Of course, I could wait patiently for his next piece of correspondence, but patience wasn't my strong suit. I retrieved the inkwell and pen and began to write.

My Dear Daniel,

I was filled with sorrow as I read the words of your last letter. What torment you must have felt as you rode away from Waterwood.

I do not believe that I would have had the strength and fortitude to do what you did. I admire your loyalty to my father so that he, in his pain, did not have to follow the path he had chosen alone.

I hope these meager words from me bring you some level of comfort and strength so that you may continue the tale of your journey.

I eagerly await your next missive.

Emma

I placed my letter to the side so that the ink could dry. I wondered how the letter I wrote in this reality traveled to the ghostly world where Daniel existed. I'd never succeeded in finding my letters to him in or on the desk. Did my handwritten words fade away in his world the way his words did in mine? Some of the blank sheets in the stack might have once held my words.

I looked out at the Lone Oak again. Seeing the area under its sheltering branches up close gave me an unsettled feeling. According to Daniel, it was a place of friendship that had grown into love and hope. Taking into account of what had happened recently, it was also a place of murder.

CHAPTER TWENTY-EIGHT

"With infinite sorrow and regret, I have to record the death of the colored woman Cassie. This is a sad bereavement to us, her death, and absence will be long felt." *February 13, 1863*

The Willis Family Journals 1847-1951
Edited and Annotated by James Dawson

I sat in the leather chair by the plantation desk, staring out the window at the Lone Oak. It was too early for dinner. I didn't feel like a nap. My eyes were too tired to do any more reading. I was relieved to hear two beeps of TJ's truck horn followed a few moments later by his voice calling my name softly.

"I'm here in the den," I sang out. "When he came down the hall, I asked, "Want a cup of coffee?" Then I remembered TJ's beautiful almost-white Lab. "Oh, what about Ghost? Is he with you?"

"Always. He's in the truck. I must admit I brought him in last night while you were sleeping. He stayed in the kitchen."

"Bring him in now. He can't stay out there while we talk."

TJ frowned. "Are you sure? He's a big dog."

"Yes, I'm sure." Then I had a thought. "But when I'm moving around…"

"I'll be sure he stays out of your way. Thanks."

I was relieved when Ghost came into the room slowly. He took his time, checking out his surroundings, instead of bounding in and jumping on me like an old boyfriend's dog always did.

"Manners," TJ intoned.

Ghost sat at my feet and extended a paw in greeting. Though we had spent time in the truck together, I had no idea he was so sensitive and well-trained.

TJ pointed to a corner. "Go and stay."

Immediately, Ghost took up his position. Oh, to have such a remarkable companion. I'd never had time for a pet. Maybe now…?

"Okay, it's coffee time," TJ announced and I followed man and his dog into the kitchen.

He whistled softly as he went about the preparations. Soon, a rich aroma filled the room. We went through the normal updates about how we'd each spent our day. For some reason, I conveniently forgot to tell him about Stephani's visit and our trip to the Lone Oak. I wasn't sure what I thought about the girl. There was something about Stephani that wasn't ringing true or maybe it was my imagination. I wanted to make my own decision about her first. Right now, I wanted to know about his connection to Waterwood.

We sat down with steaming mugs of coffee and a plate of Maria's delicious chocolate chip cookies. I had a captive audience so I raised the subject that had been occupying my mind.

"I've been doing some research about the land around here. I've come across some names. I'm trying to figure out how you fit into all the family genealogy connected to Waterwood."

He took a sip of coffee. "I don't know why you'd want to know about that. It's not that interesting."

"Humor me, would you?" I shrugged my shoulders. "Of course, if you don't want to talk about your family and land, I guess I can understand." The way I said the last words suggested that *No, I wouldn't understand.*

Not entirely convinced, but willing to humor me, he said, "Okay, where do you want me to start?"

I straightened up in the chair. Maybe now I would be able to fill in some of the gaps. "While working in the Maryland Room, I found a reference that this land was originally part of a land grant to your family before the Revolutionary War, right?" He nodded. "So, let's fast-forward to the time just before the Civil War."

He gazed out the window, but I was sure what he saw was a farm with many acres under cultivation that supported many people. "That was the glory time. Waterwood was one of the largest plantations in Talbot County, or, for that matter, on the entire Eastern Shore. Waterwood was self-sustaining, like an island unto itself. There was a lot of visiting and interaction between the families of the other plantations. I've read that they led a very active social life. It was the family in the main house that had the time for those activities. The farm operation required constant attention. The plantation manager oversaw everything. He consulted with the landowner, my great-great-grandfather, of course, but it was the manager's responsibility to make sure that things ran smoothly and the land yielded the best crop."

"Were there slaves here at Waterwood?" I asked.

His eyes clouded as he took a deep breath. "Yes, there were slaves. Remember, even though this is Maryland, part of the Union, Waterwood is still south of the Mason-Dixon Line. The economy here was based on the same elements as that of the South.

"People around here were deeply divided. Very few were in favor of going to war. They wanted to find a way to maintain their way of life." He hurried on. "I've done a lot of reading about this, and I can say with confidence that my family, my ancestors were caring people. They treated their slaves well. You won't find evidence in journals or diaries about ruthless taskmasters or whippings at Waterwood. The black folks were well-housed and well-fed."

"But they were still slaves," I interjected. It was more of a statement than a question.

"Yes, I'm afraid so. To his credit, my great-great-grandfather Benjamin Ross made sure that families were never split up. When slaves got to the age when they were too old to work, they stayed right here at Waterwood. They were cared for and lived out their days with their kin." His intensity made it clear to me that commitment to the family honor had been passed down through the generations.

I closed my eyes and shook my head. "I'm confused. How does the Emma of Waterwood play into your family?"

His forehead crinkled. "Are you sure you want to know about this?"

"Yes!" Realizing that I may have sounded a little too enthusiastic, I repeated my answer in a milder tone. "Yes, please."

"Okay then. Let me see if I can remember how the family tree works." He rubbed his hand through his hair as if trying to wake up his brain cells. Then he started ticking off points on his fingers. "Emma was the daughter of my great-great-grandfather, Benjamin F. Ross. She was a young woman, about sixteen years old, when the Civil War began. The story of her parents, Benjamin and his wife Elizabeth, has always been a favorite in the family.

"In the early 1840s, Benjamin was a young, educated man from a fairly well-to-do family. The landed gentry here on the Eastern Shore was very social. They went to Baltimore and Philadelphia for gatherings and balls. On the Shore, they visited one plantation or another for weekend events, like a hunt or a dinner, even a ball. If the portrait at the main house is any indication, Benjamin was handsome and sought after by the young ladies and their mothers.

"He avoided the clutches of matrimony and enjoyed his freedom while he learned the workings of Waterwood. That is, until he went to a glittering ball in Philadelphia."

TJ saw the smile that appeared on my face when he said *glittering ball.*

"Hey, give the guy a break here. It is the way my mother always tells the story. Do you want me to go on or not?"

"I'm sorry. It's just that...never mind." It was the kind of detail I wanted to hear. I had to tamp down my reaction to his romantic telling or I'd never hear the end of the story. "Please continue."

He inspected the expression on my face, suspecting I was making fun of him. After a few moments, he decided to go on. "Now, you have to remember that this is the way my mother always told the story."

"Got it. So, what happened at this glittering ball?"

"Well, dashing young Benjamin attended the ball along with everyone who was *anyone.* There were even people there from New York and that was a big deal back then. Benjamin walked into the ballroom. The heads of all the young ladies—and their mothers—turned his way. All, except one. She was on the far side of the dance floor, surrounded by several young men who were paying their compliments to her."

TJ held up his index finger and said, "Remember, I've heard my mother tell this story so often that I can repeat her version word for word. Elizabeth had hair the color of spun gold. Her complexion was the translucent quality of the finest pearl. She wore a silk gown the color of the pink glow of a sunrise. For Benjamin, the rest of the world faded away. He only saw Elizabeth. He had to quickly find someone to make a proper introduction because that's the way it was done. He wanted to be with her, so she wouldn't become distracted and monopolized by the young officers in uniform and sophisticated gentlemen fluttering around her."

TJ sighed. "I guess he didn't have to worry. When Elizabeth turned and saw him, it was clear that she too was mesmerized. There was no one else in the room for her, but Benjamin. The next morning, my great-great-grandparents were shocked to discover that Benjamin had proposed to Elizabeth the night before. I guess that wasn't done back then. He should have gone through the formal process of courtship, asking her father for permission, then presenting his proposal. Benjamin couldn't wait. He had met the love of his life and he wanted to spend every minute with her. This created quite a problem for my great-great-grandparents. He had violated social conventions and he was only twenty-two years old. True, he came from a well-to-do family, but men at that time established themselves before they proposed marriage. Benjamin knew that he wanted to spend his days at Waterwood, overseeing the land and he wanted Elizabeth by his side.

"According to the family story, Benjamin made a case to his father that he was born at Waterwood, wanted to raise his family at Waterwood, and wanted to be buried at Waterwood so that his body could nurture the land. He did not want to travel Europe like other young men his age. He wanted to stay at Waterwood with the woman he hoped would be his bride."

I closed my eyes and moaned. "Benjamin sounds like the answer to every woman's dream of love." I looked over at TJ and wondered if all the men in his family were like Benjamin. As much as Benjamin appealed to my girly romantic side, I wasn't sure I wanted to know. Better to go to some neutral topic.

"What was his full name? Benjamin F…?"

TJ looked away and closed his eyes. It was clear he didn't want to deal with my question.

"Oh, come on," I insisted. "You've seen *me* at my worst, learned some of my deepest, darkest secrets. We're only talking about a middle initial here. How bad can that be?"

"Oh, pretty bad," he said with a sigh. "The F stands for Franklin."

"Franklin. That's nice—" I stopped myself. "Wait a minute. Franklin? As in *the* Benjamin Franklin?" TJ nodded with a pained look on his face.

"Is the *real* Benjamin Franklin on your family tree?"

TJ shook his head and groaned. "Now, you know our family secret. We like to honor notable people we respect by naming our kin after them. It started a long, long time ago." He held up both hands. "I'm not responsible."

I sat up like a shot and paid for the quick movement with a cramp in my leg. "Wait! You go by your initials. If it's a family tradition, then your name must be…"

CHAPTER TWENTY-NINE

"Child of a frog is a frog."

— *Japanese Proverb*

It didn't take me long to figure out my new friend's name. "TJ? TJ! Your name must be Thomas Jefferson Ross."

"You got it right in one," he murmured. "I didn't grow up here, only visited during the summers. People know me as TJ, so I'd appreciate it if you didn't spread it around."

I was so surprised that my words tumbled out in a mess. "Oh wow, oh wow! Your name is Thomas Jefferson Ross! I didn't think anyone did that anymore. Now, I thought people only made up names that were hard to pronounce or gave boys' names to girls."

"The Ross family is old-school traditional. Why do you think I go by TJ?"

I stopped for a minute and realized I had offended him by making fun. He didn't deserve it. "Come on, you're named after one of the most important men in American history." I held my arms straight out from my body to emphasize my question. "How can you not be proud of that? It's an honor your family bestowed on you." Then I shrugged. "But with the name comes responsibility and pretty high expectations for anyone to meet."

"I know, I know. My dad told me that was the reason the family created the tradition. Every firstborn son is given the name of a famous person, a hero. That way, if the kid ever falters, ever second-guesses himself, he'll remember what the family expects of him and what he should expect of himself."

"That's incredible." I felt a stab of jealousy. I didn't know of any woman in history named Emma who was notable. Of course, there was Emma Thompson, a creative movie actor, writer, and producer. Not bad, but not exactly on a level of Thomas Jefferson or Benjamin Franklin.

"Yep, it's a solid concept, but not easy for a teenage boy to manage when he's having trouble fitting in. When I was growing up, I was a klutz. I was always the last one left on the bench, the last player picked for a team. My grades were okay, but nothing that would make you stand up and cheer."

He looked out the window and continued quietly. "Now that I think about it, maybe I'm more like Benjamin Franklin Ross than I thought."

I waited for him to explain until I felt like I was going to burst. "Okay, tell me. How are you like Benjamin Franklin Ross?"

He turned his face towards me and grinned. "Let me answer your question by telling you the rest of Benjamin Franklin Ross's story. Let's go into the living room where you'll be more comfortable."

In response, I followed him and snuggled into the sofa.

"Benjamin's father recognized the family's stubborn streak in his son and stopped fighting. He must have worked out something with Elizabeth's father. The young couple were married within months and set up housekeeping at Waterwood. Their daughter Emma was born during their first year of marriage. Other babies followed though they did not survive. Benjamin made sure every baby was given a name and buried with a tiny headstone marking the spot. I think Emma was nine or ten when Elizabeth gave birth to a son who survived his first two years of life. But it was at a cost. Elizabeth never fully recovered from the birth. When an illness like influenza or scarlet fever struck the Shore, neither Elizabeth nor her son survived.

"People encouraged Benjamin to marry again. After all, he had a young daughter who deserved the guidance a new wife could give her. Benjamin refused. He claimed that no other woman could take Elizabeth's place and he would be both mother and father to his daughter."

The story brought tears to my eyes. "How sad. Did Emma spend the rest of her life here at Waterwood with her father?" I read stories that it was not that unusual for an only daughter to stay in her father's home, handle the responsibilities as mistress of the plantation and act as her father's hostess.

TJ jumped to his feet and started to pace. He showed more enthusiasm now than when he was talking about the fancy ball. "This is the part of the story I think is much more interesting. There was a smaller plantation adjacent to Waterwood owned by the Collins family. Just before the Civil War, the plantation got into some financial trouble. Mr. Collins was faced with the prospect of selling off a large part of his land to pay his debts. The man was clever and came up with a different scheme that involved the Ross family of Waterwood. He suggested that Benjamin's daughter Emma should be married to his oldest son, Joshua. It would be the union of the two families in the district and would somehow solve his financial difficulties.

"The only problem was Benjamin saw through his plan. On the face of it, uniting great plantations was a good idea. But Benjamin looked at the young man who would be his son-in-law and was not impressed. He suspected he was not a gentleman and, if he had the same poor business sense that his father had, Joshua could only bring trouble to Waterwood."

"That's something I can understand," I said, as I pulled over a blue and white crocheted afghan to cover my legs. The fall season was declaring its arrival with a chill in the air.

"Benjamin talked with Emma and discovered she was

completely opposed to the idea. She had fallen in love with a young man raised at Waterwood. I don't know his name, but he was the son of Benjamin's plantation manager."

I reined in my excitement when I heard this and TJ continued.

"He was a fine young man, educated, with fine manners, but not in young Emma's class. Emma insisted it was true love. That was something Benjamin could understand."

"Of course, he would!" I exclaimed with a playful grin. "He had fallen in love with Elizabeth and proposed on the night of the glittering ball."

"This was serious," TJ insisted. "It was a difficult time for Benjamin. Tensions between the North and South were heating up. There was talk of secession. Benjamin did not want to rush into a decision that would affect the rest of his beloved Emma's life. So, he helped Joshua's father with his debts and postponed the decision about marriage. After all, Emma was young."

"What a story! How do you know all this?" I asked, my body rocking with excitement.

"The women in my family are nuts about genealogy and history. My mom found letters, or was it a diary? I don't know."

I had to take control of myself. I took a calming breath before I asked, "Do you have Emma's diary?"

"I'm not sure." He thought for a moment. "I guess we must. I can't imagine anyone throwing away something like that. Maybe Mom included it with some other stuff about Waterwood when we donated to the Historical Society. I guess I could ask and find out, if it's important."

"It would be great if you could ask." I wanted to grab the phone and thrust it at him to call the president of the historical society immediately. What an experience it would be to read Emma's words as she wrote her feelings in her diary and match them up with Daniel's letters that kept appearing on the desk. Of course, if I insisted, I'd have to explain that I was exchanging correspondence with a ghost. That wasn't going to happen. I'd have to be patient and find another way to encourage him to find the diary without raising his suspicions.

I took a small pillow and squeezed it underneath my leg, grateful that the small gesture distracted him.

"Is your leg feeling better?" he asked.

"Yes, thank you. Now, tell me why you think that you and Benjamin Franklin Ross have something in common."

"I don't know. When I think about that love story, I think it's more like two love stories wrapped up in one. Of course, it's about Elizabeth. But it's also about his love for Waterwood and that's where we match up. I was born and raised in Annapolis on the Western Shore of the Bay. I spent all my free time here at Waterwood or talking to the farmers in the area. I helped out in any way I could. My uncle who lived here called me his Little Shadow. But I would never be part of Waterwood, not the way I wanted to be."

"Why is that?" I asked.

"My uncle owned Waterwood. He planned to pass it down to his son and so on. There wasn't room for me in the line of inheritance. That meant there wasn't room for me at Waterwood unless I hired on as a farmhand. That wasn't an option. My cousin didn't want me looking over his shoulder. He didn't want someone who had a rightful place at the family dinner table doing farm work. Besides, Waterwood couldn't sustain both of us."

I tried to reconcile the story of a self-sustaining plantation that supported many families with the idea that it couldn't support two farmers today. And I failed.

CHAPTER THIRTY

"The Baltimore City Council passed a resolution unanimously to relieve the jail physician of his duties due to his failure to attend to U.S. soldiers confined there."

— *Baltimore Sun* Newspaper, January 31, 1862

TJ must have suspected my confusion and continued. "You have to remember that the Waterwood that Benjamin Franklin Ross inherited isn't the same Waterwood you see today. The custom back then was to pass down the property and its assets in one package to the eldest son, unless an arrangement was made for any other sons or family members. Emma had two sons. The oldest one inherited most of the property on his father's death, but his brother was given a chunk of rich land, large enough to support his family. That, of course, passed down through that line and was no longer considered part of Waterwood. Over the generations, more land packages were given to younger children or sold off when the owner needed cash. That's how Waterwood has dwindled to what it is today."

"But it's still a substantial property," I insisted.

"Yes, it is, but it can't sustain the land, the main house and even one family on its own anymore. Today, we rotate crops, some of which are not as profitable, to help maintain the integrity of the soil. Land-use restrictions limit the areas we can plant. Farming itself has become an expensive business. Acreage doesn't always produce enough to support it on its own. That's why I lease other fields for farming and run my custom farming business as well. In the 21st century, agribusiness emphasizes the *business* part, out of sheer necessity."

I was still confused. "So, how did you end up with Waterwood?"

TJ dropped his eyes. "That's another sad part of the story. My uncle had one son. He wasn't all that interested in farming like I was. While I was away at college, his son went out drinking one night and wrapped his car around a tree. Since his daughter didn't have any interest in the land, he deeded it to me. After losing his son, my uncle didn't have the energy or the interest to manage Waterwood. My uncle figured that some good came out of the loss. He had a chance to see some of the early improvements I made before he died. It felt good to make him proud."

We sat quietly together, each lost in our thoughts. Outside the crickets joined the frogs in their early evening concert of peeps and chirps, the sounds of early fall. They were probably the same sounds Benjamin heard as he sat quietly looking at the water, pondering his daughter's happiness and the future of his land.

Slowly, I came to the conclusion that this story didn't have a happy ending. The last thing Daniel had told me by letter was that he rode away from Waterwood with Emma's father to join the Confederate cause. Daniel's letters that appeared on the plantation desk were filled with concern that Emma thought that he didn't care about her or may have forgotten him. There had to be more to the story. I was eager to know what happened. Patience when working with children was one of my strong suits. Patience in my personal life was not.

"I hope you can finish the story, TJ. Did Emma and the

plantation overseer's son get together? Did they have to wait until after the war to marry? When did she marry the awful Joshua? Tell me what happened."

"Whoa there. You sure are interested in your namesake, even though you're not part of the family."

I shrugged, hoping to appear casual. "We girls named Emma have to stick together." I softened the statement with a wink.

"All right then. But you have to sit through the whole story." I nodded in agreement. "The plantation owners on the Eastern Shore were very conflicted about the troubles between the North and the South. They wanted to maintain the Union and continue to enjoy all its benefits, but their way of life was built on the Southern plantation lifestyle that involved slaves.

"Most landowners here wanted to avoid war and find a compromise so they could make a transition without destroying their livelihood. The men of the South, especially the Deep South, were firebrands. They thought the war was about their honor as gentlemen. States started seceding from the Union. Tempers flared in the North as well. Things started getting out of control. The Eastern Shore plantation owners were running out of options and room to maneuver." He paused and gave me a curious look. "You're sure you want to hear this?"

"Yes, I do. It's nice to talk to somebody who knows his history. Better than reading it in a book. Please go on."

He took a deep breath and leaned forward. "The year 1861 was an unsettled time. It didn't help that rumors were flying between New York, Philadelphia, Baltimore, and Washington.

"When word arrived that a group of Union Army soldiers had invaded Baltimore, everyone on the Eastern Shore went crazy. Unfortunately, this story had the seeds of truth. The first regiment to respond to Abraham Lincoln's call for volunteers came down the coast from Massachusetts by train.

"During a stopover in Philadelphia, the commanding officer heard a rumor that there would be an attack on the train while it was in Baltimore. He ordered his men to ignore any verbal abuse from the local citizens, but to load every gun, just in case.

Historians say that he told his men that if they were fired on, they were to take aim and 'Be sure to drop him.'"

"That sounds like a recipe for big trouble," I said.

"The situation was complicated," TJ went on. "The people here on the Shore were told it was a Yankee invasion of Baltimore, the port city of their grand state, Maryland. Then there was the problem of the tracks. The troop train ran to the northeast part of Baltimore where the tracks stopped. Tracks came up from Washington City but the two lines didn't connect. They had to uncouple the railcars carrying the troops and draw them through the city by horse to another station where the cars were to be hooked up to another locomotive going south. The pro-Union city fathers decided to make it an event and had a band lead the procession to the southbound tracks.

"Everything was going according to plan until a large crowd formed between the band and the soldiers. The route was blocked, so the soldiers had to get off the train and march to the other station. The crowd pelted them with rocks and bottles and anything else they could find. I guess the soldiers were pushed to the limit. They fired a volley into the crowd.

"People were killed and wounded on both sides. False reports were flying: more Yankee soldiers were on their way; the Union was going to take over Baltimore; President Lincoln was going to turn the city into an armed camp."

"I guess those were fighting words, no matter which side you were on," I said.

"They sure were." TJ looked into his mug. "Do you want some more coffee?"

"Sure."

I handed him my mug and sat back trying to imagine what it was like living in this pastoral place and hearing about armed chaos on the other side of the Bay. It would be frightening because the conflict could spread to the Eastern Shore. But there was another important reason: Baltimore was the port city for commerce. Whoever held Baltimore could strangle the Shore.

TJ returned and we settled back with our coffee, Maria's cookies long ago devoured.

He took a big drink and went on. "A wealthy Southern sympathizer over here chartered a steamer and paid for any man who volunteered to go and defend Baltimore. By the time the men from the Eastern Shore got there, the Baltimore police had the situation under control and the Union troops were on their way to Washington."

"That's like getting all ready for a football game, only to miss it. There must have been a lot of testosterone in the air."

"According to my mother, Benjamin rode off to join the Confederacy and took the plantation manager's son with him."

"That's right," I said softly.

"Oh, have you heard this part of the story before?"

I had to think fast. "Ah, no. I was, ah, just agreeing that such a crazy situation would force a person to make a decision and act on it."

"Well, that's what he did."

I put my hands over my eyes and tried to visualize the gravestones at his family cemetery. "I think I remember seeing all the Emma graves but, I'm not sure which one was hers. I was so overwhelmed by seeing my name all over the place, I didn't pay attention to the dates on the gravestones."

"I can take you back some time if you'd like to go," TJ offered.

"Yes, I'd like that. Then I could look for Daniel's gravestone, too."

He gave me a puzzled look. "Who is Daniel?"

That was a mistake. I'd have to cover it up and fast. "I think it was a name connected with Waterwood that the librarian mentioned. I don't know. There are so many names to remember."

TJ crossed his arms. "Well, Emma didn't marry a Daniel." He took a sip of cold coffee and grimaced. "All this talk about the family is making me thirsty. Why don't we head to the kitchen and I'll grab a bottle from Jack's beer stash if that's okay?" As I got myself oriented and headed down the hall, I didn't want to know the truth. I didn't want to hear the name of Emma's husband.

We settled at the kitchen table, it being a little chilly to go out on the patio. TJ picked up the story.

"According to the records, Emma married Joshua. My mother got the impression that she wasn't all that excited about the match."

"Did she read it in Emma's diary?"

"No, she found some letters written by Emma in a trunk. Mom said the girl didn't sound excited about the match the way a bride usually does."

I could barely disguise my excitement. TJ's mother had found a diary and letters. "If Emma grew up without a stepmother, she and her father must have been very close. He must have been able to tell his daughter wasn't in love," I suggested, thinking about the close relationship I'd had with Uncle Jack. When I married my high school sweetheart right out of college, Uncle Jack was all smiles at the wedding. In an unguarded moment, I caught a look on his face filled with worry and unhappiness. I ignored it at the time, but when my husband proved to be unfaithful after I helped put him through medical school, I admitted that Uncle Jack was a better judge of people than I was. Divorce was an option for me. It probably wasn't an option for Emma in the 19th century.

TJ went on. "I suspect that Emma's father knew his daughter well. Anytime anyone in our family talks about Joshua's presence on our family tree, he's referred to as the *bad seed*."

"I wonder where she got that phrase," I said.

TJ shook his head. "I have no idea. Records show that Emma and Joshua married, lived at Waterwood, and had two sons and a daughter. The girl died in her early teens, I think."

"Did Emma die in childbirth? So many women at that time died at a very young age."

"No, Emma lived to old age. It was unusual for her to have survived childbirth. It probably helped that she only had three babies." He shrugged. "I guess the fire went out of the marriage." TJ sighed. "Are you happy now that you know the Ross family history?"

"Yes, I am." I gave him a big smile. "As a thank-you, how

about having dinner with me? Maria is a great cook and she always makes enough for two. Oh!" I realized with a start. "I don't have anything for Ghost."

"Fear not, we come prepared." TJ sprinted out of the room with Ghost at his heel.

My mind was filled with thoughts of Emma and Daniel. And why hadn't I heard from him? While TJ was out of the house, I made my way to the writing den as fast as I could, hoping to find a letter from Daniel. But there was nothing on the desk's writing surface. Disappointed, I clicked off the overhead light.

There was nothing on the desk? I snapped on the light again. There was no stack of paper. How could Daniel write to me if he had no paper?

Someone had moved the stack of computer paper. Tidying up. Maria. My eyes darted around the room. Where would she put the paper? She must have hidden it away in her constant effort to keep my home neat.

I heard the front door open and close. TJ. But I had to get the paper back to Daniel or I might never know what happened to them.

"I'll meet you in the kitchen."

"Okay, I'll feed Ghost."

I had only precious moments to find the paper. Desperate, I scanned the bookshelves. Nothing. But I'd forgotten there were large drawers under the writing surface for more storage. I sat in the chair and hunched underneath. Madly, I pulled open the drawers. Nothing. Then I turned to the small file cabinet next to the desk and found the stack of paper in the bottom drawer.

"What are you doing?" TJ asked.

I almost cried out in surprise. I had to think fast. "Found it!" Gripping the stack of paper, Daniel's paper, I sat up slowly and returned the stack to the desktop. "I remembered I needed some paper and I didn't know where Maria had hidden it. You know, she is always saying *Everything belongs in its place* only I don't always know where that place is." My laugh sounded weak, but it was the best I could do. "Let's eat!"

I hustled TJ down the hall and smiled when I heard Ghost crunching happily in the kitchen. Soon, we too were enjoying our dinner.

CHAPTER THIRTY-ONE

"The Secret of Happiness: A mind always employed is always happy. This is the true secret, the grand recipe, for felicity. The idle are the only wretched."

— Thomas Jefferson in a letter to his Daughter

TJ and I shared a delightful dinner of delicious food seasoned with some laughs. Ghost had his kibble that TJ carried in his truck. Afterward, I was ready to crawl into my bed for a good night's sleep. As I walked TJ to the front door, Ghost stopped and growled. TJ stopped as well, heeding the alert from his dog. He motioned me to stand still and put his finger to his lips for quiet. My heart thudded in my chest. The PTSD threatened to trigger. The man and his dog crept down the hallway.

We all jumped when sharp knocks hit the door.

"Who is it?" TJ demanded.

It felt like forever before a man's voice answered with a question. "TJ? It's Craig. Detective Craig Mason. What's wrong?"

I leaned against the wall and started breathing again.

Before answering, TJ turned to Ghost, who stood rigid, hackles raised. The stripe of gray fur standing up on his back, a sign he was unsure or angry. TJ said in a stern voice, "Friend." The dog tore his eyes away from the door, stared at TJ for a long moment then lay down on the floor by his feet, calm, but ready.

TJ opened the door then lowered his voice, but I could still hear him say, "Craig, don't sneak up on us like that, not with a murderer on the loose. Think, man!"

As the detective stepped over the threshold, he whispered an apology to TJ then greeted me. "Evening, Ms. Chase."

I tried to steady my voice. "Good evening, detective. Let's go into the living room."

As I sat down, I noticed TJ's look of concern. I nodded and braced to hear bad news. "What can we do for you, Detective?"

"Well, ma'am, you both know that I'm investigating the incident at the Lone Oak. I was wondering if either of you might know where Josh Collins is?"

"I'm not surprised to hear his name," TJ said. "When there is trouble, Josh is usually right in the middle of it. A bad seed is a bad seed."

Bad seed made me remember the man named Joshua of long ago. "Why would you say that?" I asked.

"It is what it is." He shrugged. "When families have been in the same area for a long time, they intermarry and the kids often act like they own the place. They strut around like the entitled elite. Isn't that right, Craig?"

The detective grimaced. "Well, I wouldn't want to put it like that. But I have to admit, it is a problem. So, have either of you seen him?"

I shook my head. "The only time I saw him was here at the Cottage."

TJ shot out of the chair. "What was he doing here?"

"He showed up one day," I began hesitantly, not sure why TJ reacted so strongly. "He said he wanted to welcome me to the neighborhood and make sure I was okay. He thought it could be unnerving for a city girl to be living alone here at Uncle Jack's

Cottage in the middle of nowhere." I casually added, "He knew that Stephani had come by the Cottage. His sister is the library intern I'm working with, remember?"

TJ narrowed his eyes. "Was she here too?"

His reaction, of course, triggered a defensive response. "Yes, as a matter of fact but they didn't come together. And when was I supposed to give you a list of everyone who comes to the Cottage?"

Detective Mason stepped in. "Okay, okay. You two can discuss that later. Ma'am, when did you see Josh?"

"I don't know, yesterday maybe? Why don't you talk to Stephani?"

"I have and she claims that she doesn't know anything."

Claims? There was more going on than I thought.

The detective pressed. "Did he say anything about where he was hanging out or tell you if he was leaving the county?"

"No, nothing like that," I answered him while I kept my eyes on TJ. "It was nothing long and involved. He showed up to say hello, introduced his friends, and left. That was it."

The detective followed up. "What friends?"

I scratched my head, trying to recall the details. "I only remember their funny nicknames, Tin Man and Toad, I think."

The detective made a note while TJ sat down again. His body language of legs crossed away from me showed he was closing me out of the conversation. And he did.

"Craig, what have you got?"

"TJ, you know Josh. He's always interested in getting the most for the least amount of effort. If there's a get-rich-quick scheme, Josh is on it."

I wasn't going to let them shut me out. "He struck me as a bully masquerading as a regular guy.

"I wish I could confirm the real names of these boys," He looked at his notes. "Tin Man and Toad."

I closed my eyes, trying to call up the memory of that afternoon. "Tin Man was a thin young man, really thin, who looked like his hips could barely hold up his pants. His blonde hair was cut with weird bangs. He seemed to hang on every word the bully said."

The detective looked at TJ. "This Tin Man sounds like Donnie Sawyer." TJ nodded in agreement.

I continued. "And the other young man was tall, had brown hair and deep dimples. He was the best-looking guy in the group. Why would they give him the ugly nickname, Toad?"

"Edward Ray, Jr. We know about him," said the detective.

"I swear that kid would do anything to be with the cool guys," TJ declared.

"Do you think he's the one who murdered the young man?" I was so surprised. "He didn't look the type." I looked down at my hands. "I guess there isn't a type or you could sweep up all the offenders and put yourself out of a job."

"You're right about that. I don't think the boy did it." The detective sighed. "He is like that comical character in the movies. He talks tough. You know, says the words, but you don't believe him. When it comes to doing something illegal, like trespassing on somebody's land, he gets nervous."

"Sounds like he's earned the name Toad. All bluster, but happy to sit on his pad," TJ said with a chuckle.

"I think he's our snitch," the detective said softly as if revealing a secret.

"Snitch?" I asked.

"The caller on the Tip Line," Craig said. "I'd bet money that whoever called was there when the attack went down. I listened to the recording. The male tried to disguise his voice, but now that I think about it, it sounded a lot like Toad. I could see him calling the Tip Line to get help for Kid Billy. Leaving a friend out there under the tree bleeding must have upset him. I need to talk to him again and push harder."

"So, is he a good guy or a bad guy?" I asked.

"He was a good kid, but he has taken up with some bad company," TJ chimed in. "Josh is a bad seed. He wouldn't hesitate to trespass on somebody's land or something worse. He had one run-in with the law while he was a minor." TJ frowned. "I don't think it was anything serious unless you can be thrown in prison for being annoying. Was it drugs?"

The detective shook his head. "TJ, you know I can't answer that. The kid was a minor. The word is that the system worked. We thought we scared him straight. Now that he's an adult, it gets serious if it escalates."

"Something tells me he is guilty of being a Class A manipulator," I added. "What about the victim? Was he part of the posse too?" I asked.

"Yes, Kid Billy, Tin Man, Toad, and Josh all grew up together. Kid Billy got into some trouble when he was a minor, too. Nothing serious. Word is he got straight. But recently, I heard that he got upside down about money and needed to score quickly. That could be why he started running with Josh again."

TJ leaned back and closed his eyes. "Let's say, they heard that old story about a treasure buried under the Lone Oak and thought they should dig it up. Let's say, they went out with their flashlights and shovels. Josh tells them where to dig, but there's nothing there. So, he points to a different place. They dig again. Nothing. And that happens again and again."

"That would explain all the different holes around the Lone Oak," I said.

TJ shot me a look. "How do you know about them?"

I wanted to ignore him, but we were talking about murder. "Stephani took me for a little ride to the Lone Oak. I saw the holes the police filled in, sort of." To deflect any response, I quickly picked up the thread of his scenario. "The guys were out there digging and got frustrated because they weren't finding anything. Things started getting tense and Bam!"

"Or try this." The detective's gaze drifted toward a window. "They're all digging, all but Josh. Heaven forbid he should get dirty. Kid Billy starts to get nervous. After all, they're trespassing on private land in the middle of the night. An arrest could mean trouble for him. He says they should leave, do some research and come back when they have a better idea where the treasure might be.

TJ continued the story. "Josh goes all macho on him. There's a lot of posturing, normal for guys that age. Kid Billy holds his shovel out to Josh and says he can dig if he wants to, but he's going home."

The detective turned to TJ. "Can you hear Josh saying, 'You're not going anywhere till I let you. If I say dig, you dig.'" TJ nodded. Craig continued. "Josh asserts that he's the boss and he demands to hear Kid Billy state that fact."

And Craig played out the rest of the scene for us. "Kid Billy says yes, Josh is the boss, but Josh didn't believe he is sincere. They get into a fight of words. All the Kid can think of is getting away. Josh can't let this insubordination go unchecked. He takes the shovel and halfheartedly swings the shovel at the Kid to scare him. But the Kid is quick and jumps out of the way. But what infuriates Josh is that Kid Billy doesn't show any fear. Now, it is a contest of wills and male pride. Josh won't let anyone else come out on top, no matter who or why. He swings again and connects with Kid Billy's head. Battle over and won."

I was surprised at the detail the detective used to describe what may have happened under the tree. "How do you know all that? I thought the victim never regained consciousness."

"Imagination helps in this job." He winked at me. "And so does experience. It was a head wound. Even a small cut would bleed like the dickens. I think the guys got scared when they saw all the blood and peeled outta there, leaving Kid Billy on the ground. They couldn't call 911, because of questions they'd face: what they were doing on the land, why they were digging holes, and the rest."

A shudder ran through me. "Do you think the boy would have survived if they had gotten help right away?"

The detective shook his head. "The doctor doesn't want to speculate, but I think Kid Billy was doomed when the shovel slammed into his skull." He slapped his thighs with the palms of his hands. "That's all I've got right now. I need to find Josh. If either of you sees or hears anything, be sure to let me know right away."

He pointed his index finger right at my nose. "And no more neighborly conversations for you. If Josh did this, he is dangerous. He'll do anything to protect himself. So, call me. Don't engage. No friendly chat. You call me."

After the detective left, TJ said, "You need to listen to Craig. You're not to get involved. You should've told me he came to the Cottage." Then TJ let out a long sigh. "I guess I should have told you the negative things about living here."

"You mean things like not having good cell phone coverage, being a half-hour away from civilization, and living across the creek from a witch's den?" I said, trying to lighten the mood.

But he didn't respond to my humor. "About Josh. Jack had run-ins with the boy since he was young. One time, Jack caught him stealing a tool from the garage and got angry. It wasn't the value of the tool. It was the principle of the thing. The kid was disrespectful and threatening. He said Jack *owed* him." TJ shook his head. "Jack didn't owe him anything."

"Did Uncle Jack call the police?" I asked.

TJ shook his head. "Josh returned the tool… by lobbing it into the woods. It took us an hour to find it. What that kid needed was a father to whack some sense into him." Anger made his face flush red.

"Okay, I get it. Not a good neighbor," I said quickly to defuse the situation. "I'll watch myself. Anyone else I should know?"

"His sister Stephani is no prize."

My eyes grew wide in astonishment. "Stephani? The library intern who is helping me?" Then I shook my head.

He looked away as if trying to make a decision then he turned back. "You do know she is Josh's sister."

"Yes, but she's nothing like her brother," I insisted.

He shrugged. "Pardon the cliché, but the apple doesn't fall far from the tree. They are brother and sister, brought up in the same house."

"I'm afraid I can't agree with you. I've worked with Stephani. She is meticulous and respectful, almost to a fault. No, maybe she was wild when she was young, but now, she has her act together. I think I'll give her the benefit of the doubt."

His mouth clamped shut, but I could see the strain on his face. I wasn't going to change his mind so, I opted not to try.

Instead, I voiced the question that was rolling around my brain. "I know I'm probably jumping to conclusions, but is this Josh any relation to the man who married Emma a century ago?" He didn't answer right away. "Do you know? You must know."

He cast his eyes to the floor and finally answered with one word. "Yes."

He was embarrassed. Why? Then it hit me like a bolt. If you went back far enough, Josh, Stephani, and TJ were on the same family tree.

TJ stood up. "I gotta go. Thanks again for dinner." He was out the door with Ghost on his heels and they were in his truck in a flash.

I leaned against my front door until it closed with a quiet click. My hands were shaking like leaves in a light breeze when I set the deadbolt. *A bad seed*, I thought. *A bad seed can grow into an apple that doesn't fall far from the tree.* It was a cliché, but, in this case, a truism. I may have met a murderer, right here at the Cottage.

CHAPTER THIRTY-TWO

"When you are about to write a letter to a friend, think what you would say to him if he were at that moment with you, and then write it. We all like *talking* letters – good talking, of course."

How to Write Letters
by Professor J. Willis Westlake, 1883

I was tired and stressed by all the talk of murder. I wanted to lie down and sleep comfortably in my bed upstairs instead of on the sofa. But there was something I had to do first. With fingers crossed, I turned on the light in the writing den, and heaved a sigh of relief. There, on top of the stack of papers was a short letter from Daniel.

Dearest Emma,

I wanted to write a letter in response to your note, but the paper was gone. I panicked as I ransacked my father's desk. There was always a fine stack of paper to be found there, but now it was gone. There was not a page or a fragment to be found.

I've been waiting quietly for someone to bring more. Again, my patience paid off. More paper appeared and I am able to write to you once again.

I pray, do not break the connection we have made. Your presence and love are all that allow me to exist in this world. Without you, I would be like the leaves of corn grown from the soil of our beloved Waterwood in autumn. Golden, but dried out. Brittle. Ready to be carried off with the next breath of wind. Scattered into the unknown.

Emma, I beg that we remain joined, even if only through written words until we are together again.

I am, my dearest friend, most affectionately and kindly yours,

Daniel

Relieved, I made my way upstairs for a peaceful night's sleep.

The next morning, I was *up with the birds,* as Uncle Jack liked to say. I had time to revel in Mother Nature's morning activities before Stephani arrived and I had to begin my human chores and errands. I stopped on my way to the kitchen and was delighted to find a long letter from Daniel. After capturing his words in photographs, I took it out to the patio with a fresh cup of coffee and sat down to read.

Dear Emma,

You are such a dear and sensitive woman. I hesitate to write of events, in fear that you might be overcome by their import. I ask that you forgive me. I send these words only because you asked. Be brave, my dearest Emma. Your strength fortifies me.

Of when I last wrote, your father and I were in Virginia. The men of the unit we joined were trying to set up batteries at Mathias Point to threaten traffic on the Potomac River that runs up to Washington, D.C. It was an area that favored us. There were dense undergrowth and tall trees that would make it hard for the U.S. forces to see what armaments we had in place, if any.

I guess the goal was to disrupt the movements of the federal government troops and supply lines in any way possible while the South organized itself.

One morning, a stiff breeze snapped the flag as it hung from its pole. It was not the Stars and Stripes as we have known our flag to be. It was the flag of the Confederacy. The breeze brought us sounds of shelling

shelling in the distance. It wasn't long before some pickets reported that one of the Yankee commanders was using the guns of his flagship to bombard Mathias Point. The men stationed to protect our encampment had run away in the face of the men who came ashore from the ships. It was not a large force, but deadly. They were seen clearing away the foliage from the land and building fortifications.

The call went out from the officers that every man must rush forward to counter the incursion. It was confusing. Horses' hooves thundered around us as men rode back and forth, yelling orders. Infantrymen ran between the tents and cooking fires, their bayonets flashing in the sunshine. We moved through a thick forest area. When we neared the shore, there was a grand vista of the Potomac River.

It was easy to see why it was an important fortification. There were sweeping views both up and down the river and one could observe activities on the far shore.

What we saw was chilling. In the middle of the river, a large ship was anchored. Someone said it was the flagship of a commander. Some of the men of its crew were gathering up their tools on our side of the river.

Our boys opened fire and the crew ran to their boats and pulled hard on their oars to get to the safety of their ship. Seeing them on the run, our boys ran to the shoreline and kept firing.

Your father and I watched the action from the rear line as we were expected to do. We were not part of this fight. It wasn't long before the flagship's guns were brought to bear and started firing back at us.

Facing superior fire, our boys moved back, the zing of bullets chasing them. Then, they ran to avoid the shells. There was chaos for a time as the boys ran by us seeking safe shelter. Stay low and follow me, your father ordered. I did not see him leave. It was the first armed conflict I had ever observed. I was mesmerized by it. Then, I heard him call my name and it was enough to remove the fog from my brain.

I started running to find him. I must have tripped on a tree root because I was face down in the dirt. I started to get up, but somebody pushed me down hard. I must tell you I was scared that it was one of the Union sailors.

Then, I heard the man's voice near my ear. He called me by name. I was sure it was a friend, someone who knew me, someone who would help me. But he was sitting on my back. I couldn't get up. I pondered that he wanted to keep me out of the line of fire from the federal guns.

He said that he'd been looking for me and was glad he'd found me. I was relieved and stopped struggling to get up. The voice was one I had heard before, of that I was sure. I did not know who it was. I turned my head around as far as it would go to see the face of my friend and savior.

I was shocked to discern the identity of the man sitting on my back. Of all the people I knew at home, I would not have thought he would help me. I was wrong. He was there, in the midst of the battle, trying to protect me. You know him as well.

It was Joshua Collins.

Yes, it was a surprise, but I can only tell you that I write of events as they happened and is the truth.

Then, he leaned down close to my ear and yelled above the noise. He said that he had something for me. I saw the flash of the metal barrel of his gun.

I am sorry to say that I am not certain of what happened next. It is a muddle. Know that it was not long before I was moving away from the fighting. The only thought in my mind was you. Oh, how I have longed to be back at Waterwood with you.

Again, I apologize that I am still confused about what happened. Was I wounded? Did your father bring me home? The next thing I knew, I was here at my father's desk in the plantation office. I was sitting in his chair as I did when I was a boy.

I want so much to run and find you, but I cannot leave. It is as if I am chained to this desk. But I am home and safe. I am sure that your father or mine shall appear at any moment to explain all. Dare I hope that you might come as well? I have settled down to wait.

Until that day does come, you will be protected. Always remember that you have two things that can stand between you and ill fortune ~ my admiration and that which is secret, placed under the Lone Oak by your father and me for you. You must use it to keep yourself safe and independent until we are together again at Waterwood.

Your loving servant forever,

Daniel

My hands shook, making Daniel's letter flutter in the growing warmth of the new day. His revelations were almost too much for me to take in. Yes, I was being silly. A man alive in the 1860s was no longer walking the earth, but his letters, personalized as if written to me, had made him a vibrant part of my life.

It was hard to think of him as dead. Seeing his grave marker in the cemetery would have helped make that fact a reality. I had looked for it. It was nowhere to be found. Now, I understood. If he had fallen in battle, his body would not have been transported back to Waterwood. Like so many others, he might be in a single or unmarked grave.

It's one thing to die at the hands of an enemy in war, but the real shock was that he died at the hand of someone he knew. Someone who claimed to be his friend.

Was there a possible connection between events of his time and what was happening today? The sages say that history repeats itself. Could that be true in this small corner of the world here on the Eastern Shore?

I reread that portion of Daniel's letter where he recounted the attack by Joshua. Here was a written statement that Joshua Collins, who lived in the 19th century, had committed murder. His descendent, known as Josh, was suspected of another murder. It seemed that the Collins family had a stain of a bad seed that survived the generations.

I scanned the letter again for the mention of what Emma's father had done to protect her. It read: two things that can stand between you and ill fortune ~ my admiration and that which is secret, placed under the Lone Oak by your father and me.

Whatever they had buried under the Lone Oak was meant to keep her safe. I could only imagine it was money or valuables. Why would they bury it? Why wouldn't her father have given it into the hands of someone he trusted? Were the times too unsettled? Were loyalties in question?

Stephani would be here soon to drive me to my Pain & Torture session. Afterward, I'd ride with her to the library and do some more research in the Maryland Room. I went inside and quickly typed out a copy of Daniel's letter. All of his letters were valuable to me, but this one most of all.

As I dragged myself upstairs to dress, Daniel's words thundered in my mind:

Until we are together again at Waterwood.

Daniel had written those words to me—*to Emma*—only moments ago. This wasn't like finding a letter written decades ago stashed in a drawer of a desk. He'd written to Emma trying to make sense of things. He didn't know what happened after Joshua had attacked him. He didn't know anything until he was sitting at his father's desk. My desk.

He believed that he was wounded and sent home. I didn't understand the why's and how's of metaphysics, but I knew the strength of a tie forged from love. I felt it every day with Uncle Jack. I knew the power of the desire to live, survive even a most horrendous event.

Daniel's love for Emma and Waterwood was strong. Stronger than any action Joshua could have taken against him. That's when I came to a chilling understanding:

Daniel didn't know he was dead.

CHAPTER THIRTY-THREE

"If, when writing letters, we would keep before our minds the question, 'How would this look one year or ten years hence?' we would save ourselves from writing a great many foolish things."

How to Write Letters
by Professor J. Willis Westlake, 1883

Somehow, I set aside that realization. I couldn't deal with it quickly before my ride arrived. I needed the comfort of bright sunlight and a peaceful time to figure out how to proceed. As I made my way to the bottom of the stairs, I vowed not to let my mind wander down the dark corridors of What If.

Stories abounded about what ghosts did when they realized they were dead. Horrible tales of anger, retribution, retaliation directed at people who were still alive and well. How many were true, if any? I didn't know. I didn't care. I had come to Uncle Jack's Cottage for peace and healing. So far, Daniel, or should I say Daniel's ghost, had behaved, had added a surprising dimension to my new life here. I didn't need that spirit to go into a rage.

What to do? What to do? I wondered, as I waited for my ride. Then a thought hit me and I grabbed my phone. I'd see if TJ could pick me up at the library, then we could go back to the cemetery. Stephani arrived right on time. I quietly wished she had a more accessible vehicle. While the Jeep was cute, it proved harder for me to climb into than TJ's truck. It took some maneuvering and some muscle from Stephani, but I was finally ready to go.

At my P.T. appointment, it seemed that the exercises were getting easier. Was I getting stronger? It wasn't worth double-thinking the question. I was glad I wasn't craving a fistful of painkillers when I was done.

Later at the library, I settled at one of the tables to resume my research. Stephani, as usual, was eager to help. I craved the freedom to wander the stacks and poke around in the file drawers where unbound local historical information was cataloged. It would be fun to thumb through the files, open one at random, and page through its contents, hoping to find a gem. I found just such a gem in one of Stephani's miscellaneous files about the Civil War. Someone had typed out a short paragraph about money using an old typewriter with worn keys.

It was all about money.

Evidently, as tensions grew between the different political factions on the Eastern Shore, the wealthier families worried about their deposits in the local banks. The valuation of currency was fluctuating. Also, there was the question of access to safe deposit boxes that held other valuables in the bank vaults. The author of this short historical piece raised the question I had: Where did families hide their valuables if they removed them from the banks?

Could it be true? Did Emma's father bury a chest of treasures under the Lone Oak?

I didn't have to speculate in the silent, dusty corridors of history. I only had to raise that question with Daniel as soon as I got back to the Cottage.

"Did you find anything interesting?" asked Stephani as her eyes eagerly searched the papers spread out in front of me.

I calmly moved my right hand to cover the page about buried

treasure. I didn't want to share any information yet. "Oh, there are so many interesting things in your research files. I could get lost in them for hours. These files alone would be a great inspiration for a novel."

I noticed Stephani's eyes were racing over the labels on the file folders. Quickly, I shuffled the papers into an organized stack.

"Or" I added, "The information would be a great jumping-off point for a nonfiction book." I gently pulled more folders toward me. I felt like I was playing a shell game. "There are some wonderful drawings of ladies fashions in these folders."

After I showed her a few, I rested my hands on the files. "You have all the information and answers any writer might need for a book." I gently leaned against the back of my chair. "I don't know, Stephani. I'm in a real quandary about what story I want to tell. What story the kids would enjoy."

Stephani lit up as she glanced down the aisle and mused, "I remember being mesmerized by stories my grandmother used to tell."

"Oh, tell me."

"No, they were nothing special. Just family stories. I'm sure you can come up with something much better than hers." Her bright expression had closed down tight. She wasn't going to share anything with me.

Disappointed, I gently pushed myself away from the table when I saw TJ making his way through the bank of computers toward me. "It's time for me to go. Thanks again for driving me around. I appreciate it."

Stephani watched while I collected my things. "I don't mind carrying you around."

I had to smile at her use of a favorite local phrase, *carrying you around.*

Stephani continued. "I'm happy to do it. If you need any more research help, you know you can call on me. I'm learning more every day about what is here in the Maryland Room. You have my telephone number. Just call me and let me know what you need and I'll look it up."

TJ walked in, but his eyes were following Stephani as she went into a back room. "What were you talking about with her?"

"And hello to you, too," I said with a little sarcasm.

He drew his eyes back to me and laughed. "Okay, hello. How was P.T.? How was your research time? Have I focused my attention on you now?"

I playfully punched him in the arm and said, "Yes, I think it's time for us to get going."

I handed my things to him. "Come on, I have plans for you." He followed me as I moved right along. I was feeling pretty good.

"You don't have to make a mad dash to the truck," he warned.

"I know," I whispered as we made our way through the library. "I'm not pushing myself. I'm just feeling stronger. I'm hesitant to say it out loud, but I feel like I've turned the corner."

We walked through the automatic doors into the small, landscaped courtyard of the library. The sun shone brightly without the scorching heat of summer.

TJ walked closer to me and lowered his voice. "Did you hear? Craig caught up with Josh and has him in custody."

"That's a relief." And it was. I hadn't realized how worried I was about running into Josh again, especially on my patio. "Could you put my papers in the truck, then take a short walk with me?"

"Part of your research?"

"Yes," I said. "I've made a discovery."

After he stashed the papers, we crossed the street and followed the brick walkway to the front of the county courthouse. I found a bench and sank down on it.

"Okay, before you lecture me, that was too far to walk, I'm happy to rest here awhile."

"Why did you want to come to the courthouse?" TJ asked as he sat down next to me.

"I wanted to see where it happened. This is where Union soldiers marched on the Eastern Shore. The story was in one of the library books we took out on your card."

"Tell me more," TJ said.

It was a pleasure to talk with a history buff as avid as I was.

"The soldiers came from Baltimore to arrest a circuit court judge suspected of being a Southern sympathizer. He had directed a grand jury to investigate some arrests made during the 1861 election and issue indictments. They pulled the judge right off the bench while he was conducting a trial. When he resisted, they pistol-whipped him and hauled him off to Fort McHenry on a charge of treason, punishable by death."

TJ took off his hat, ran his fingers through his hair, and reset the hat. "And I thought today's political maneuverings were getting outrageous."

"Remember, the nation was being torn apart by civil war. It didn't help that the federal troops stayed here to keep the peace, which only outraged both Southern and Northern sympathizers." I thought for a moment. "Maybe that was the event that forced Benjamin to choose sides."

"You might be right," said TJ.

"And to think that it happened right here," I said, taking in the graceful red brick courthouse, surrounded by a plaza landscaped with old gnarly trees and flowering shrubs, outlined by a tall black wrought iron fence. It was hard to imagine such violence in such a peaceful place.

TJ chuckled. "There is a lot of history here on the Shore, much more than we can tackle today. Ready?"

I nodded and we made our way back to his truck. Fortunately, it was all downhill.

CHAPTER THIRTY-FOUR

"I made a coffin for our little baby Elizabeth. She died awhile before day this morning and was 20 days old. I carried her to Oxford and put her in the ground alongside our other infants, now 5, 3 girls and two boys all buried in a row next to the garden fence." *December 12, 1857*

The Willis Family Journals 1847-1951
Edited and Annotated by James Dawson

As we made our way out of Easton, I said, "It's such a beautiful day. Do you think we could take the long way home?"

"Sure," he said. "Do you want to drive around or do you have a specific destination in mind?"

"Well, I'd like to…" I looked at him and realized something was different about him. "What have you done to yourself?"

He glanced around. "What you mean?"

"I don't know. Did you… you got a haircut!"

He glanced in the rearview mirror and smiled. "You noticed! I clean up pretty good for a farmer, don't you think?"

"Not half bad for a farmer or anyone else."

"It's getting to the time I have to climb into the combine. I figured I'd better get a haircut or I'd look like a shaggy mountain man by the time I finished the harvest. Now, maybe you won't mind being seen with me."

I shook my head. "I never mind being seen with you. Of course, we've never really gone anywhere," I said with a laugh.

He placed a hand flat against his chest. "Oh, you know how to wound a guy."

"You've given me an idea," I said, as I ran my hand over my hair. "Do you think there might be somebody available now to shape up my hair? We cut it when I was in the hospital and rehab. It was easier that way."

"And you've been cutting it yourself since you were released," he said as he turned toward one of the shopping malls.

How embarrassing. It must look worse than I thought.

"Well, I wasn't gonna say anything. You struck me as a woman who paid attention to her looks, but I can understand, with everything else going on…"

I used both hands to smooth my hair back and straighten my bangs. That's when I noticed that my bangs were so long, they almost covered my eyes. "So, you're saying that where there are shaggy mountain men, there might also be shaggy mountain women?" I didn't wait for his response. "Kind Chauffeur, please drive straight to a local hair salon. I fear this might be an emergency."

He had me wait in the truck while he ran inside the shop that advertised Walk-ins Welcome. It only took a moment for him to negotiate an appointment for me with a stylist who looked like she had just stepped out of a fashion magazine. Seeing her perfect hair, makeup and cute outfit made me feel even worse.

I sat in her chair and saw a dowdy woman in the mirror. My handiwork with the scissors had only made it worse. "Can you do anything to salvage it?" I wailed.

She frowned and went to work, snipping here and combing there. Soon, she swiveled the chair around so I faced the mirror. She had performed a miracle. My hair was just above my shoulders, much shorter than I'd worn it in ages. It moved when I did but was long enough to pull back for a P.T. appointment. I looked as good as I was beginning to feel.

Back in the truck and driving down the road, TJ kept stealing looks at me. At this rate, I was afraid he was going to drive into a tree.

"Okay, okay, you were right. I must have looked a fright. Your girlfriend did a great job."

He grinned. "Yes, she did." He redirected his attention to the roadway. "And she isn't my girlfriend."

Somehow, that piece of information pleased me. *Stop that!* I ordered myself. It wasn't a good time for me to get involved right now. I had too many issues, too much baggage to burden someone else. No, a new relationship could wait for a while. With that decision, the bright sunlight lifted my spirit.

TJ must have noticed the change in me. "I think you've kept me in suspense long enough."

I perked up. "What do you mean?"

"When I picked you up at the library, you said you wanted to take the long way home. You never answered my question if you had a specific destination in mind."

I appreciated the fact that this man could get me back on track so quickly. I decided to meet his playful attitude. "You are absolutely right, kind sir. I guess I got distracted by the horrible realization that I looked a fright. Now that all is right with the world, I was wondering if we could drive by your family cemetery one more time."

His face scrunched up and he said slowly. "You're very interested in that place. Is it because you're preoccupied with death or—"

"No, that's not it at all. I've been doing a lot of research, as you know. I'm beginning to feel like I know one of your ancestors named Emma. I want to look around again if you don't mind."

"No, I don't mind taking you there at all. I might even learn something that I can share with my family. I might even surprise them."

We headed off to the main driveway of Waterwood. He parked by the stone wall of the cemetery enclosure. Ghost jumped out and took off running and sniffing at top speed. Seeing the streak of his white coat weaving around this quiet place was a little unsettling. After all, his name was Ghost. I got out of the truck and made my way to the gate without any help, for once. I paused to take in the atmosphere of this serene spot while TJ pulled out the key to the iron gate hidden behind a loose stone.

"Are you coming?" TJ asked.

The gate swung open and again, I entered the place that held family secrets tied to Waterwood. Daniel's letters had shown me that there were connections and betrayals, masquerades, and riddles.

I headed over to Emma's grave, navigating the ground carefully. Her white marble headstone was in excellent condition, a sign of a loving family. Next to it, the gray granite headstone, marking the grave of her husband Joshua who died in 1890, was cracked and growing lichen. Neglected. What he deserved, I thought with a stab of anger.

There was a small marble block nestled close to the foot of her grave marked *Baby Boy* 1867. A miscarriage or stillborn child? Lost, but not forgotten by his mother.

I checked the dates on Emma's stone:

BORN MAY 11, 1844
DIED JANUARY 10, 1895

The dates spanned the time of the Civil War. I felt sure that this was the grave of *the* Emma who should be receiving the letters coming through the old plantation desk. I couldn't imagine the loneliness she must have felt as she waited, dreaming of Daniel's return. I wondered if she ever learned the truth.

I'd found the final resting place of Daniel's love. A shudder ran through me as I remembered that Daniel didn't know he was dead. I couldn't imagine how he would react when he found out that his Emma was long gone. Thinking about the strength of his love for her and how it had transcended death soothed me.

I wished I had brought something, a small bouquet, to pay tribute to this woman who had inspired such strong feelings. What a joy it would be to read letters she had written to Daniel, to learn about her the way I had gotten to know him.

"TJ, before we leave, would you look again for a gravestone with the name Daniel on it, please. It's kind of important to me."

Steadying myself, I reached down to remove some fall leaves from her grave. Bushes with needle-like leaves of soft blue were planted on either side of her marble headstone. It was their scent that caught my attention. Minty, yet lavender-esque. I closed my eyes and reveled in the fragrance. I broke off a twig.

TJ returned. "I didn't find any stone carved with the name of Daniel."

"Do you know what kind of bush this is?" I handed him the twig.

He crushed a leaf between his fingers, held it up to his nose then held out his hand so I could take a sniff. "It's rosemary, symbolizes remembrance. You'll find it in many cemeteries."

"It smells so wonderful. I had no idea it could grow to such a size."

"The city girl speaks. I bet you've only seen rosemary grown in those itty-bitty herb gardens people have in the windows of their condo kitchens," he teased.

"You're right." I held my hands up in surrender. "I bow to the farmer, master of all plants."

"You were lost in thought looking at her grave. Care to share?"

"I wish I knew what she looked like." I caught him looking at me. "What?"

"She has really snagged your attention. Why?"

I wanted to tell him about Daniel, but I was afraid he would think I was crazy. Instead, I said, "Oh, I've always been interested in women, how they lived during that time in our history—Civil

War. I'd like to think she was beautiful and feminine and strong to run a plantation when everybody was away fighting."

"Not everyone went away to war," he said with a little disgust as he pointed to the grave next to Emma's. "The word in the family is that the only cause *he* believed in was himself. I have no idea how he got such a beautiful woman to marry him."

"How do you know she was beautiful?" I asked with a hint of humor. "Or are all the women in your family beautiful?

"I know because I've seen her," he said calmly.

Was Emma's ghost walking? Was she as unsettled as Daniel? "Where?" I breathed.

"At the main house."

"When did you see her? Was she...?" My voice trailed off when TJ gave me a look filled with growing confusion.

"I see her anytime I want," he answered, then a little groan escaped his lips.

"What, what is it?"

"Nothing," he grumbled.

But it was clear, something was going on. "Tell me."

"There's a picture." He mumbled.

"What?"

He dropped his arms by his sides as if surrendering to the inevitable. "In the 1800s, if a family had the means—and mine did back then— it was traditional to have portraits painted of certain members of the family."

When I realized what he was saying, I screamed. "There is a portrait of Emma." I pointed to the grave. "This Emma, at the main house?"

He slowly shook his head. I was so disappointed. He waited another agonizing minute, then said, "There isn't one portrait. There are two."

CHAPTER THIRTY-FIVE

"Florence Willis death at 16 was an especially heartbreaking loss to parents Nicholas and Susan. They lost nine other children at much younger ages. November 15, 1868" (Typhoid Fever)

> — *The Willis Family Journals 1847-1951*
> *Edited and Annotated by James Dawson*

T WO PORTRAITS!
I swatted him in the arm out of excitement and frustration and almost lost my balance.

He grabbed me before I could go down. "Hey, girl. Easy does it." When I was steady again, he dramatically rubbed his arm where my weak hand had made contact. "What was that for?"

"You didn't tell me about the portraits."

He took off his ball cap, ran his fingers through his hair, and reset the cap. It was a gesture I now recognized as nervousness. "I didn't want to push my family on you as some people do. I didn't think you were that interested."

"Yes, yes, I'm interested. Where are the portraits?" He wouldn't meet my gaze. "They're at the main house, your house, aren't they?" It was more of a statement than a question. "You could take me to see them right now." Again, a statement.

"I'm sorry, I shouldn't have said anything. The house is in no shape for visitors. I still have a lot of work to do before I can have you over. After the harvest, I was planning to spend the winter working on the house. Then maybe in the spring—"

"I can't wait that long," I whined. "Please, where are the portraits?"

"One is upstairs." He sighed. "The other is in the foyer by the front door."

"The foyer?! I could just slip inside the front door. I promise I wouldn't look in any other room. I won't even look up the stairs. Please, TJ, this is important to me." I sounded like a brat pleading for a piece of candy, but I couldn't help myself.

Finally, his eyes met mine. He settled his cap on his head again. "I don't know. I'm not the best housekeeper—"

"That doesn't matter."

A cloud crossed the sun. "My farmer instincts tell me there's some rain in that cloud," TJ said, as if hoping I'd forget about seeing the portraits. "I think we need to get you home."

"No!" My resistance made him stop. "Please take me to the main house to see at least one of the portraits."

He looked up and a fat raindrop splashed on his cheek. "All right, if we leave now."

I took off for the truck while he rushed to lock the gate and stash the key away. He whistled for Ghost, who came running. We all made it into the truck as the heavens opened. In the deluge, we drove to the main plantation house of Waterwood.

TJ's truck navigated the wide gravel drive easily. "Now, don't judge the house from what you see from this angle."

"Okay," I said slowly. I didn't quite understand what he meant by *this angle.*

"The house is almost two hundred years old. They sited houses differently back then. Today, the front of a house faces the driveway, because people usually arrive by car or truck. In the early days here on the Shore, people usually came by boat. So, the main houses usually faced the water." He pulled up to a door and an umbrella materialized to ward off the rain. "We'll walk around the front so we can go into the foyer. Don't worry about getting muddy. There's a stone walk."

As we made our way around to the front of the house facing the river, I got my first look at the heart of Waterwood, the place that had captured my imagination. It wasn't the typical majestic plantation house with *two* levels of porches depicted in the Old South, but it was impressive. The large brick house with seven second-story windows across the front was built to withstand the cold winters and nor'easters that could make life challenging on the Eastern Shore. The airy porch was perfect for spring afternoons and warm summer evenings. The four chimneys rising above the slate roof confirmed that the designer set out to create a *home* of warmth and comfort.

We went up the front steps and through the heavy wood door painted with black enamel that I imagined had welcomed many family members and friends over centuries. It was a relief to be inside, out of the pelting rain. TJ flipped some switches. Light from a huge crystal chandelier and several wall sconces flooded the foyer.

"I need to clean the chandelier…"

His words of apology and excuse faded into the background as I quickly scanned the walls. When my eyes fell on a painting in an ornate wooden frame, I knew I'd found Emma at last. It was not a painting of a startling young beauty. This Emma had experienced life with its storms and happy moments. The hint of a soft smile on her lips suggested she had found contentment and peace. Her eyes were the color of the deep blue waters of the Chesapeake on a sunny day. Her flaxen hair was drawn up softly under a straw hat that gave her flawless pale skin a little protection from the sun. She was painted in a soft blush-pink gown. Its sleeves were full at the shoulder then drawn in tightly at the elbow. A gauzy white flounce trimmed a dipping neckline. TJ was right. She was a vision of beauty.

"And here is the other portrait. It's more of a family portrait. I don't like it as much as this one so, I keep it out of the way."

He carefully placed the painting of the family on the hardwood floor under her portrait hanging on the wall. The difference between the two was shocking. I had to look twice to be sure that it was the same woman in both paintings. In the family portrait, her husband Joshua stood in a fine suit with one hand firmly planted on his hip, master of all he surveyed. A young boy and girl gathered around him. Emma sat separated from them on the other side of the painting. She had a baby on her lap. She looked worn and unhappy.

"Oh, TJ, I agree with you. It's hard to believe it's the same woman in these paintings."

"I guess the artist who did the family portrait wasn't very good," he suggested.

"I'm no expert, but an artist is supposed to make people look even better than they do in real life."

He frowned as he looked at the two pictures again. "She must have been miserable at the time of the family portrait."

"Do you know when they were painted?"

Grinning, he hopped into action. "Yes, thanks to my aunt's work on the family tree. She attached little notes to many of the paintings." He looked at the back of each painting. "The family portrait was done in 1871. Her portrait was painted in 1892."

I remembered the dates on a headstone. "That was two years after her husband died."

"Guess she blossomed after he was gone. Are you done with the family portrait? I'll put it back, out of the way, where I think it belongs."

While he was gone, I quietly communed with the lovely Emma. *I don't think you ever knew what happened. But Joshua didn't make you happy, did he, Emma? He wasn't Daniel.*

The artist had painted her walking next to a narrow span of calm water that reflected a deep blue sky with a few wispy clouds above. She stood to the right side of the frame to show some of the surrounding landscape.

I peered a little closer as TJ returned. "Is that the Lone Oak in the background?"

He looked closer, too. "Yes, I think you're right. I never noticed it before."

I took a couple of steps back so I could better take in the whole scene. "Do you think Emma is walking close to the place where the Cottage stands today? I wonder if that's significant."

He moved to stand next to me. "Again, I think you may be right." He shrugged his shoulders. "I don't know a whole lot about paintings. Don't artists make up backgrounds for their portraits? After all, the subject, the person, is the important part of the picture."

"That's often true, but this looks too familiar," I mused at the scene for a few moments while the rain beat down outside. "I think the artist did it on purpose."

"Or the subject wanted to be shown in this spot."

"You're on to something, TJ. Maybe this spot was important to her." Silently, I added, *as the Lone Oak was valued by the young lovers, Daniel and Emma.*

I was lost in my thoughts when TJ said, "Are you okay?"

"Yes, why?" I stammered.

"You're doing it again. You're touching that place where your necklace used to be."

I jumped a little when I caught my hand resting at my neck.

"I guess it's an Emma thing," he said. "She is wearing a locket in this painting."

He was right. It was a beautiful locket or…? I tried to stand on my toes and squint at the oval pendant hanging from a silver chain.

"There is something unusual about her locket. Look here." I pointed.

TJ walked up close to the painting. "It's not clear, but it almost looks like a tiny portrait of someone."

"Do you think it is a miniature?" I asked.

"I'm no expert, but it could be."

Was it a product of the artist's imagination? Or was it a valued possession from her jewelry box?

CHAPTER THIRTY-SIX

"When you are about to write a letter to a friend, think what you would say to him if he were at that moment with you, and then write it. Such a letter should be unstudied, free from affectation, and as nearly as possible like good conversation."

How to Write Letters
by Professor J. Willis Westlake, 1883

TJ leaned his long, lanky body against the wall by Emma's portrait and folded his arms. "I think it's time," he said with a solemn expression on his face.

Slowly, I said, "Time for what?"

"Time for you to tell me why you're so interested in Emma."

I started to open my mouth, but a flash of lightning, followed by a clap of thunder, rattled the room.

"And you need to tell me about this fellow Daniel. I don't remember anyone by that name on my family tree. I think I deserve an explanation."

I sank onto a step of the grand staircase with a sigh. "You're right. You do, but it's not quite that easy."

"Sure, it is. You only need to tell me. That's all. Simple English. I'll understand."

"What if I show you?" I asked.

"Tell me. Show me. I don't care. I just want to know what's going on." His voice was strained.

He deserved to know. His steely eyes bore into me. This was about family, his family, worthy of his interest, his defense. I had no choice. I had to tell him, but in a way he would believe me or, at least, give me time to prove that Daniel was real, as real as a ghost can be. I had to tell him in a way that didn't end up with me being carted away in a straitjacket...or losing my friend.

I pulled myself up on my feet. "Okay. We have to go back to the Cottage."

His brow furrowed as if he was about to object. He glanced out the window over the front door. It was still raining. It didn't matter. "Okay, let's go."

In the few minutes it took us to get to the Cottage, the storm had moved off. The rain had stopped. The sun, low on the horizon, peeked through the clouds. The sunset would be impressive, but we were both focused on something more compelling. He toweled the dog dry so Ghost wouldn't track mud through the Cottage or have to wait in the truck. I offered TJ coffee, which he refused. I suspect he knew I was stalling. With no other option, I led him into my writing den and we sat down.

I began the story at the beginning--that first next morning here at the cottage—when I'd found the first letter from Daniel.

"I thought at first," I said with a nervous laugh. "That you had broken into the Cottage and left it on the desk to spook me."

He didn't even smile. "That's why you had me change all the locks and took my key."

I averted my eyes and nodded slowly.

"So, who left the letter?"

"The letter was signed *Daniel.* Since I couldn't figure out how the writer had gotten into the Cottage, I wrote a response demanding to know who would address me as *My Dearest Emma* and left it on the desk by the stack of paper. The next morning, I found the reply."

"Can I see it, read it for myself?"

This is where it got complicated. I opened the door to the cubbyholes and pulled out the transcribed copy I'd made and printed.

"Yes, here you go. I didn't know the words were going to fade away so I wrote down everything I remembered."

It only took him a moment to read the short missive. "This is a bit of fanciful writing. It could have been a practice writing assignment." He flung the sheet toward the desk, but it missed and fluttered to the floor. "I trusted you. Now, you have two minutes to tell me the truth."

This was the moment, the moment when he could decide to walk out or I could earn an ally and discover all I could about Emma and Daniel. It would not come again. I had to take the chance.

With the door to the desk open, I reached up to the cubbyhole where I'd stashed all the letters and copies. I opened my photo gallery on my cell phone. With my file and my phone in hand, I confronted TJ. Confronted him, so he'd know I wasn't being polite or trying to mislead him.

I took a deep breath and began. "As I said, the morning after I moved into the Cottage, I found a letter here on the desk addressed to *My Dearest Emma* written in black ink. I think they used to call the handwriting style Copperplate—flowing, a little ornate. Only calligraphers write that way today. I had to show you the copy I made of that first letter because the words disappeared without warning." I flipped through the papers in my hand. "But I can show you the most recent letter I've received. The words haven't faded yet."

TJ took the paper and shook his head a little in disbelief. "You mean you have received more than one letter from this Daniel?"

I held up the papers. "Oh, yes."

"How is that possible?"

I cringed because this admission would make me sound crazy. "I've been answering Daniel's letters. We've been corresponding since that first morning." I thrust the papers and phone at him. "They're all here, pictures of his letters and copies of mine. There are copies of the letters that faded away. Go ahead, read them. Tell me what you think. I'll be in the kitchen." I turned and walked out of the den, leaving a mystified man in my wake.

I had time to make a fresh cup of coffee and sit with my thoughts while I finished it before he stumbled into the kitchen and fell into a chair.

"This is unbelievable," he began. "How do I know you didn't concoct this whole thing?"

"Why would I do that?"

He shrugged, but not in an angry way. I think he was as mystified and confused as I had been when Daniel's letters first began appearing.

"I don't know." He shrugged again. "Boredom, maybe?"

I straightened up, ready to defend my sanity and honor, but he reacted before I could say anything.

"No, I'm not saying I don't believe you. It's all just, I don't know, incredible."

I relaxed a little. "But you're not convinced that Daniel is a ghost." I wasn't sure if it was a question or a statement. "I don't know what else to tell you."

"You have to admit it strains reality as we know it. Don't we need to know more?"

My hackles went up again. "Whoa, you're not going to suggest that we bring in those crazy ghost hunters with equipment, microphones, and eerie green lights, are you?" I started shaking my head. "Because I—"

He held up a hand for me to stop. "I'm not suggesting anything. I'm still trying to wrap my mind around what you've shown me. Can you give a guy a break?"

I knew I should. He had earned it. I put my elbows on the table and ran my hands over my face. We sat quietly together as the reds and violet of the sunset faded to the deep blue of night. In the growing darkness, I made TJ an offer.

"It's my turn to write a letter. I was going to leave it on the desk tonight. If he continues the routine, his reply should appear on the desk by morning. Why don't you watch me write the letter then I'll go upstairs? You sleep in the den. When we find his letter in the morning, you'll know I didn't sneak into the room to swap out the letters in the middle of the night. Then maybe you'll believe me."

He thought for a few moments. "That's a good way to resolve things. We'll have dinner, write the letter and call it a night." Then he added in a voice that put distance between us. "By morning, I'll either know the truth or know to tell Mr. Saffire that you need more help than I can offer. Do we have a deal?"

If Daniel didn't write back by tomorrow morning, I'd lose TJ as a friend and have to deal with an attorney who'd been told I was crazy. It was a gamble, but I knew it would be when I decided to tell him the truth.

I held out my right hand. "Deal."

CHAPTER THIRTY-SEVEN

"Don't be afraid to write of little things. ...Things that are worth talking about are worth writing about. When absent from home, we gloat over the simplest details. Anything and everything that calls up the picture of home with all its dear associations and makes us forget for the moment that we are scores or hundreds of miles away."

How to Write Letters
by Professor J. Willis Westlake, 1883

We scavenged our way through the fridge and cabinets to stretch the meal Maria had left me into a dinner for two. Our conversation was stilted. Ghost could feel the tension in the air. He kept watching us, looking first at TJ, then me, then back to his master. Finally, he gave up with a snort and found the perfect spot for an after-dinner nap. I thought how much easier it was to be a dog than a human.

"Shall we write the next letter?" I suggested as we finished putting the dishes in the sink.

"I thought you were going to do that?"

"I am, but, from this point on, I want you to walk every step with me until you either accept what's happening or you walk away convinced that I'm crazy. I thought that was our deal."

He stretched. "You're right. If I walk away now, Daniel, whatever he is, will bother me forever. Let's get to work."

I sat at the old plantation desk with TJ hovering over me. It was curious that I didn't feel like he was intruding or judging what I was doing. Instead, it was comforting that I had a partner in this adventure. At least, he would be a partner if I proved that Daniel was on the other side of our correspondence. It was time.

"I try to respond to Daniel's most recent letter. I think it's safer than introducing a new tangent," I explained.

"That's fine. Do what you think is appropriate. I'm new at this so, I'll watch."

I slipped a sheet of paper in front of me. After removing the cover of the inkwell, I dipped the old-style pen into the ink and began.

Dear Daniel,

Please tell me more about the secret buried by the Lone Oak. I know you and my father believe that it will keep me safe. These are unsettled times. Knowledge shall be my shield.

I turned and looked at TJ. He was frowning.

"What's wrong?" I asked.

"It's short and sweet," he said.

"Yes, and…?"

"Let's ask something specific. You were wondering about the miniature Emma is wearing in the portrait. Ask him about it."

I turned back to the letter, thinking. What could I say that wouldn't reveal I wasn't *his* Emma? I picked up the pen again, dipped it into the ink and added the line and closing to the letter so it read:

Dear Daniel,

Please tell me more about the secret buried by the Lone Oak. I know you and my father believe that it will keep me safe. These are unsettled times. Knowledge shall be my shield.

I will keep the secret as close to my heart as I do the miniature.

Yours most sincerely,

Emma

"Yes, that's good. Let's see how Daniel responds to the mention of the necklace."

And, I thought, *it's something I know nothing about, which will help prove I'm telling the truth. And if the necklace was a product of the artist's imagination, Daniel might be confused or even angry.*

I'd been so careful about what I'd written up to now, but I couldn't argue with TJ. I hid my unease as I signed the letter, moved it to the center of the desk's writing surface, and covered the inkwell.

"Now, what?" TJ asked.

"Now, we wait. Usually, I go to bed and find his response on the desk in the morning. You can sleep in the spare room upstairs, but it might be better if you slept here. That way, you'll know I didn't sneak in a reply while you were sleeping. I can give you a comforter and pillows. What do you want to do?"

"Have you ever been in the room when his letter appeared?"

"No," I said slowly. "I never thought of that."

"I have a sleeping bag in the truck I use during the harvest when I can't get home. I'll close the door and stretch out in the hallway. I don't want to scare away this Daniel, this ghost."

"But—"

"It's okay, it's only one night. Ghost and I have slept in worse conditions."

It didn't take long to get them settled and for me to go upstairs and put my head down on my pillow. I'd sounded so positive when I was telling TJ about Daniel. This was the test. Would Daniel reply?

CHAPTER THIRTY-EIGHT

"A person's social, intellectual, and moral culture are indicated in his letters, as plainly as in his manners, dress, and conversation."

How to Write Letters
by Professor J. Willis Westlake, 1883

The next morning, something woke me at dawn. My first thought made me close my eyes again and snuggle into my pillow. This was the morning of truth: Had Daniel responded? Was he angry about the mention of the miniature? Would TJ believe me?

Life would be so much simpler if I could stay in bed. But curiosity made me swing my feet to the floor. The house was silent except for the usual, random creak. Was TJ still sleeping? Quickly, I pulled on a sweatsuit and made my way downstairs, calling out his name.

Nothing.

I headed straight to the den. I looked at the desk and my

stomach clenched. My letter was gone, but there was no reply in its place.

No TJ. No letter.

There was nothing for me to do, but make a cup of coffee, sit on the patio and stare at the Lone Oak. That's where TJ found me with an empty mug.

"There you are. I've been looking for you." The man was out of breath. His shirt from yesterday was wrinkled. "You were right. I never would have believed it, but it's all here." He held up a white piece of paper with the smooth handwriting I'd come to recognize. Daniel had answered our letter.

Dearest Emma,

I read your most recent letter with dismay. Do you not remember what your father told you?

In the high emotion of war and displacement, I can understand why you might not be able to recount the details.

Therefore, I am writing to you with great concern. It is of the utmost importance that you have this information clearly at hand so that you can take care of yourself. I would never forgive myself if any delay on my part put you in danger.

Harken back to the late afternoon that the horse and rider galloped up to the house with news for your father about events at the bank in Easton. As you know, everyone was very nervous at that time. No one knew what would happen between the North and the South or if the Union would survive. Unsettled times are never good for a bank. The rider brought news about a board meeting at your father's bank. A vote by the board of directors showed a split of six to five in favor of the Confederacy.

My father knew that your father was very nervous about his deposit at the bank and was pacing all night, trying to puzzle out the best thing to do. The next day, he went into town and converted all of his money deposits to gold and silver and brought them home. He had me bring down a strongbox from the attic and he filled it with the precious metals and other valuables he collected from around your house.

Late in the night, the three of us went out to the Lone Oak. By lantern light, your father carefully walked off a complicated pattern, stopped at a spot just beyond the branches, and told me to dig a deep hole. We buried that strongbox together. After we covered it over with dirt and concealed the disturbance with grasses and leaves, he swore us to secrecy and gave us a sacred charge. If anything happened to him, we were to make sure that you, his beloved daughter Emma, had the valuables for your use.

Remember, your father put the strongbox there for you.

If you require it and I am not near at hand, take someone you trust and a shovel to the spot below the limb where we loved to sit and dream. Look to the dawn and walk, counting out the day of your birth. Turn toward the place you loved to play in the mud across the water.

Walk again, counting out your birth month, and pray as we did as children before bed.

I am sorry to be so opaque, but one never knows into whose hands this letter may fall. You and I share a history that began when we were small children.

Knowledge of these places is part of us and can never be forgotten. They are ours alone. No one else can interpret these direct actions and steal what is rightfully yours.

Your mention of the miniature brought a smile to my face. I remember how you cajoled me to sit for you. It was almost painful to watch you struggle with the painting. You had taken only a few lessons when you announced that you wanted to create a miniature of me. When it was finished, you were unhappy with the result, but I thought it was a fair likeness. I rejoice to think that you have it now to remember me.

I want you to know that my whole being yearns to see you. I fear it is not possible right now. I shall content myself with thoughts of your sweet face. As I sit here at my father's desk, I feel a connection so, here I shall stay, waiting.

As always, your obedient servant,
Daniel

We had our answer about a time long past and today's mystery of the many holes dug around the Lone Oak. There was buried treasure somewhere here at Waterwood. I even had instructions on how to find it if it hadn't been dug up already. Daniel had encrypted the information in a very basic, but effective way. I had seen the month and day of Emma's birth on her tombstone only hours earlier at the family cemetery. I understood that the first direction was to the east, but from where? The reference to a limb of the Lone Oak was clear, but which one. Where was her favorite spot to play in the mud? And how did they pray as children? Those words conjured up an old lithograph of a child praying by her bed, on her knees. Could that be what Daniel was suggesting?

TJ was still trying to catch his breath. "Before sun up. Something woke me. There it was on the desk. What he said about the miniature reminded me... I had to run up to the house and that is where I found this." TJ held out his hand and opened it. A painted oval miniature with a silver chain lay in his palm. "I remembered my mother put a jumble of things in a small box. It took me a while to find it, but here he is. Daniel."

Daniel.

My fingers trembled as I picked up Emma's necklace. The painting wasn't refined, an effort by a fledgling artist. Even though it was small, it was easy to see that the face of the dark-haired young man was handsome, filled with compassion. His dark brown eyes were alive and his full lips were about to draw up into a smile. Emma had added some redness to his cheeks that may have been a result of his time working on the plantation. He had a well-shaped chin and a nose that blended with his other features. I thought she had captured the essence of the young man who was writing letters to me.

"Emma?" TJ spoke softly. "Emma?"

"Oh, I'm sorry," I said with a start. "Thank you for finding the necklace. It's amazing to see a portrait of—"

"A ghost."

I raised my eyes to TJ's face. The mask of disbelief and suspicion was gone. "You believe me?" My words quivered.

"I think I have to. If this is a hoax, you deserve a gold star for pulling off such an elaborate deception. But I don't see how you could have known about the necklace. Yes, I do believe you, but I think we should keep this between us, don't you think?"

Looking back at the miniature, it took me only a moment to agree. It was good to see Daniel's face, finally. I wasn't surprised that he had a sweet expression. Somehow his personality—his compassion, his loyalty—came through in his letters. "I wish…"

He waited, but finally had to ask, "What do you wish?"

"I wish there was some way to reunite them."

TJ took off his ball cap, ran his fingers through his hair, and resettled it on his head in a gesture born of nerves or deep thought. "I don't know how to do that. Usually, people who loved one another in life are buried next to each other, that whole idea of spending eternity together."

"But Daniel was murdered someplace in Virginia during the Civil War. His body was probably tumbled into a mass or unmarked grave." I could hear the tears of regret in my voice.

"So, that's not an option. I suppose we could put a headstone next to hers in the family cemetery," TJ suggested. "What do you think?"

I sighed, looking at the Lone Oak across the creek, my fingers playing with the chain.

"Emma? What do you think of the idea of a headstone for Daniel?" TJ asked again.

"Sit down and let me talk through a jumble of thoughts."

He settled into a chair and Ghost rested his head on TJ's thigh and they waited.

"The idea of a headstone is a nice gesture," I said. "Only, it's obvious that Daniel's spirit is restless or he wouldn't be writing these letters." I looked up at the man and his dog and said gently, "TJ, I don't think he realizes that he's dead."

I noticed a little shiver run through TJ's body. He was as unsettled by the thought as I was.

I went on, thinking aloud. "What if Emma's spirit is still out there longing for Daniel? What if there was a way to reunite them?"

His eyes grew wide as the significance of my words hit him. "You want to have a séance?"

I shook my head. "I didn't need a séance to connect with Daniel. No, it might be something simple. Remember Daniel seems to be chained to the desk. What if Emma is..." my words trailed off. I had run out of ideas.

Thankfully, TJ carried the idea along. "What if Emma is connected to something, too?"

"Or some place. Remember the background of her portrait." I pointed to the Lone Oak.

He craned his head. "Yes, and there was a stand of crepe myrtle. But the perspective is all wrong." He looked at his watch. "Look, I've got some things to do today including a trip to the Western Shore. You keep thinking about what we might do. I'll walk along the shoreline and see what I can see." He stood and pointed a finger at me. "Don't you go traipsing around in the grasses and weeds! If you fall, I might never find you. We can talk again tomorrow." He pulled out his phone, ready to get on with his schedule. "I think you've accomplished a lot for one day." He added softly, "You made me a believer."

I held out the necklace with the miniature to him. He shook his head. "No, you keep it safe. Maybe it will inspire you."

CHAPTER THIRTY-NINE

"If an invitation is issued, an acceptance or regret must be issued if it includes *R.S.V.P. =Repondez s'il vous plait – answer if you please.*"

How to Write Letters
by Professor J. Willis Westlake, 1883

I spent the rest of the day puttering around the Cottage, racking my brain for an idea of how to reunite the lovers. I was tempted to walk along the shoreline to find the perspective where Emma's portrait was painted, but TJ was right. If I fell, he'd never find me in the thick foliage. If I fell in the water, well, I didn't want to think about that outcome or the tirade I'd have to endure if I survived. Besides, the wind was picking up, a sign that a storm might be coming. I avoided taking a nap during the day so I'd get a good night's sleep. But my plan didn't work.

I wasn't surprised that I felt a headache starting to spin up from the back of my neck. The best way to salvage the night was to take some aspirin with some warm milk and head back to bed. I put Daniel's last letter into the cubbyhole.

On my way to the kitchen, a loud knocking at the front door made me stop. Someone was here at the Cottage in the middle of the night? I quickly reached into the pocket of my robe for my cell phone, but it wasn't there. The base station for the cordless phone was in the living room. To get there, someone could see me walk past the little windows on either side of the front door. The phone might not be there. I ducked into the den. My breath was coming in gulps. What to do?

I stood silently in the dim light, hoping this person would go away. The knocking stopped. I strained my ears to hear a car engine. Funny, I hadn't heard a car drive up. But the sounds of the wind could have masked it. I stood still. Minutes went by. The person must have left. As I relaxed, the knocking started again.

A woman's voice called out. "Emma? Please open the door. I need to talk to you." She knocked again. "Emma. It's me, Stephani!"

Stephani? Here? At this time of night? Something must be wrong.

I got to the front door as fast as I could and threw it open. Stephani stood in the dim lamplight. Her usually perfect hair was running with rainwater. Mascara and eyeliner smeared her right eye. Mud splattered her stylish red boots.

My fists clenched in fear. "Stephani, what's wrong?"

Panting, she marched past me into the hall and left puddles in her footsteps. I knew there was a murderer out there somewhere. Maybe in the shadows? Was he stalking her? I slammed the door and threw the deadbolt.

"Stephani, tell me what's going on," I insisted. "Is someone after you?"

"No, it's nothing like that." She gulped some air. "At least, not yet. We don't have much time." She looked around first towards the living room then towards my study. "Where are they?"

"Where are *who*?" I snapped. Her anxiety was contagious.

She heaved a big sigh. "Not who. What. The papers. I have to see the papers."

Now, I was truly confused. "What papers? Why don't you

come and sit down?" I pointed toward the kitchen. "Tell me what's going on while I make some coffee."

She caught my arm and stopped me. "I don't have time for that. Stop playing games. If you had been straight with me this afternoon, I wouldn't be here now. In fact, I'd probably be long gone."

I stared down at her hand on my arm. She got the message and removed it. Even though I was tired, the rush of growing anxiety had fired up all my senses. Anger was building. I didn't want to upset her any more than she was, but she couldn't push her way into my house like this. By instinct, I started turning on the lights. Lamps, ceiling lights, it didn't matter. Later, I'd have to go around and turn them off, but it felt right. Then I remembered TJ's instruction: *If you need anything, turn on all your house lights and I'll come.* What I needed was to calm this young woman. I can do that, I thought, as I clicked on another overhead light switch, just in case.

Stephani followed me into the living room. "What are you doing? Why are you turning on the lights?"

I had to think fast. "I've found that when I'm upset, light can be comforting, especially in the middle of the night," I added pointedly. "Why don't you tell me why you are here?"

"You really don't know. You are truly a piece of work." She crossed her arms. Her eyes traveled from the top of my head, down to my feet, and back to my face. "You got your hair cut? About time."

She walked around me, checking out the cut. That gave me hope that I could distract her and get the woman out of my house.

"It's not bad. But not great." She huffed out of exasperation. "I don't care. Whatever game you think you're playing, but you can stop right now. Give me the papers and I'll leave."

I shook my head slowly. "I'll tell you one more time. I don't know what papers you think I have. The best thing is for you to leave. You can come back in the morning." I started toward the door.

Instead of following me, she headed into the study and turned on the light.

"What are you doing?" I said as I tried to race after her. *Daniel's letters!*

"I'm turning on more lights," she snarled as she opened the door to the plantation desk to expose all the cubbyholes, slots, and tiny drawers. She started to ransack the desk, pulling down papers and shuffling through them. In the rush of air, my folded blue butterfly fluttered down to the desktop and was smashed by a flying file folder.

"Stop it! Stop it right now," I ordered. I slammed the door of the desk. I couldn't let her see his letters, especially the last one. She'd know about the Lone Oak treasure. I didn't want to look up to that cubbyhole. If I did, she would go right to it.

"All right then, give me the notes that you made today at the Maryland Room and I'll stop going through your things," she demanded with a snarly attitude that she had kept hidden until now.

"My notes from the library?"

"Yeah, the ones you made today. The ones you wouldn't let me see. I know you found something. I know you found the key to the buried treasure."

Treasure! I was right. That's what this was all about. I had to get this girl out of the house. I wasn't strong enough to fight her off. I needed the police. My brain kicked into overdrive. If I lied to her, she'd know. I remembered that the best lie was based on truth. I turned to look at her, my eyes boring into her. I made my voice as stern as I could.

"Stephani, what I found wasn't important—"

"Don't you lie to me." She glared. "I saw you."

I took a quick breath and began again. "You don't know anything. The information I found today was about plantation life. TJ took me for a walk one day to his family cemetery. I was surprised that I shared a name with many of his female ancestors. I know Emma is—"

"Stop stalling. Spit it out. What did you find?"

"I learned about life on the plantation here for those women. How hard they worked, slaughtering pigs, smoking meats, making clothing for everyone, including the slaves. No wonder they all died young."

Her eyes narrowed. She took a deep breath and started to pace. She was weighing the truth of what I said. I hoped I'd passed the test. "The notes wouldn't do you any good. You don't have your glasses."

She let out a shrill cackle like witches are supposed to do. "You are so gullible. I don't need glasses. I can see just fine."

"Then why do you wear them?"

"To make me look studious," she sneered. "People take me seriously when I wear them." She paced back and forth then stopped in front of me. "I don't know if you're telling the truth or not. I don't need those notes. I only need you. You're going to show me where that treasure is buried." She slipped her hand around the upper part of my left arm and squeezed.

Did the detective get it all wrong? Is Stephani the real treasure hunter? If her grasp of my arm was any indication, she could easily swing a shovel and kill somebody.

I had to free myself. I asked Stephani a ridiculous question about having dinner to distract her while I reached behind me for something to use to defend myself. My fingers found Uncle Jack's heavy metal stapler.

I closed my hand around it. I raised my hand to swing the stapler with all my might. She seized my wrist and drove it down on the corner of the desk. My fingers were shocked straight and I dropped the stapler. It clattered to the floor. Pain shot up my arm.

"Okay, no more." I said, sucking in air. "I'll do what you want."

CHAPTER FORTY

"It is advisable to keep copies of all important letters, as a protection against possible misrepresentation, fraud, or malice."

How to Write Letters
by Professor J. Willis Westlake, 1883

We stood there as if suspended in time: Her grip on my arm tightening. My body in her control. My breaths coming in shallow gulps. It was crushing to face the truth of how weak I was. The look of triumph on her face sickened me. Her lips stretched into a smirk that made me look away in disgust.

"Look at me!" She jerked my body hard. "Look at me, I said!"

I turned my head as she commanded and her scornful smile broadened. "That's better." In a singsong sweet voice, she said, "If you do everything I tell you, you won't get hurt. That means, don't even think about being brave or doing something silly." She shrugged. "You won't win. You're a cripple."

I wanted more than anything to slap that smug look off her

face. But I knew she was right. The only one who could get hurt would be me. I'd have to wait for my chance… and take it.

She must have sensed my defiance and leaned closer. The smell of garlic and crab went up my nose. My stomach turned over. "If you try something, I can't be responsible for what might happen to you," she said with menace. "It wouldn't be my fault if you fell and broke your other leg."

She brought her face so close to mine that I could feel puffs of the air and spittle on my skin as she spoke each word. "That's your worst fear, isn't it? No more running, dancing, and all that stuff you used to do. And this time, it would be *your* fault." She waited for a reaction, one that she could revel in.

I wasn't going to let her see how her words had struck at my core. Instead, I tried to look contrite and dropped my eyes so she couldn't see them burning with hatred. Hatred, born of weakness and fear.

That sickening sweet voice spoke again. "Now, you're going to find the treasure for me. After that, we'll see what happens. Now, move!" She jerked my arm. I almost fell. "You're pathetic," she sneered as she rattled the walker. "Get moving."

I thought she was behind me as I rolled it down the hall and out the door to her Jeep. She shoved me into the passenger seat. I didn't put up a fight. What could I do? The woman was younger, stronger, healthier than me. It didn't help that I thought of Kid Billy. Did Stephani plan to leave me at the bottom of a hole?

What if the treasure chest was gone? Emma's father had put it there about 150 years ago. Somebody might have taken it in all that time. Stephani would blame me. I tried to hide my shock that she was after the treasure, not Josh. She must have gotten the boys to do the digging for her. She knew them. They'd grown up together. A shiver ran through me at the next thought. In a fit of rage, *she* must have swung the shovel at Kid Billy's head.

No, she couldn't let me go. I had to think of something, *fast*.

"Sit still" she snarled, "and hold on." Gravel flew as she spun the wheels and headed out to the main road.

I clung to the bar in front of me until my knuckles were white.

At the main road, I expected her to turn right toward the Lone Oak. When she turned left, I wet my lips and looked around trying to hide my surprise.

"Don't worry," Stephani said. "I know where to go." The glow of the dashboard lights lit up her self-satisfied smile.

"This is another way to the Lone Oak?"

Stephani slammed the brakes. I stiffened my arms to keep myself from flying into the windshield. The Jeep fishtailed. It came to a stop, straddling the roadway. Stephani slapped the steering wheel. "So, it *is* at that big old tree! I wasn't absolutely sure."

I'd served up the location without being asked. Why, oh why, hadn't I kept my mouth shut?

She rammed the stick shift into reverse and hit the gas, almost sending us off the side of the road. She yanked the stick into first and we flew down the road in the other direction.

"So, he was right." She slammed her fist into the steering wheel again. "I hate it when he's right."

"Who?" I asked so quietly that I wasn't sure she heard my question over the engine.

"Nobody. Never mind. He won't be bothering us anyway," she jabbered.

"Who?" I asked again.

"Sit and be quiet," she spat back. "Let me think."

You can't do two things at once? I thought. *That can't be good.*

As we raced toward the Lone Oak, I tried a new tactic. "Stephani," I said calmly. "You don't have to do this. Your library work—"

"Shut up! You think I want to spend my life buried with dusty shelves and moldy books?" She flicked her hand at me. "I'm pretty, too pretty for the reference room. I need to go where my passion takes me."

That wasn't exactly what I said, but now was not the time to quibble.

"I was working in that horrid place to find clues. It took its toll, I'll tell you. They keep the dehumidifier turned on all the time. I have had to use a ton of moisturizers to save my skin. My nails dried out so much I couldn't keep a decent manicure. It was horrible."

"Did you find what you were looking for?" I had to keep her talking while I figured out what to do.

"No. Then, like a gift from heaven, you walked in. You took a different approach and I'm gonna follow it to get what belongs to me—to make my dream come true."

"And what dream is that?"

"I'm going for the glitz and glamor. I'm going to be a famous hair and makeup designer. I've got the education and experience. Look at me." She held her arms out. "I know what I'm doing. I only need to take the final step."

"And what is that?"

"New York City."

I was surprised. "Not Los Angeles?"

"Nope, too common. New York has class and so much more: TV, movies, Broadway, and the women with money who want to look fabulous. I can do it all. I just need the treasure to get me there. Then I'll make my dream come true." Her expression changed in an instant, making the pretty girl ugly.

I put my hands in my lap, trying to appear calm. This girl believed the treasure still existed and it belonged to her. The truth didn't matter. Her perception was her reality. If I humored her, I might get out of this mess in one piece. "Well, if that's the case, I could help you find a lawyer and—"

"HA!" She laughed again. "The law doesn't always do what's right."

"Stephani, you have accomplished so much. No one, not even the law, can take that away from you. Why would you throw it all away on some crazy notion? You can still—"

"SHUT UP!"

And I did.

I remembered the confrontation with Josh on my patio. Brother and sister. The apple doesn't fall far from the tree. They both wanted something for nothing. Without some easy influx of money, he would end up laying concrete into his fifties, wearing nothing but an old t-shirt and dirty jeans. He would have to bully people to have any friends at all. They'd stand around making fun of other people. His beer belly would be so big, he wouldn't be able to see his feet.

We sped down the road. The lack of light pollution from houses and streetlights was an advantage. Once my eyes adjusted to the darkness, the moonlight made it easier to see the shape of the land. Stephani pulled hard on the steering wheel and sent us careening into the field surrounding the Lone Oak. It took what little strength I had to keep myself from being jostled right out of the vehicle.

In black silhouette against the star-filled sky, the Lone Oak loomed large. For more than a century, it had guarded a treasure that had cost two lives and ruined more. Would I be next? I glanced over at Stephani and could see the lust for riches that consumed her. No amount of logic could reach her.

CHAPTER FORTY-ONE

"Every oak tree started out as a couple of nuts who stood their
ground."

—Henry David Thoreau

Stephani slammed the brakes and we stopped in a cloud of
dirt. "Get out!"

I fumbled around, trying to move my leg, hoping for a
miracle.

"Stop stalling!" She came around to my side, seized my arm,
and yanked me out of the Jeep. Her iron grip was the only thing
that kept me from falling to the ground. When I regained my
balance, she let me go. Teetering, I groped for the Jeep's fender for
support.

She scanned the area. "Okay, where is it?"

I rolled my eyes. "Look, I keep telling you. I don't know."

"Liar!" she roared. She reached into the back of the Jeep then
held a bunch of manila folders from my desk triumphantly in the
air. Folders, that included the yellow one.

No! It was the yellow folder where I kept Daniel's letters or what was left of them. She must have grabbed it when I wasn't looking. I had to get it away from her before she could paw through the pages. I didn't know if the letter with the coordinates for the treasure chest had faded away yet.

"Those are mine," I declared with a false sense of bravado. "Give them back."

She held the folders high over her head and sang out to the universe. "She wants her papers back!" Then she whined. "Poor baby, I took her things." She lowered her head and drilled her eyes into mine. "But the information in them isn't yours. It belongs to me. You know where the treasure is buried." She shook the folders in the air again. "It's all right in here."

She took a couple of steps toward me and held the folders under my nose. "Go on. Deny it. I dare you," she sneered.

I wanted to move away, but I didn't. I fought down the fearful trembling that was welling up in my body. If this person saw proof of my fear, I had no idea what she'd do. She had shed the persona of a studious young woman as easily as she'd tossed away her fake eyeglasses. Now, she was a frantic madwoman. Her cobalt blue eyes flashed with rage. I couldn't reason with this monster she'd become. But if reason didn't work, maybe attitude would.

"You're a thief," I snarled right back at her. "I trusted you. You stole those files and you have the nerve to threaten me." I felt like a fool, but the tactic worked. She was thrown off when my bullying attitude met hers.

"Y-yes, and it's all your fault," she sputtered. "You shouldn't have cut me out."

"Cut you out?" I let out a crazed laugh to the sky. "You're an idiot. Everything in those folders came from your precious Maryland Room." That wasn't exactly true. I held on to the slim hope that she hadn't seen the transcriptions of Daniel's letters.

"It was all right there, under your nose, and you didn't even know it. Stupid girl."

"I knew it!" She held up the folders again. "It's all right here." She laid them on the hood of the Jeep and started rifling through the papers. Her forehead wrinkled. "You know, this is inefficient. You're supposed to use the tabs on the folders to label what's in each file."

"Ha! Still the mousy librarian," I was feeling the role and sneered. "You have to cut me in on the treasure or find it yourself. And we both know how well that's worked for you."

I must have touched a nerve. She put both hands flat on the hood and slowly pushed herself up straight. Then she cocked her head and twisted her lip.

"I'm not going to read through everything. You're going to tell me where the treasure is."

Fear rippled through me. Her swagger was back. She gave me only a second to respond, which wasn't fast enough. She held up the yellow folder and swept the others on the ground.

"Is it in this one?" She raised one eyebrow. Her eyes bore into me, watching for my reaction.

The wind caught one of the papers and pulled it out of the file. It danced it up into the branches of the Lone Oak high above our heads.

"Is that the one that tells where the treasure is?" She demanded, her eyes never leaving the paper.

I looked at the paper floating above, tantalizingly close but out of reach. Was Daniel keeping the secret safe? I dropped my eyes and fired back. "Are you crazy? How should I know? I—"

She thrust a pointed finger in my face and squealed in triumph. "You know where it is." She yanked me over to the tree's wide trunk.

"What? No. I... Get it! Get the paper," I ordered. Playing a bully was better than being the simpering, pleading little person I felt I was inside.

But Stephani stood as if she was made of stone, watching the page dance on the wind in the glare of her Jeep's headlights.

"GET IT!" I ordered again. "If you're so sure that's the one with the clue."

This time, Stephani sprang into action. She ran after the paper, jumped and flailed, as it swirled out of reach. She watched the soaring piece of paper, not where she was stepping.

"OW!" Down she went with a heavy thud. All I heard were moans, then a crybaby's voice. "My ankle. I hurt my ankle." She touched it. "Ow!"

Stephani had stepped in a freshly-filled hole and twisted her ankle. But she wasn't my concern. Not now.

I looked up to locate the missing sheet of paper. My eyes followed each gyration as it made its escape. The breeze swirled and pushed it around. It did somersaults between the branches of the mighty tree.

If I only had wings, I thought in desperation. *Even two good legs.* I had no choice. I couldn't keep up with it. I could only stand and watch it escape. A sudden gust caught it like a mighty hand and slammed it to the ground in front of me. I snatched it up, folded it, and stashed it in the back pocket of my jeans. I had no time to celebrate its rescue. The night still held surprises.

CHAPTER FORTY-TWO

"To write a good letter of condolence requires good taste and fine feeling...do not call up the harrowing details of the sad event."

—*How to Write Letters*
by Professor J. Willis Westlake, 1883

"You should watch where you're going, Fanny." The voice came out of the darkness, deep and gruff and sarcastic. "You could hurt yourself out here." His tone changed to mock concern. "Oh, you did hurt yourself. Too bad."

"Shut up!" She snapped as she struggled to her feet.

"That's not a very nice way to greet your beloved brother," said the man, mewing as if she had injured his feelings.

"I thought you were in jail," she snarled.

"Not anymore," he said, singsong. The tall young man walked into the pool of light coming from the Jeep. It was hard to believe they were related. His solid, chunky build was so opposite her willowy figure.

"Josh, how did you get out?" Stephani demanded.

"Mom, of course." He cocked his hip and looked at his fingernails. "She does everything I tell her to do."

My head swung back and forth between these two people, sparring like children. They had forgotten I was there. Tentatively, I slipped my right foot toward the line between the light and darkness.

Josh crooked his head to the side, considering her, judging her. "You should be more like Mom and do what you're told. Fanny." He said her nickname with great relish.

"Don't call me that." Her voice was low and threatening.

He snapped his fingers. "Oh, that's right. You hate my nickname for you, big sister. I forgot, Fanny." Each word dripped with sarcasm.

"Mom said it was cute when you were little. I hated it then and I hate it now. You know that," she shot back. "Now, go away,"

He took a step toward her and held out his arms in submission. "Why would I leave my sweet big sister out here in the dark to…"

I stopped listening to the treasure hunters squabble and concentrated on getting away. I knew I couldn't outrun them. I thought if I could hide, maybe I could save myself. I took another step.

Stephani fired back at Josh. "I have every right to be here. This was my idea. I was here first. You think you can swoop in and finish what I started? I'd be long gone if Kid Billy hadn't been such a wimp." She made her voice high and whiny. "I don't want to do this anymore. I want to go home. I won't tell anybody, I promise."

She went on in an icy cold voice. "I told them I was the boss. I ordered him to dig. I told them all to keep digging."

"I know, I know, I saw the whole thing." Josh clasped his hands together as if in prayer. "Oh, when will you realize you need me to get anything done?" Josh dropped his hands in disgust. "Thought you could use my posse and cut me out? Never happen." He started to pace with a swagger in front of Stephani. "You taught me how to be a bully, but I added the finesse that inspires loyalty. Something you fail to understand."

"You knew?" she said in disbelief.

He shrugged. "Of course. They're my boys. *Mine.*" He planted his feet and pulled up his jeans. "I watched you do the hard work, getting dirty and all. But you surprised me, Fanny. I didn't think you had it in you."

Fanny didn't say a word.

Josh shook his head. "The Kid only wanted to go home."

This was my chance. Slowly, I shifted my foot backward and took one step then another, and another. I hoped Josh would start talking again to cover any sound I might make. And he did.

"You could scream to the heavens that you were the boss, but that wouldn't make it true. You came up with a great line. 'Can't you get it through your thick skull?' Josh chuckled. "The Kid promised he'd tell nobody, but you didn't believe him."

"I was so close. And they were going to run away." Stephani's explanation sounded thin.

I kept moving.

"I had to prove to them that I was in control," Stephani insisted. "I grabbed the shovel and swung it. I only meant to scare him."

Josh's words dripped with disgust. "You're weak, Fanny. You can't control nothin'. Especially your temper. When he ducked and you missed, it made you mad."

I took another step back and slipped into the shadows.

"What would you have done?" Stephani said, trying to salvage her pride.

"Physical violence is no way to treat your posse. I use finesse." He gave a little wave of his hand, preening over the use of such a word. Then he dropped the façade. "But I must admit, you had a good idea."

"Whacking Kid Billy in the head?" Stephani said.

"Yeah, you didn't have the guts to carry it out the way you should. He would never have kept your secret about the treasure. He had to go."

"So, you picked up another shovel…" Stephani stated.

Josh shrugged.

"Somebody had to finish what you started. It wasn't my fault that he couldn't get out of the way a second time."

She gave her head a little shake. "Why didn't the other guys turn you in?"

He held his hands up in the air. "Isn't that obvious? I never used violence against any of them."

"Until that night," Stephani added.

"That's right. I had to teach the Kid a lesson. I had to teach them all a lesson. If I could kill once, I could do it again."

"You're a hot mess, Joshua Collins."

The truth of the murder was worse than I imagined. Together, who knows what they could do. I had to move.

Josh stepped closer to his sister. "None of this matters. I came to this godforsaken place for one thing, Fanny. And I will have it, Fanny. Then I'll be happy to disappear and leave you here, all by your lonesome self, Fanny. Oh, wait! You won't be alone, will you? Once you get ole TJ to knock you up, you'll make it to the Big House," he scoffed. "Imagine, my big sister Fanny, will be Miss Stephani of Waterwood."

TJ… The Big House… Miss Stephani of Waterwood!

I almost blurted out my surprise but clamped my lips together. Keeping my balance was something else. The world gyrated as my leg decided if it was going to hold me up or collapse. Finally, the muscles engaged and I was stable again.

Josh wasn't done with his sister. "You'll really come up in the world, Fanny. And you'll do it the old-fashioned way, on your back." His laughter filled the night.

I stifled a yelp when I bumped into the fender of the Jeep. I'd worked my way around in the shadows and came up from behind on the driver's side. Strength was draining out of every muscle. All I had to do was pull myself up in the seat. I knew how to do it on the passenger side. This would be harder. I had to rely on my bad leg. I raised it into the Jeep, gripped the steering wheel, and pulled myself up and in. Thankfully, my leg didn't give way.

Josh was still lecturing Stephani. "All I want is what's coming to me, what our family should have had a long time ago. Then everything would have been different and nobody would be dead. I'll even give you some." He took two steps forward so they were almost touching. "Now, tell me where it is, Fanny. Then I'll be out of your way."

Stephani started to say something and choked. She cleared her throat and started again, trying to sound innocent. "Where is what?"

In the Jeep, I was stiff with dread. I hadn't been behind the wheel of a car since the accident.

The sibling argument raged on. Josh declared, "I want the same thing you want, Fanny."

"You'll get nothing," she pronounced.

"And who's going to stop me?"

"I am."

"You?" he sniffed. "That's a joke."

I could see the siblings clearly in the headlights. Stephani pulled something out of her coat pocket. It glinted.

A gun.

Now, I whispered to myself.

"Give me that," demanded Josh as he took a step toward her.

"No way!"

He grabbed for the gun. She shrieked. The night herons screeched in response.

I started the Jeep's engine, drowning them out. My foot stabbed the accelerator. My hands pulled hard on the wheel. The tires ground through the soft dirt. The headlights swung madly. There should have been two surprised persons caught in the beams.

But there was only one standing under the Lone Oak. She was waving the gun in my direction and screaming for me to stop.

Kerrackk.

The shot sounded like the end of the world, but I couldn't let it stop me. I steered away. The wheels caught the loose dirt in a hole.

She ran and got ahead of me. The gun was pointed right at the windshield. Certain she was blinded by the lights, I kept going. But one lucky shot would end it all.

Something roared in the darkness. A waterman's truck with no muffler like a workboat on land. Was it a savior or a threat? I couldn't wait to find out. The only way to save myself was to do it all by myself.

I steered the Jeep right at the girl who'd lied to everybody, used everybody. Invaded my home. Threatened me.

How are you at a game of chicken, FANNY?

I pushed the pedal to the floor and ducked down in case she got off a lucky shot. She leaped out of my path. I was on my way to the road and out of this nightmare.

But not quite.

Lights flared behind me. The truck. Josh.

He was coming up on the right to bar my way to the road. I couldn't outrun him. I pushed the pedal to the floor. The Jeep shuddered as it crossed the rough ground. It was built more for fun than getting out of trouble.

I stole a look over my shoulder. Josh was gaining.

I had only one choice. I gripped the steering wheel. My timing had to be perfect. Stones kicked up by his big tires dinged my pathetic beach ride. It was my only weapon. I had to make it work.

He was closing in.

NOW.

I yanked the wheel hard to the right and aimed for his door. The shock on his face was the last thing I saw. The last thing before everything went black. Just like in the accident.

CHAPTER FORTY-THREE

"The best domestic letters are dictated by the heart rather than the head. Loving word is precious, filling the soul with sunshine, and making it for a time oblivious of pain."

—*How to Write Letters*
by Professor J. Willis Westlake, 1883

"Emma?" A man's soft voice called me out of the darkness. "Emma, come on. Wake up."

I felt a touch on my shoulder.

"TJ! Don't move her," someone instructed. "Her neck, be careful of her neck. Watch her head. That windshield is spiderwebbed. She must have hit it hard."

Slowly, I recognized one of the voices. TJ. He was here. I didn't want to open my eyes. I didn't want to face what I had done to myself. It was enough to know that TJ was there. It meant that Fanny and her brother Josh couldn't hurt me. Couldn't hurt me anymore than I'd hurt myself.

Someone pried open an eyelid. A strong white light filled my eyes. Was this the light at the end? Had I survived one accident only to lose my life in another, one of my own making?

I was drifting back into the great fog when his words called to me. "Emma, come on. Let me know you're here." His voice was filled with anguish.

Pain was starting to register. I wasn't sure who was hurting more, him or me? The man said I hit the windshield and broke it. But my head didn't hurt. I thought it should, but it didn't.

What about my leg? I thought in a panic.

I tried to flex. *It moved.* Maybe it's okay. I took a deep breath in relief and moaned. *My chest! Oh, no!*

"Emma! Thank the Lord! You're here!" TJ said in great excitement.

I might be here, but I'm in a world of hurt.

The real world formed into a mass flashing red and blue lights. Strangers poked me. Asked me inane questions, like what was my name? Then I was bundled into an ambulance for a heavenly ride to the hospital on a comfy cloud of drugs.

Later, I found out that it wasn't my head that had broken the windshield. It was the sheer force of the impact. The airbag had saved me, but at a price. I had to remember to move slowly and carefully until my ribs felt better.

In those crazy few moments at the Lone Oak, I had saved my own life. Josh hadn't walked away from the accident. He was someplace else in the hospital, handcuffed to his bed. In my statement to the police, I repeated what I had heard Josh say.

To avoid a charge of accessory to murder, Stephani had corroborated my testimony and agreed to testify, if I wouldn't press charges for breaking-and-entering my house and kidnapping. They worked out something with the insurance company about her mangled Jeep.

My stay in the hospital was tense at best. I was worried about Daniel. What if he wrote to me and I wasn't there to answer his letters? Finally, I persuaded TJ to bring me some paper from the stack on the plantation desk and any letter that might appear.

Fortunately, Daniel wrote in his first letter after that awful night under the Lone Oak that he was tired and wanted to rest a little. That worked for me. I assured him that I would respond when he wrote again.

I struck a compromise with the doctors that I would be their best patient, if I could go to rehab for intense therapy for my battered body. I was haunted by a deep-seated terror. I'd convinced myself that as long as I stayed in the hospital, they could amputate my leg. They agreed and moved me to a place that didn't have an operating room. The physical therapy sessions were a challenge, but they got easier as my body healed. The following weeks did me a world of good.

Whenever TJ took a few hours off from the harvest, he came to visit. Of course, Ghost was by his side and became a favorite with the other patients. I began to look forward to his frequent phone calls with the combine rumbling in the background. We had lots to discuss. There were the official statements and the gossip about the case involving Stephani and Josh. And I learned more than I ever thought about the details of a harvest.

The one thing on our minds the most was the question of Emma and Daniel. We agreed to wait until I was released from rehab before making any final decisions, but Daniel wouldn't be denied.

CHAPTER FORTY-FOUR

"When we see ourselves in a situation which must be endured and gone through, it is best to make up our minds to it, meet it with firmness, and accommodate everything to it in the best way practicable. ... while fretting and fuming only serves to increase our own torments."

—*Thomas Jefferson*

Just a week before my release date, I knew there was a problem when TJ didn't respond to my bright, welcoming smile. His eyebrows were drawn together. His mouth hung open a little.

"What's wrong?" I asked, reaching for his hand. Afraid, I looked behind him for Ghost. "Where's..."

"He's coming. Mr. Tomlinson is giving him cookies."

Relieved, I thought of something else dear to me. "Is something wrong with the Cottage?"

He shrugged and handed me a letter.

My Dearest Emma,

I am suffering. The loneliness I feel sitting here at my father's desk is draining me of life. I don't understand why I never see my father. Why can't I go out and find you? You know that I'm here, but you do not come. Have I offended you in some way? Did you find what your father left for you in our special place? Have you slipped the hold that I thought Waterwood had on you? Please, tell me.

Perhaps I should break the invisible chain that keeps me here and find you. I cannot survive much longer. Tell me what to do. I must relieve this pain.

Now and ever yours,
Daniel

We huddled in the corner of the sunroom and spoke in riddles in case someone overheard our conversation. We tried to persuade ourselves that Daniel could be appeased by a letter to buy us a little more time. After the nurse delivered my one pill, I suggested we walk outside.

"It's a little chilly." TJ was always thinking about my comfort and well-being.

"This is a heavy sweater. I'll talk fast." I zipped up the white cable-knit sweater, grabbed my cane, and headed for the door. Outside and out of earshot, I summarized the situation. "The way I see it, we have only three choices. Two of them involve dealing with Daniel by letter."

"What do you mean, deal with him?"

"The first way is to placate him. Tell him not to do anything yet."

"Okay, we've discussed that," TJ said. "But after reading this letter, I'm not sure that will work."

"That's why there's option two. Tell him that I, I mean, Emma has found someone else."

TJ drew in a quick breath. "That's risky."

"I know." I waited because TJ took off his cap, ran his fingers through his hair. When he replaced his cap, he said, "Or we could tell him the truth."

"What?" The word came out in a whispered scream. "Are you crazy?"

He shrugged. "Or we just ignore this letter and take away the stack of paper from the desk. If he doesn't have paper, he can't write to you. Then we put the desk back under a tarp in the garage and forget all about this."

My breath caught in my throat. That was probably the easiest solution. But, somehow, I couldn't see myself doing that to a man I'd come to know and admire, even though he was dead. I searched TJ's face, but there was no comfort or resolution there. His furrowed brow told me that he wasn't happy with any of the options.

A shiver ran through me. It was either from the chilled breeze that had picked up or the thought of possible consequences of our decision. I was about to tell TJ we could wait no longer when I touched my neck and remembered the miniature Emma wore in the portrait.

"There is one other alternative, TJ." He gave me a hopeful look. "We could try to reunite them."

"Let's go inside. You're shivering. But first, will you tell me how we're going to do that?"

I laid out my plan. When we went back to the sunroom, he was smiling and I was shivering with excitement and a little anxiety.

TJ must have been a Boy Scout because he came prepared, just in case. We found a quiet spot with a desk in the rehab facility where I could use the inkwell and write a letter to Daniel.

Dearest Daniel,

I read your letter and my heart broke. I cry, knowing how lonely and confused you must feel. Many things here at Waterwood have changed since you and my father rode south. There is only one thing you must know. I believe you know it in your heart. You must have faith in my constancy of affection.

My dear Daniel, I beg that you be patient only a little while longer. I beg that you stay at the desk of your father. It is the key to our happiness. It is the way I can come to you. Trust me in this.

Think also of the miniature I painted to capture your dear face so I'd have you with me always. I know it is no great artistic work as I was a fledgling painter. To me, it is the dearest portrait ever created. As you sit at the desk, think of it and remember the wonderful times we spent by the water.

Be patient, my love. I'm coming.

Sincerely and entirely yours,

Emma

TJ read the letter over my shoulder as we waited for the ink to dry. I heard him clear his throat.

"Is something wrong?" I asked, worried.

"No. It's just that…are you promising Daniel that Emma will join him? I mean…"

I gazed at the letter again. "Yes, I guess I am." I felt a shiver go down my spine.

"Isn't that a big leap? What if... What if this doesn't work?" he said with great reluctance.

"You're right. What we're doing requires a great leap of faith. I think we have to give him hope so, he'll give us time to put our plan into action. If we don't, he could go on a rampage now while I'm still in rehab. I wouldn't want you to deal with that alone. I'll be out of here soon. In the meantime, you have some renovation work to do."

"And what if our plan doesn't work?"

TJ spoke so softly I barely heard him. But his concern was clear. I had to calm the unease of both men in my life. "Let's trust our plan. If it doesn't work the way we hope, we'll deal with it together."

CHAPTER FORTY-FIVE

"The butterfly I folded when I first came to the Cottage helped me transform my life. I can only wish the same for Daniel."

—*Emma's Journal*

On the day before my release from rehab, I sat down at the desk in the out-of-the-way corner I'd used before. With paper, inkwell, and pen, I began to write what I hoped would be my last letter to Daniel. I wanted it to be ready when TJ came to visit so he could put it on the plantation desk tonight.

My Dearest Daniel,

At last, all is in readiness. I am coming to you. Stay by the desk. Remember the miniature I wear on a necklace. I yearn to stand with you by the water of our favorite creek and to gaze at the majestic Oak Tree where we've spent so many happy hours. Know that I believe with all my heart that love transcends all. I am coming to be with you for all eternity.

Your Beloved Emma

The next day, my day of independence, TJ picked me up. I was eager to get home to the Cottage. It would be my first opportunity to see the results of TJ's labors. He'd spent a lot of time walking the shoreline of the creek, looking for the spot where Emma had stood for her portrait. We were both surprised that it was at the dilapidated cabin down the way from the Cottage.

As we drove down the main road to St. Michaels, he took his right hand off the steering wheel and gestured towards the back seat. "I know you're anxious to get out of rehab, but you're coming home with only a cane. Is that wise? Are you rushing things… again?" He gave me a crooked smile.

I too remembered that awful night after the writers group meeting when I had fallen. The night he had taken care of me. I smiled again. His concern touched my heart. "I am much stronger. Not to worry. There is no way I want to go back."

Carefully, he made the turn for the long driveway down to the Cottage. It was wonderful to see the field of golden stalks that surrounded the Cottage. He pulled up at my front door and I released my seat belt.

"Just leave my things in the truck." I scrambled out with my cane. "Let's go to the cabin. I can't wait to see it."

"I hope you like what I've done. The guys will be here soon to move the desk." He hustled behind me. "Hey, wait up! Be careful. The path isn't like the smooth floors at rehab."

"I'm sure you've done a great job, but it doesn't matter what I think," I called back over my shoulder as I scooted along. "It's all up to them."

At the curve in the path, I stopped and gazed at the cabin that was no longer in danger of collapse. It looked better than it had during my years visiting Uncle Jack. I could feel a tear tracking slowly down my cheek.

Catching up to me, TJ asked with a little hesitation, "What do you think?" He saw the tear on my face and his face crumbled. "Oh no, you hate it," he declared, his Southern accent clear which signaled how much he cared. "I'm sorry. I'll—"

"It's perfect!" I wiped away the tear. "TJ, you're the best!"

"Hey TJ!" a gruff voice called out. "We're here and ready to work."

It was time to put our plan into action.

I made my way back inside to my writing den to prepare the plantation desk for its new home. I gathered the stapler, scissors, and ruler along with the modern pens and pencils. I emptied the drawers of the thumb drives and chargers, anything from the modern world. If everything worked out, there would be no need for such things. I put the inkwell, bottle of ink, and what was left of the paper that had started it all in the box. I had a plan for them, too.

The men transferred the parts of the plantation desk down the narrow path and reassembled it in the restored cabin. I think we convinced them that I'd be working on a book at the desk there.

"I'll go with the guys and pay them. Be right back," TJ said.

Finally, I was left alone in the renovated cabin in the middle of the woods by the water. This was the place I'd spent many magical hours as a child. Where I sat in an antique dining room chair just months ago feeling lost. Now, I felt like I'd not only found myself again, but discovered I shared my love of this place with another

Emma. I had to tackle one final task to complete before we'd lock the cabin.

I wanted to leave an origami shape in the cabin for the young lovers. Research showed that the butterfly symbolizes a soul set free. Color is always meaningful in origami as well. I found that dark red was often used to represent love and a bond with a special someone. What could be better than a crimson butterfly? I'd practiced folding the butterfly in the final days at rehab. Now, with confidence, I calmly folded a butterfly for Daniel and Emma. Now, it sat on top of the things in the box that TJ carried down to the cabin for me.

TJ soon returned and we looked around the renovated cabin, now solid and watertight. "You did a beautiful job, TJ. I'm so glad you added the window. It frames the view of the Lone Oak perfectly."

TJ beamed with optimism. "What do we do with these things?" He pointed at the box.

"You'll see." First, I put the bottle of ink in a cubbyhole. The inkwell and pen went above the short stack of paper on the desk's writing surface.

"Is that enough paper?" TJ asked.

"Hopefully, Daniel won't need any."

"Why?" TJ asked, then he brightened. "Of course, if he is reunited with Emma, he won't write letters to you anymore."

And if this doesn't work, I thought, *an angry letter will appear.* But I didn't say anything. I wanted to stay positive that our plan would work.

"And now, for the other vital piece." I opened a small jewelry box I'd found in the Cottage to keep the miniature safe. "I'm so glad you unearthed this necklace." I gently laid it on the sheets of paper and whispered a plea for Emma to come to this place to be with Daniel.

TJ and I stood quietly for a few moments. There was nothing else to say. Then we headed out through the door and TJ locked it. It was time for us to go on with our lives.

I led the way down the path back to the Cottage. At the front steps, I picked up my cane, put it on my shoulder like a rifle, and went up the steps, holding on to the rail.

"Wait! You're walking," he said in surprise.

I turned back, laughing. "Yes, I have been since I was about a year old."

"No, I mean you're walking without the cane."

"The doctor and the therapist both said I don't *need* the support, but it would be nice to have it for the next week or so to build my confidence."

"You're walking, well, like a normal person," he said. He put his hands in his pockets then took them out again. TJ was fidgeting with embarrassment.

I took a small bow. "Thank you, thank you very much. Walking feels better now even though I'm not quite ready for dancing." I shrugged. "Not that there's a rush. I was never very good at it."

He spoke the next words so quietly that I almost missed them. "I am."

"You are—?"

"I'm good at dancing. Mom made me go to Cotillion when I was young. Later, when I found that girls like boys who dance, I took more lessons at that famous dance studio."

"You didn't." I burst out laughing. "I've never met anyone who answered those ads and signed up."

"Well, I did and, I must say, it paid off. In fact—"

Quickly, I held up my hand. "Stop, stop! I don't need to hear details."

He took a step toward me. Always distracted by pain and then the activities at rehab, I'd forgotten how handsome he was. A hunk of light brown hair bleached blonde by the autumn sun fell over his forehead. His shirt sleeves were rolled-up, baring his muscular arms that had rescued me after my fall. But it was his sparkling eyes—hazel green like his land—that drew me in.

He held out his hands to me. "If you need motivation, keep on getting better and, when you're ready, I will take you dancing."

A wave of warmth moved through my body. I tried to keep the

giddiness out of my voice, "You don't have to worry. I doubt that will be anytime soon."

As I put my hand on the doorknob to go inside, his words stopped me again. "In the meantime, may I take you out to dinner tomorrow night? As friends. Not a date. We wouldn't want to do that."

The air around me seemed to shimmer. A great calm feeling came over me. "That would be nice. We can talk about things other than…" I cocked my head toward the cabin.

He chuckled. "Yes, that would be nice." He called out as he started walking back to his truck, "Pick you up at seven-thirty."

I called after him. "Why didn't you ask me before?"

He stopped and turned slowly toward me. "I don't normally like city girls. Had my fill of them at college. Grad school was the worst. As soon as they found out I had some land, they were all ready for me to sell up and buy some fancy condo in the city or a big McMansion in the suburbs. No, thank you. But you're different. I figured I'd wait."

I couldn't let it go. "Why?"

"I didn't think you were ready."

"And now? What changed?"

He smiled. "You're ready to start living again."

A slow smile of satisfaction played on my lips. I nodded gently. "Yes. Yes, I guess I am."

Turn the page for a
Sneak Peek of Book Two
in the Letters Series

Letters Across the Miles

By
Susan Reiss

LETTERS ACROSS THE MILES
(CHAPTER ONE)

I t started as a rumble in the distance. Then, the noise and vibrations rolled over the land scoured flat during the ice age. Acres of fertile land soaked up the pelting rain. I suspected the Chesapeake Bay, two hundred miles of pleasant waters, was whipped up to four-foot waves. It would not be the place to be tonight. This storm was unsettling enough inland at the Cottage on a creek. As the storm moved closer, white-hot lightning followed by booming shock waves reminded me of a cannon firing in war, the Civil War. And of Daniel and Emma or the cabin TJ had restored for the lovers. I'd have to check it in the morning for damage.

I stood at the window watching the storm's flashy pyrotechnics. I'd heard that this kind of violent storm could spawn a tornado. People say the sky turns a sick green if a twister is in the area, but who could tell at night? Man was a sitting duck for Mother Nature's tantrums.

A splintered lightning fork streaked across the sky. I felt awe. The fork split and stabbed the earth. My muscles tensed. Close, that strike was close. The flash drilled through my eyes to my brain, blinding me. Thunder rattled the window and thudded against my chest. Driven back from the window, I wanted to run.

Instead, I inched my way across the floor in the dark. The last thing I needed was to trip over something. My leg, mangled in the accident months earlier, was much better, even close to normal most days, but I wouldn't tolerate even a stubbed toe. Besides, there was nothing to worry about. The Mid-Atlantic area of the United States was never hit by tornados. Except for the one that screamed across Southern Maryland almost twenty years earlier, causing more than a million dollars in damage. Or the whatever-it-was that skipped through a wooded area bordering a luxury area known as Kenwood outside of D.C. It cut off trees at an even height of about eight feet. One expert called it a tornado and had to walk back that designation. The damage, they said, was caused by *straight line winds*. Of course, it wouldn't harm the beloved Japanese cherry trees that lined the streets of Kenwood. Mother Nature must have known who lived there. But those were instances on the western shore. This was the Eastern Shore of the Chesapeake Bay. It wouldn't happen here. It was a phrase I'd heard the locals say many times.

The storm struck again, lighting the room in eeriness. Thunder pounded my little house. There was nowhere to hide except… Lightning cracked again. Forget caution. I sprinted across the room, launched myself into bed, and pulled the covers over my head.

Emma, I lectured myself, *stop being foolish. You're safe here in the Cottage that has weathered storms for more than a hundred years?*

I was shaking, actually shaking. *I'll never get to sleep with all this racket. I'll never get to sleep. I'll never…*

Rays of sunlight warmed my face. I had fallen asleep and now it was morning. Slowly, I remembered what had happened in the night.

The thunderstorm.

The lightning strike.

The cabin!

I threw off the covers and scrambled into a pair of sweats and sweatshirt. *Slow down. Slow down,* I reminded myself as I walked down the stairs. It hadn't been that long since my release from rehabilitation to heal my body after the car accident that almost took my life.

Safely on the main floor, I slipped into my rubber moccasins, went out the front door, and skidded to a stop. For all the noise and fireworks of the night before, Mother Nature had created a breathtaking morning. The tall pines sparkled in the sunlight as they swayed gently, sending out puffs of pine scent through the air. The birds greeted me with a lively symphony of song. Not just one bird, but a forest full of those who had not yet flown south for the winter. There were Blue Jay squawks and Chickadee chirps plus the voices of those who came for the winter, robin trills, crow caws, and the Canada goose honks. And over it all was the cloudless sky dome of an achingly gorgeous blue. But it was the air that impressed me the most. Scrubbed clean by the storm, the air must have been as Mother Nature intended it to be in the beginning.

I took in a deep breath and scurried down the path toward the cabin. Scurried wasn't the right word. The thick mud and puddles made it slow-going, giving my brain plenty of time to concoct all kinds of possibilities of what I was about to see. The wind had pulled off the roof. The cabin was a burned-out shell destroyed by the lightning strike. Or…

I rounded the bend in the path and saw the cabin nestled in the cove of crepe myrtle and wild grasses, safe. It stood strong and untouched, just the way TJ had built it. With a deep sigh of relief, I retrieved the key from its hidey place and opened the door.

From the outside, the little cabin of wood planks had literally weathered the storm. On the inside, a maelstrom had struck. I only had eyes for the old plantation desk, Daniel's desk. Thankfully, it seemed to be untouched, but the sheets of white paper we'd left on its flat writing surface were strewn everywhere as if someone had thrown an almighty temper tantrum. It was exactly what I'd hope never to see.

When I inherited the Cottage from Uncle Jack, I'd discovered the desk used by the plantation manager of Waterwood, the land surrounding the Cottage. When I had the antique moved into the den from the garage where it had been buried under a blue tarp, an extraordinary experience had begun. Daniel had left letters addressed to Emma on the plantation desk. Why was this unusual? His letters were dated 1862 and this was the 21st century. Daniel wasn't writing to me really. He wanted to contact his true love, Emma. In a moment of silliness or boredom, I'd responded. And our correspondence had begun. His desperation and loneliness had made me want to help reunite them. I figured anything was possible since I was corresponding with a ghost.

My friend TJ repaired this cabin to shelter the desk. I put a miniature portrait Emma had painted of Daniel next to a stack of paper and we closed the door. We assumed that the only way we'd know if we succeeded was if Daniel never left another letter addressed to Emma on the desk.

And now this! Paper scattered everywhere, as if flung into the air in a fit of rage. Did Emma fail to join him? Was this another betrayal in his life, one that had finally broken his heart and ignited eternal grief and fury? I could feel the salt of my tears sting my eyes and my skin as they trickled down my cheeks.

"There you are," the male voice stated with some relief. TJ had come as if I'd called him. "I thought I'd find you here. Did you know you left your front door open?" he said in his calm, laid-back way. "I see we had the same idea. I was wondering how the cabin… whoa!"

I knew he'd taken in the papers strewn everywhere and he'd realized what it probably meant.

"It looks like… did Daniel… does this mean…" TJ touched my arm as I continued to stand with my back to him. I didn't want him to see me crying. "Emma?"

"I'm so sorry," I wailed.

He turned me toward him, put his arms around me, and let my tears soak into his Oxford cloth shirt. He didn't say a word. What could he say? The evidence was clear that we'd failed to reunite the lovers of old. After all the research to uncover the true Emma of Daniel's world and their connection. After the discovery of who had torn them apart. After the search for a treasure that was rumored to be rich enough to be life changing. After the terrifying murder of a young man in our time. After TJ rebuilt the cabin and…

It had all ended in disappointment and rage.

"I'm sorry," I murmured as I looked up at TJ.

"Okay, time to dry your tears." He pulled out a cloth handkerchief from the back pocket of his jeans. "Let's see what happened here."

"Isn't it obvious. I-I-I failed them," I sputtered.

"Sh-h-h, we don't know that yet." He went around the small cabin interior, collecting the papers flung everywhere. "Didn't you say that if our efforts to reunite Emma and Daniel failed, he would write a scathing letter about betrayal and being abandoned?"

I nodded, sure that if I spoke, I'd start crying again.

TJ held up a fistful of white sheets to me. "Emma, every one of these pages are blank."

I took the sheets and inspected them. What he said was true. "Maybe his words have already faded as they did with his letters to me?"

"You have been checking the cabin religiously several times a day for the past two weeks.

"How did you know…"

"Because you're not the only one who wants them to be happy. I've been anxious to know if what we did worked. I haven't found any evidence of correspondence from Daniel. You've told me you haven't found anything either, right?"

I nodded.

"So, I don't think Daniel did this. I don't think he made this mess. I think the storm…" he paused, his green hazel eyes slowly inspecting the ceiling, the door, the window… "Ah ha! Here's your culprit." He pointed to a partially broken glass pane in the window overlooking the creek and the Lone Oak tree. He looked outside. "Yes, there's a branch on the ground. Probably broke off in the storm. "And if Daniel were sending you a message, he probably would have shredded that." He pointed to the origami butterfly I'd folded from crimson paper and left in a cubbyhole for the lovers, to symbolize a soul set free and a bond of love to last forever. It sat just where I'd left it weeks ago. "Stop your worrying, please. I think we succeeded."

TJ was ever optimistic, and I decided to follow his lead. It was so much better than the alternative. I folded his handkerchief and stuck it in my pocket. "I'll put this through the wash."

"OH! I almost forgot." He reached into his shirt pocket. "I wanted to check on the cabin and to show this to you, a letter I found last night."

He handed me a small envelope, a little discolored, with a heavily-cancelled one-cent stamp in the corner. There was a letter inside.

"You'll see by the cancellation that it was written during the Civil War and addressed to Emma Collins, Daniel's Emma, I think."

Carefully, I took out the letter and unfolded it, eager to read it.

"Be careful," he said softly. "Look at the notation there at the bottom. I suspect Emma wrote it."

The letter signed *Sally* (*Sarah Lowndes*). The notation written in a different hand read:

Which is worse... to live without the man you love as I do or to live with your beloved, the man who so many revile and despise ... and now suffers their hatred as well.

Curious, I asked, "Who was Sally?"
"I'm not sure. But I suspect you have a new research project."

Are you intrigued?
Visit *SusanReiss.com* to be notified when Book Two is released!

ACKNOWLEDGEMENTS & NOTES

Betty Dorbin, librarian and lover of history, traces her family roots on the Eastern Shore back to the 1600s. One area of the family's estate that continues to exist is the family graveyard. She has meticulously researched her family history and was kind to share what she'd learned during a leisurely stroll on a brilliant fall day.

Keith Shortall of Shortall Farm on the Eastern Shore, a man with rich soil under his fingernails, was so kind to share his time and expertise so TJ could be presented honestly and correctly.

University of Maryland Extension Service was a wonderful source of farming information.

Heartfelt thanks to James Dawson, owner of the Unicorn Bookshop, Trappe, Maryland and editor of *100 Years of Change on the Eastern Shore: The Willis Family Journals 1847-1951*. Not only was it a wonderful source for chapter quotes, reading the entries helped bring alive the times when Daniel and Emma lived.

Though Stephani was an interesting character, the real Maryland Room of the Talbot County Free Library is staffed by Becky Riti. She presides over a treasure trove of information, everything from maps and books to original journals and photographs from long ago. She knows how to find things and is eager to help every visitor to her domain.

ACKNOWLEDGEMENTS & NOTES

The fact that cursive writing is no longer taught in many schools is a shame, in my opinion. So, here's a tip of the hat to teachers and parents who take the time to teach the next generations. It's faster than printing and can be more legible. If nothing else, it gives a person the means to develop a distinctive signature.

Many thanks to the St. Michaels Fire Department, Station 40, especially Kevin Smith, Firefighter Engineer and Kristen Jones EMT/Firefighter for help in getting the "fire in the field" scenes right!

I think all dog lovers dream of having a well-trained companion. I'm fortunate to live with Leo, a yellow lab, who has qualified as a therapy dog. Before the lockdowns of the pandemic, he was the reading dog for kids at the St. Michaels branch library. His training became a little lax during our at-home time. Whenever someone came to visit, he was out of his mind with delight. One day during a particularly exuberant greeting, I said, "Manners." Much to everyone shock, he sat and extended a paw. Since Ghost is so well-trained in the story, I thought I'd add this little detail to his behavior in honor of Leo.

We don't really write letters anymore. We write emails. Writing good letters to clearly convey information and how we truly feel is fast becoming a lost art along with cursive writing. I often thought of good letter-writing as belonging to times centuries past. Then I found the little book in the public domain and online called *How to Write Letters: A Manual of Correspondence Showing the Correct Structure, Composition, Punctuation, Formalities, and Uses of the Various Kinds of Letters, Notes and Cards* by J. Willis Westlake, A.M., Professor of English Literature, State Normal School, Millersville, PA 1883. Quite a mouthful, I know. It was printed 138 years ago, as of this writing. Of course, some of the advice no longer applies, I was surprised how much of the information would be useful today. For example, the author suggests that a letter written in anger or extreme emotion should be set aside for at least a night, if not several days. I'm sure we all have hit *Send* before we should have.

ACKNOWLEDGEMENTS & NOTES

Many thanks to my writing buddies, Jen and Donna, who are always willing to read and comment. You are great companions on this writer's journey.

And as always, thanks to my family for your support always. Barry, Erin, Zoe, Matt, Maggie and our newest addition, Joey, I love you all to the moon and back!

Susan Reiss
St. Michaels, Maryland
2021

St. Michaels
Silver Mysteries

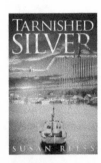

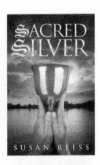

St. Michaels
Historical Novellas

available now   coming 2021